First Time, Long Time

First Time, Long Time

A novel

Amy Silverberg

GRAND
CENTRAL

NEW YORK BOSTON

Grand Central Publishing
Hachette Book Group
1290 Avenue of the Americas, New York, NY 10104
grandcentralpublishing.com
@grandcentralpub

First Edition: July 2025

Grand Central Publishing is a division of Hachette Book Group, Inc. The Grand Central Publishing name and logo is a registered trademark of Hachette Book Group, Inc.

The publisher is not responsible for websites (or their content) that are not owned by the publisher.

The Hachette Speakers Bureau provides a wide range of authors for speaking events. To find out more, go to hachettespeakersbureau.com or email HachetteSpeakers@hbgusa.com.

Grand Central Publishing books may be purchased in bulk for business, educational, or promotional use. For information, please contact your local bookseller or the Hachette Book Group Special Markets Department at special.markets@hbgusa.com.

Print book interior design by Marie Mundaca

Library of Congress Cataloging-in-Publication Data

Names: Silverberg, Amy, 1988- author
Title: First time, long time : a novel / Amy Silverberg.
Description: First edition. | New York : Grand Central Publishing, 2025.
Identifiers: LCCN 2025006864 | ISBN 9781538726471 hardcover |
  ISBN 9781538726495 ebook
Subjects: LCGFT: Bildungsromans | Novels
Classification: LCC PS3619.I55234 F57 2025 | DDC 813/.6—dc23/eng/20250306
LC record available at https://lccn.loc.gov/2025006864

ISBNs: 9781538726471 (hardcover), 9781538726495 (ebook)

Printed in the United States of America

LSC-C

Printing 1, 2025

For my parents, who are not the parents in this book

"Just once in my life—oh, when have I ever
wanted anything just once in my life?"

—Amy Hempel, "Memoir"

1.

One strange Tuesday evening my mother called and said, "The Problem wants to visit you." That's what my mother called my father: The Problem. As far as my mother was concerned, he'd always been a problem. And the worst kind too: one without a solution.

I didn't want to talk about The Problem. "I'm on a date," I lied. I thought this would be the fastest way to get my mother off the phone—my mother, who so often worried about her only daughter being alone. That's what my mother always said: I'm worried you're all alone.

"You answered the phone on a date?" my mother asked.

"He's in the bathroom."

In the pause before my mother, Carrie, spoke, I knew she must be deciding if I'd lied, and then, if she should say, "I know you're lying." Maybe it was an act of kindness or only because she was distracted, but my mother moved on. "So your father hasn't called you?"

"No," I said. "Why?"

In Arizona where my mother had relocated, I imagined the shadows of the cacti stretching long and ominously across her condo's sand-colored patio.

"Oh," she said offhandedly, as if it was suddenly nothing to worry about. "I'm sure he's fine. But when he came to pick up Peter in the truck, he was acting strange. Your father. Not Peter."

Peter was the family dog—an elderly standard poodle who loved my father to the point of obsession, and only tolerated my mother. My parents shared haphazard custody.

"What's wrong with him?" I asked.

"Well, I don't know. He just said he wasn't feeling well. Mentally. And that he thought visiting you would help." She'd become defensive; I could hear the edge of it in her voice. "He's not my problem anymore, is he?" But that wasn't really true. He'd be her problem forever, and mine too.

"Well should we call someone? If he's doing badly."

"I am calling someone," my mother said. "I'm calling you."

My parents had separated as soon as I'd left the house at seventeen— so quickly, in fact, it was as though I'd stepped off the lowly, floating raft the three of us had shared and threw the balance off so completely the two couldn't keep it steady alone together, without me. One of them had to get off—or they both did. And so they separated. Now, eleven years later, neither one had bothered to file for an official divorce, even though my mother had been living in Mesa, Arizona, with a man named Raj for the last six years.

Who needs the paperwork? my father said. I get home and she isn't there. Why would I need a paper to prove it? My father had always been a difficult man, but the difficultness had calcified into something else recently, something harder and shinier, with much less give.

2.

In sixth grade, I asked my mother what was wrong with my father and she said, "Nothing," and then said, "Well. Why do you ask?"

She'd left her job at the clinic early to pick me up from school—a rare treat—because I normally took the school bus, and we'd been on our way to Hot Dog on a Stick at the mall food court, another treat, where I would have her undivided attention, something I wanted so badly at the time it was almost like money, or water even, its own kind of currency or resource.

My mother worked at an inpatient clinic for girls with eating disorders and often came home exhausted from begging other people's troubled daughters to just swallow the yogurt on the spoon. I tried not to be any trouble.

I'd been picturing it all day, in math class and at recess: the time alone with my mother, sitting across from her in the airy, fluorescent food court, her attention like a spotlight, attention that was normally so hard to come by. In the car, my mother's face had looked unusually tense (by then, I had a finely tuned antenna for the moods of every member of my family) and I felt acutely disappointed that the lunch wouldn't be what I pictured. It would be hijacked. My mother would be distracted by other things. My father probably, whom she referred to as The Problem even then, or my older brother, Jack, who had begun to become *problematic*.

Like some daughters do, I made myself into a miniature of my mother: someone younger and shorter who could help her out—help her "take care of things." It wasn't hard to do: I have her same straight, lank hair, the ends of which sometimes break off when it's cold, and I, like her, have always referred to myself as "a good listener."

It was then, on our way to the mall, that I asked if there was something wrong with my father.

A simple reason: the night before, a neighbor had come over to play, and we were hiding in the hallway closet from some unknown entity, a game for which neither of us had specified the rules. I thought something might happen between us, a kiss maybe, right there in the mothball-smelling darkness of the closet, beneath the winter coats nobody wore, when my father started yelling. He wasn't yelling *at* anyone, more like yelling at the sky, or yelling at the room.

If I could tell you what he was yelling about, trust me, it wouldn't make a difference: his obsessions were odd and mystifying. Why had my mother bought potato chips he hated? Why did the painting of a farm in the hallway look so ugly, and why hang it there, where everyone could see it on their way in the house? Why were Legos so goddamn hard to put together, and what the hell was *Star Wars*? Who was going to war? The stars?! And why did they live in this house anyway, in this shit neighborhood? Why was the yard shit brown? Why was his life shit brown? Why?!

His yelling was not scary exactly, but pained, like he could barely take it, and the neighbor, a redheaded boy with freckles even on the backs of his knees, whispered in my ear, "What's wrong with your dad?"

What *was* wrong with my dad? I hadn't known until that moment that other people could see it too.

"I don't know," I said. "He just gets overwhelmed."

He'd gotten "overwhelmed" for as long as I could remember. Sometimes he got "worked up." Sometimes his nerves were just "frayed." He was from a different generation! my mother said. Men weren't allowed to go to therapy. They couldn't even picture the word "therapy" in their minds.

Somewhere along the line I had inherited my mother's problems. I'd also inherited her straight, thick eyebrows and squarish jaw. You can get away with it, my mother said, until you turn my age, and everything starts to drag.

Watch out for jowls! she said, as though I would see them arriving in the distance and then duck out of the way.

I'd inherited things from my father too, but they were harder to articulate.

"Maybe The Problem will just show up," my mother said now.

"Well if he plans on that, he hasn't told me."

I talked to my mother almost every other day, though long gone was my pure and unadulterated need for her attention. (When I was a kid, I'd cup her chin in my hand and drag her face toward me, hold it there!) Now, there was something else between us: an understanding that we were cut from the same, stained cloth.

"Hey," I said, "my date's back."

"Oh, right," my mother said, the joke of it in her voice. "Your date."

I wasn't on a date—far from it. I was technically still at work. At a junior college, I taught people who only sometimes wanted to learn. Sometimes they wanted to talk about sports or television or who they'd slept with the night before. Those were the young ones.

Occasionally my classes were filled with busy people tethered to responsibilities—children to raise and rent to pay and sick parents who required care. They just wanted a higher degree that the complications of life had not allowed them to obtain. I taught Intro to Fiction. Plain old "Reading and Writing" was what I called it. Before this, I'd taught English lit at a private high school up north. I'd traveled south—like a bird! my father said—and the junior college was supposed to be a better job. Now I understood that what constituted a better job from a worse job was more complicated the older you became, the more jobs you worked, the more life you lived. In fact, what constituted better or worse in general had become difficult to decipher. Most things were not bad or good at all, but both at the same time.

I didn't know if writing was teachable. I still don't. If someone taught me to write, I don't remember who they were. It had something to do with the lack of novels in my home. There were only ever biographies of famous people and magazines and the *Guinness World Records*, which my father sometimes read aloud when he was in a good mood ("seventeen corn dogs in one minute!") and that made novels more interesting, taboo even. Like pornography.

At the junior college, I only tried to sell the students on how a good novel might change their lives, or at least, make their lives easier, more livable. On the first day of class, I always said the same thing: "I'm selling you a new way of seeing the world." It was corny, and I knew it, but sometimes corny worked. Sometimes they took it as a challenge, turning away from me, or rolling their eyes. They acted as though they wouldn't be changed by a novel no matter what it was, no matter if I found a writer that spoke so wholly to who they were—some unarticulated version—that they'd wonder if they'd written it themselves. Sometimes I was able to surprise them.

Now, three weeks into the semester, I was trying to unhook myself from my own agenda, to listen to what they actually wanted, and give them that.

Teaching wasn't my only job, though it was the least excruciating. I also facilitated book clubs for wealthy women in Los Angeles. Some were sweet elderly women who pressed baked goods into my hands when I left, told me how smart I was, how pretty. Did I have a boyfriend? Why not? they wondered.

Others lived in homes as large and secure as fortresses, tall hedges like curtain walls blocking the view from passersby. Men in uniforms brought the women icy martinis on silver trays. These women wanted me to talk quickly, to get on with it, so they could discuss the people they knew. Who was getting ugly, who was getting fat, whose kids were rejected by Princeton and Stanford. Pick something entertaining to read! Not boring. But not sad! And not weird. Too weird—that they didn't like. We're busy, they said. They were busy with important lunches they had to attend and charity boards they had to sit on and tennis matches in which their backhand gave them a much needed edge.

When I arrived, one woman shouted, "The book girl is here!" because the woman had never bothered to learn my name. "How's our book girl?"

"Allison," I'd say, though nobody was listening.

"They take something from me," I'd told my mother on the phone, "they take something from me I can't get back."

"It's not their fault," my mother said when I complained. "Some people are born into it."

"Money?" I'd asked.

"Selfishness."

I worked other jobs, too. In Los Angeles, so many jobs were required to cobble a life together. What would my life look like to other people? A disheveled pile, a tattered quilt. If I saw my own life in the window of an antiques shop, I'd turn away from it, disgusted. Who'd buy that thing? I'd say to myself. The patterns, the texture—it all clashes. This life makes no discernible sense.

Sometimes I wrote copy for a high-end lingerie website (Diana waits for her lover by the fire, lounging temptingly in our sheer black Seductress Two-Piece for $265), and before that, I'd written horoscopes for an astrology app (available on both iPhone and Android).

Virgos, I'd write, *Mama said there'd be days like this.*

Aries: Keep on truckin'.

Unless it was the month my brother died, October, then I'd allow myself something poetic and abstract: *Scorpio: Nothing gold can stay.* Eventually I got fired for that—too much poetry, not enough fortune-telling.

"Horoscopes aren't good," my boss said, "when they only make sense to you."

3.

Before my mother called that strange Tuesday, I'd agreed to meet with a student after hours in my office at the Glendale Community College.

I'd been sitting in my small barren room with nothing on the walls. I'd meant to decorate, to put a clever *New Yorker* cartoon on the wall, or a framed poster of my favorite novel's cover. In the year I'd worked there, I hadn't been able to decide on anything. My indecision had become pathological, paralyzing. And anyway, there was always someone standing in the doorway, asking if I could print a syllabus, or sign a form, or teach one more intro class in which I might—this time—convince them to read.

The student I was supposed to meet with, an eighteen-year-old named Julie (short for Juliette), sent an email canceling, so I decided to take myself to a bar. It seemed like a good way to start a short story, and I hadn't written for so long: a woman walks into a bar.

I tried not to think of my father, though I was *always* thinking about my father. He was the planet around whom everything orbited.

No, I'd decided, I wouldn't worry about him tonight. And anyway, soon he would surface, in the way he always surfaced, shoulders barely above water, bobbing ruefully.

I knew how the conversation would go: I'd ask, Why haven't you been in touch? Mom was worried about you. And he'd say, She was worried? She has Raj, as though my mother had such a small vat of worry, it could only belong to one man at a time. And, my father would say, Why haven't you been in touch with me? You could've called.

It was the same stalemate we found ourselves in again and again, like a dream you keep having, in which you're naked in a high school classroom.

"You think you're the only one who misses him?" my father might say. "The only one who feels like this?"

No, I'd say. We're in it together.

4.

I was sitting at the bar with a book in front of me, when a famous man sat next to me. I'd brought a notebook, but I hadn't taken it out of my purse. I didn't have writer's block so much as writer's dread. I couldn't face the pages, their hideous blankness.

"What are you reading?" the famous man asked.

I looked at the cover, suddenly unable to answer. It was a book I read about online, something about magical realism: a father turns into a lamp. I showed it to him.

"Haven't read it," he said. "I don't even know why I asked. I'm not much of a reader."

I knew immediately who he was, of course. I'd known about him for what seemed like my entire life—as long as I'd known about my parents, about myself.

"I wish I were a reader," he said. "I know it's something I should be."

He was more handsome in person, somewhere in the shallow end of his sixties, wearing a soft-looking black sweater and smelling of expensive soap. I could picture the place where the soap was purchased: one of those quiet, ritzy stores that only sells artisan toiletries, a striking woman at the cash register, a handsome gay man in an intimidatingly stylish outfit by the door. Probably this famous man had never set foot in that store; probably someone else did that kind of thing for him. He sort of looked like one of the monied, liberal dads that sometimes showed up at the expensive private high school where I once worked, dads who drove expensive electric cars and wore hats that said *The Future Is Female*. Still, those dads showed up a lot less than moms. No-Dad's-Land, the staff called it, joking.

"I think everyone means to read more," I said.

"Even you?" he asked.

"Okay," I said, "not me. I already read a lot. I read at stoplights. I read all the time." I felt his nearness in my pulse now, speeding it up. I'd heard his voice all my life. All my life, he'd been in the background. I couldn't figure out a way to say this out loud without sounding absolutely demented.

I've been listening to you all my life!

He was the most famous radio personality in the world, the most famous radio DJ to have ever lived. How many radio DJs was he competing with? That wasn't the point. He changed the form, everyone said that. Also, this man served as my father's conscience, the cricket on his shoulder forever whispering rights and wrongs. The Problem's hero. The god of my house. Rather, my father was the god of my house, and he was the god of my father. I'd inherited my father's gods, just like I'd inherited his knobby knees and an allergy to shellfish.

This man, Reid Steinman, was saying something now, and I asked him to repeat it. Goddamn it. I was a bad listener! The membrane between my thoughts and my words was still dangerously thin. My brother died two years ago. The light in every room still looked changed.

"May I ask what you do?" Reid repeated. I felt struck by the "may"—the politeness, the formality. "For work I mean."

People in this city were always asking what I did for a living! Even famous people wanted to know! I bounce around, was what I wanted to say. No, "bounce" sounded too easy, too fun. I don't bounce so much as slide down the wall like something splattered or spilled. But I couldn't say that— it made no sense! I was having trouble accessing what people said when they met someone attractive, what to say when you wanted to win someone over. "Deep down I'm a good person," maybe. "I have sex enthusiastically." These things must be conveyed with subtext of course, but I couldn't figure out what that subtext might be.

Also, I thought he might be waiting for me to impress him—to make him laugh with the strangeness of my small and singular life. Or maybe asking about my life was just a pickup line, to show that he understood women want to be asked this kind of thing—what do you do, what are you interested in—as opposed to just being looked at.

I'd read that in a magazine profile of him once. He'd said, "Yes, I ask women about their sex lives on the radio, but I also want to know what they do every day, and more so, what they do in private. And not even sexually, just what they do when they're alone."

Like a writer, I'd thought, when I read that. Turning rocks over and seeing what's beneath.

"Before you got here, I was sitting next to someone weird," I said. I didn't *want* to talk about what I did every day. Honestly, I didn't think I could describe it if I tried. The days passed without my consent. I barely got to look at them. One morning, I kept thinking, I should grab one of my days by the shoulders and look it in the eyes and ask, What's been *happening*?!

And what I said was true: I had just been sitting next to a weird man. He left only moments before Reid sat down. This man tapped me on the shoulder to show me his phone, more specifically an Instagram account, which depicted an Asian woman grilling what looked like a skewer of hamsters on an outdoor flat top grill. He laughed when I recoiled.

"Isn't the world crazy?" the man said.

I wasn't sure what he found crazy: that people grilled hamsters in an Asian country he surely hadn't bothered to learn the name of? Or the fact that he had access to that knowledge—a video of it!—at a bar?

I'd just said "huh" and looked back at my book. I'd been trying to shut the door on the conversation. I always wished I looked like the kind of woman a man might be intimidated to talk to at a bar. Instead, I looked like the kind of woman to whom strangers on airplanes often told secrets. "Approachable" is probably the word.

Reid nodded and I felt embarrassed at letting the story of the weird hamster man spill out like that. I need to talk to more men, I thought. I need to *practice* talking to men.

Now Reid wore a puzzled expression, as though I might have something on my face—an eyelash or a stray piece of dryer lint.

"I'm glad I came and saved you," he said. "I don't normally have such impeccable timing."

I knew without a shadow of a doubt he wanted to sleep with me. Even if you are a woman whom not every man wants to sleep with (maybe only some men, maybe even only a fraction of them), you still knew this look. You are born knowing.

And listen: I do not think most men want to sleep with me. But some—some definitely do. And yet, the way he was looking at my face—closely, not lecherously—felt intimate, rather than invasive. I'd always found the idea of being with an older man a little sinister. Don't older men want to control you? Or was that just a leftover scrap from something my mother had said?

Meanwhile, I'd never dated a bald man; had never even slept with one. I'd turned twenty-eight just last week.

"And what do you do for work," I said suddenly. I'd pretend I had no idea who he was. It felt good to render him anonymous, like I'd grabbed a little power back.

"I'm on the radio," he said.

"You have a radio show?"

"Yes," he said. "I have a show. I've had it for a long time."

"What's your name?" I asked.

"Reid," he said. He stiffened a little, having to say his name in a bar. "Reid Steinman."

"Reid Steinman." It was a thrill to say his name back to him, right to his face. I repeated it slowly, as though I were sounding out words in a different language. Then I said it again. "Reid Steinman," like it was suddenly becoming familiar to me, lyrics from some long-forgotten song. "I think my dad's a fan."

He smiled. "Is that good or bad?"

"Neither," I said, though I couldn't decide if that was true. "I think he listened to you when I was growing up."

"A lot of dads like me," he said.

I could picture these dads, on the other side of the proverbial hill, saggy-faced and beer-drinking men who liked to hear a dirty joke in a bar. But I knew that was only a stereotype. If I knew anything about dads: They were complicated.

Reid smiled again, but there was a tightness. Maybe this was a tired ritual. How many times did he have to sit and listen, his face as open as a menu, while a fan recounted the many hours they spent listening to him growing up, or their parents had. Or maybe this felt exciting to him, the way something you were good at—that always ended well for you—was exciting, like teaching sometimes was for me. Like writing used to be. I didn't want the conversation to end and suddenly I felt very worried about what I might say next. I wanted to extend the moment. Surely it was just a moment. I thought around for something to say.

"Do you have any kids?" I said. I knew he had one. He almost never spoke of her on the radio. When he did, it was only in passing: I visited my daughter in college. Oh, my daughter plays the guitar.

"I have one," he said.

I knew from listening to the show for so long that his family was off-limits. And maybe his daughter would've been, had he known I was a fan. But luckily I wasn't. I was just a girl in a bar.

"And what does she do?" I asked.

"She's in between things," he said. "She's back from college."

I wondered how old he was. My father's age? I'd google it as soon as I was alone. He looked sort of ageless, in the way well-tended bald men sometimes look, shiny and smooth and elaborately moisturized. In the dim, buttery lighting of the bar—beneath those stylish naked bulbs I some-how associate with lonely geniuses—his edges appeared softened. It was romantic comedy lighting. There was a doglike quality to his face, a sort of turned-up nose, like a pug. But he was not unattractive. Probably he had spent a lot of time looking at himself in the mirror, at different angles, in different clothes—testing, trying. And so much could be improved with money! Could be massaged and papered over. Had he gotten plastic sur-gery? I'd google that too.

"So your father listens," he said. "But you've never heard me?"

Of course my first instinct was to continue to lie. Lying had always been my first instinct, for as long as I could remember. Something to do with my dad—I'd take any pains to hide a truth that might upset him. But where had my instincts gotten me? And what could I lose from telling the truth? Dignity, maybe, but I didn't have that much dignity to start with.

"I've listened before," I said.

"A casual listener," he said.

"Something like that."

"So you do know who I am." He raised his eyebrows in an exaggerated way. I remembered he played a role in a superhero movie once, as a bank teller, but he wasn't very good, and had never been cast in anything again.

I kind of liked that he'd already caught me in a lie, at least a small one. He's getting to know me! I thought.

"I know who you are," I said. I grinned, like I'd wanted him to find me out.

"Good," he said. "If you didn't—" He touched his head as though miming a headache. "It can be difficult to explain."

The bar was uncrowded, but I could feel the static of other people's eyes on us. Uh-huh, someone whispered, that's him. A few people craned their necks to look. But at other tables nobody cared. Life in this city went on: a script was purchased, a dream was crushed. "That was her fourth affair!" someone shouted, to an eruption of laughter. I was always getting distracted by other people's lives.

"I'm a teacher," I said, "in answer to your earlier question." I liked how noble it sounded, and humble too. I wanted to *help* people! I did not mention the other strung-together jobs: the horoscope app, the lingerie website, the book clubs. Then, I thought I noticed some slight change in his face: a drooping around his mouth. Teachers were boring. They did not *do*, and that was why they *taught*. "I'm a writer too," I said and immediately regretted it.

"What have you written?" he asked.

"Nothing you've read," I said. And if he knew that meant things had not gone well, writing-wise, he didn't show it on his face. "But I'm working on something new," I lied.

"I'd love to read it," he said.

"Maybe someday," I said. I meant it: I found the whole idea of him reading something I wrote terrifying and exciting both. I might even say arousing.

"And do you like teaching?"

I was not used to being asked so many questions, to being the center of someone's attention. "Yes, well. Yes, I do. But sometimes I wish I was doing something else."

He smiled, and I noticed his teeth were unnaturally white and straight. Capped? Veneers? These were things I hadn't known existed until recently. I'd moved to Los Angeles one year ago, after I'd gotten tired of the private high school where I worked up north. (I liked calling it that: *up north*. It made me feel like I was a frontierswoman, or an explorer.)

"There are a lot of things you don't know," an ex-boyfriend had said, "for someone who reads so many books."

"What else do you wish you were doing?" Reid asked now, flashing his much younger teeth.

"At this moment?" I said. "Nothing." I was flirting now, leaning closer to him. It was trite choreography, but I was relieved I remembered the steps.

"Instead of teaching," he said, but he was leaning closer too. "Did you always want to be a teacher?"

No, I thought. "Sort of."

"I sort of wish I'd done something else," he said. "I guess that's easy for me to say now, right?"

A man approached from behind Reid, and I wasn't sure if I should say something. I liked the idea of giving Reid some sort of signal: like we were on the same team, two people colluding. The guy was middle-aged, in a baseball cap, its brim optimistically stiff. Before he reached Reid, he turned the cap backward in one fluid motion. When I first moved to LA, I couldn't believe how many of the men wore backward baseball caps and frequently asked for help.

"Are you from the Midwest?" a coworker had asked when I'd said this.

"No," I'd said, "I'm from the middle of nowhere," which wasn't really true. Of course it wasn't true—everywhere was somewhere, but I was from somewhere very specific: outside of Reno, Nevada. The town has a name but I won't use it. The whole place still feels difficult to explain, in the same way it is difficult to explain the taste of food, or your own childhood.

5.

The closest city to where I grew up is Reno, Nevada, and it still requires a drive long enough that you could get lost and end up surrounded by endless farmland.

I'll say this: Everyone in my town knew a kid who owned a horse. Everyone also knew a kid whose uncle had a lot of land where you could host keggers or séances or paintball matches, and another kid who'd died tragically in some unspeakable way. The kid who owned the horse could often do tricks (like barrel jumping or shoulder stands), and the kid whose uncle had a lot of land usually had a story about a wild orgy that happened there (twelve people at least, with someone famous even, like Sharon Osbourne or Tony Hawk). The kid who'd died tragically was always used as the moral of a story, a kind of small-town allegory ("that's what happens when—"). The whole town had a whiff of violence, like the chemical smell from a factory where angry fathers worked.

Everyone knew how to gamble. In fact, so many kids' parents worked at the casinos that when you took your first summer job there, everyone already knew your last name.

Every teenager was perpetually looking for a pool in the summer and a ride to Mount Rose in the winter.

And most of all, everyone was waiting to leave.

Another thing about the town: it became famous for a court case involving a real estate dispute.

In a house just down the street from my childhood home, a man in his twenties broke in and killed his parents. When that house went on the market, the seller didn't disclose this bit of grotesque information. After the buyers found out, they insisted it wasn't worth the money they'd paid and they sued the seller.

(Why had the man broken in and killed his parents? What had they done to him? Was he crazy or deeply aggrieved? We didn't know and we never found out. We only knew that he lived in New Hampshire and sold herbal supplements at a kiosk in the mall. Imagine driving all the way from New Hampshire to kill your parents with the herbal supplements you couldn't sell still in your car, buckled into the seat next to you for safekeeping.)

If the family who accidentally bought the house (for a remarkable price!) had asked anybody in the town, we could've told them: that place is haunted. Something unthinkable happened in there, inside that one-story ranch house that looked like any other house on the block. When they sued, the family who'd purchased it had even hired a guy from New York whose whole job was to evaluate how the psychological stigma of a property affected its value.

"This house has no value," is pretty much what he'd said. "Though," he'd explained to my dad, who was a dealer at the craps table, "what the seller must disclose varies from state to state."

"Is that so?" my father asked, while he moved the long craps stick deftly around the table, pushing dice to the next unlucky roller.

"In California, for instance, the seller must disclose if a death happened in the house within three years."

"How about three years and one day?" my father asked. (He could easily carry on a conversation while he worked. He was very good at multitasking.)

"Then, that's okay. They don't have to disclose it. Sometimes the buyer even has to ask, 'Did someone die here?' But your house," he said, meaning the one very close to where my family lived, "that kind of brutality? That kind of murder? They should've disclosed."

At least that's what the jury said in the civil suit: that the sellers should've said "a terrible murder happened here." Who wanted to live in a house like that, with those sorts of ghosts?

✻   ✻   ✻

But wasn't every lived-in place haunted by something? Or someone?

When my father arrived home that night, he'd only said, "I should've gone into real estate! You can charge people an arm and a leg for a job you just made up."

6.

"I can't believe you're here," said the fan in the backward baseball cap. He was talking to Reid, of course, not to me.

"I can't believe you're standing right in front of me." He looked like he might be on the verge of tears. "You are like my hero, dude."

Reid greeted him with alarming neutrality. "I'll sign something quickly," he said, "but I'm in the middle of a conversation."

"Great," the man said. He was smiling so hard it looked painful, like he'd stepped on a piece of glass but was too embarrassed to tell us. Reid spread out his empty hands as though to say, "What should I sign?" and the man looked stricken. "Umm," he said, looking around.

"Here," I said, and handed him my book, the one about the father who turns into a lamp. "You can have this."

An old childhood instinct: to prevent a problem before it snagged on a thorn and began to drag, unspooling itself all over the room.

"Thanks," the man said. "Are you guys—"

"Maybe," Reid said, to a question that had not yet been asked.

If he was being forward, I didn't mind. Lay it on thick, I thought. Slather it on me.

I knew Reid's reputation: that he was the most charming man on the radio, that he slipped information out of celebrities like a pickpocket slipped money from a purse, even as those people thought they were being tight-lipped. And it was true what everyone said: His voice was lovely, even in person, without any sort of technology to enhance or modulate the tones.

It was not the low, smooth, syrupy voices of the radio DJs that came before him; but rather reedy and higher pitched, like the voice of a professor in some remote but sought-after field—linguistics or archaeology. Distinguished. How many times had I heard this voice? If I closed my eyes, I could be back in my father's truck. I could be somewhere else entirely. Outside of Reno, Nevada. With my brother. Creeping through the Haunted House that was rotten to its core.

Yes, it made me feel special to be charmed by this man, or for him to *attempt* to charm me. He saw something particular in me, something hidden. Maybe that something was only sexual, but that was something, nevertheless.

"Who shall I make it out to?" Reid asked the fan.

"Oh hey actually," the fan said, "can you sign my hat?" He handed my book back. "Sorry," he said. When he removed his hat, he, too, was bald, though he had a medical condition that left his head red and scaly. I looked away, to give his head privacy.

"See," he said to Reid, pointing to his own baldness. "I'm part of the club."

"That's what I'll write," Reid said, though he didn't pry his gaze away from me. "Part of the club. Your name?" he asked, still looking at me.

"Jay," the man said, and Reid repeated, "Jay." Did he feel a thrill hearing Reid say his name? Could he, too, close his eyes and pretend he was in his car or his childhood bedroom—anywhere else? Suddenly this man, this Jay, couldn't help but look at me too, as though he'd previously missed something significant about me, whatever it was that Reid saw. They were both staring at me while Reid gestured at the man for a pen. I pulled one from my purse.

"Thanks," the men said together.

On the other side of the bar, the group of people the man came with looked excitedly on. Was the woman in a matching baseball cap the man's girlfriend, or his wife? She smiled at me and gave a tiny quarter-moon wave. How strange, she must have been thinking, that this famous man is sitting at the bar with someone so ordinary. Or maybe, she was thinking, someone so young.

Maybe the woman was trying to place me—had she seen me in a movie or a TV show? I think I look like I could play a woman in a digestive yogurt commercial if they had hair and makeup on set, someone to make my lank hair look fuller, wind-blown. More likely, I'd be offstage, handing a yogurt to the woman in scene. That's what I looked like: a background actor who accidentally wandered into the foreground.

Often, I had the feeling that my life was somehow moving on without me, as though I had no say in it at all. I'd even recently took up jogging. I used an app on my phone called Couch to 5K that was supposed to train you how to go from sitting on your couch to running a 5K. Believe it or not, I was still in the couch phase of the process. Suddenly, on that Tuesday in that bar, I wanted to take control of my life. I wanted to make something happen. It was for this reason that when the fan walked away, I turned to Reid and said, "Should we meet here again tomorrow?"

"I work tomorrow," he said.

Of course! Tomorrow he'd be back on the radio, back to his normal life. We were merely having a brief encounter. This was not meant to extend. I felt so embarrassed the shame came to me as a bodily sensation: a hitch in my stomach.

Then Reid said, "How about the day after? But not a bar. To tell you the truth, I don't really drink."

"Of course," I said. I already knew he didn't drink. Only sparkling water, and never the flavored kind. There were so many things I already knew about him.

"Do you have a card?" he asked.

"A card?" Did people even carry cards around anymore? And even if they did, why would I have had one? What would it say? *I'm trying* embossed in smooth red lettering. *Can't you see that I'm trying?*

Instead, I ripped off a piece of the menu, with the hard, starchy good-quality paper restaurants like that used, the kind of restaurants with flattering, soft bathroom lighting, where influencers took photos of themselves in the mirror's golden light, a restaurant where Hollywood types took meetings, swiping at their cell phones in the high-backed booths, lying about their projects—it might just get made. The menu offered sixteen-dollar deviled eggs and whimsical drinks with names like the Blue Desperado. I lived thirty-five minutes away, in a studio apartment in the armpit of the valley, in a place called Van Nuys. I'd never laid eyes on the apartment before I'd arrived—I'd seen none of its boxy stucco glory.

"I'll take it," I'd told the landlord, a woman with a buzz cut who seemed forever in a rush.

"You've already paid," the landlord said. "You have no choice."

Now I took the scrap of paper and wrote my name and number down in the neatest lettering possible. It didn't look like my handwriting at all. It looked like the handwriting of someone organized and dependable.

"Last name?" Reid asked and I wrote that too.

"Jewish?" he said.

This question, in a small town outside of Reno, Nevada, would have made me nervous. But with him, I felt it might give me a leg up, or at the very least, make me seem familiar to him in a way I hadn't seemed before. We shared something—some secret, bubbling historic anxiety.

"Sort of," I said. "On one side." Enough to wreak a kind of havoc on the nervous system.

"I have to go," Reid said, looking at his blank wrist. I looked at it too, noticed his long fingers, his manicured nail beds. Pianist's hands. Though I'd read somewhere that "pianist's hands" was a myth—that actual pianists have gnarled hands, often large, with swollen knuckles from playing so much.

Still, I knew—Where had I heard it? From Reid himself?—that even though he just played piano for fun, that he was actually very good at it. In fact, he took piano so seriously he almost wrung the fun right out of it, like an old towel, practicing for hours every day. This is the problem with modernity maybe, you never know how you know things.

"I wish I could pay for your drink," he said, "but I didn't bring my wallet." He'd walked into the bar with no wallet, no plans. Was this what it was like to be rich and famous? Wandering and restless? Loitering in bars and chatting women up?

"That's fine," I said, clinking the ice in my now-empty glass. "I already paid."

"What did you drink?"

"An old-fashioned." My father's drink. Though he just as often ordered a piña colada or a strawberry daiquiri, a man filled to the brim with contradictions.

Reid leaned forward and plucked the cherry out of my drink, holding the stem gingerly between two fingers, jiggling it slightly to let the residual whiskey drip off. It was a strange gesture, compelling in its complete and utter lack of sexiness.

"May I?" he said, and ate the cherry before I could respond, tucking the stem into his front pocket.

I watched as Reid moved through the arched doorway—he was very compact, almost a whole head shorter than me—and thought about calling my father.

"Atta girl," he might've said, as though it were an accomplishment to be able to attract men, to carry on a conversation with one I wasn't related to. But he wouldn't have really meant it that way, more like, Atta girl, letting your life unfurl so far away from your mom and me, whatever that life had become. And anyway, this wasn't just any man—it was a man my father would've liked to attract, though not in a sexual way.

My life seemed to bewilder my dad, not just because of its bookishness, but also the way it seemed to have paused suddenly, at least my writing-life, stunned like a snake in the sun, or an opossum frozen with fear, having narrowly missed being run over by a car. I had started over in a new city for this very reason: to use phrases like "I'm starting over." Sometimes all you needed was a phrase to repeat aloud, one you might speak into existence.

"You were such a smart kid," he'd recently said. "All those books. Notebooks you'd fill and fill. We thought you were the smartest kid we'd ever seen. Je-sus Christ," he said, "even your brother thought so."

*   *   *

The only book other than the *Guinness World Records* I'd ever seen my father read was Reid Steinman's autobiography. He never read novels, though he could recite whole scenes of movies by heart, and not just *The Godfather* either, but romantic comedies too. Show business impressed him, in the broadest sense of the phrase. You could hear the exclamation point in his voice: Showbiz! Surely this had influenced my brother, who had become a stand-up comedian.

Reid wasn't just a famous person, he was a man my father admired more than his own long-dead father, who died when he was only two years old, and about whom he knew almost nothing, always invoking his memory in a reverent whisper.

"I bet he'd be so happy to know you're out in LA. Starting over," he'd said.

The fact that I'd never met the man was beside the point. My father's gods were my own.

7.

A week passed before Reid called me. When I heard his voice, my heart banged in terror. Romance can feel so much like a scary movie.

"Are you happy I called?" he asked.

I felt elated. "I'm not unhappy."

I was out to drinks with some of the other adjuncts at the junior college. She goes to a lot of bars, I could picture him thinking. This was a tiki place in Glendale, with fake birds hanging from the ceiling, carved statues in every corner, charming in its clutter and too-muchness. I walked outside to take the call. I'd worried it would be my father, calling on a strange line, which he sometimes did, after his phone had fallen in the gutter or down a slat in a wooden floor, and he'd ask to borrow some strange woman's phone. Now I allowed myself to feel relief.

"How was your day?" Reid asked.

"Just grand," I said. I wished I had a lie at my disposal—a funny story, an odd fact. "I taught Shakespeare." I didn't. I taught an author he'd probably never heard of, someone relatively little known, whose three books I loved ruthlessly, defiantly. It was a mistake to teach words so familiar to me, so beloved.

"Did they like it?"

"Who doesn't," I said, "it's Shakespeare." The class was a failure, mostly. The students didn't get it, weren't that interested. "I'm out with my coworkers," I said. "Are you still at work?" It felt presumptuous to say "the studio" or "on the radio" or any other indicator that might reveal how much

I knew—how much I thought about him there, talking into a microphone. I was still trying to pick apart the radio version from the real version.

My brother had explained this: it's called a persona.

At the beginning of his stand-up career, he'd used the nickname Little J. He'd ditched it as soon as he left home, but that's how our hometown still referred to him: Little J. His jokes were bad at first, I remember that. Crass, hacky. He never talked about himself, not anything truthful anyway. He talked about dicks and tits and vaginas. (No wonder he, too, also loved Reid!) It would take years before he mastered the alchemy, before he could pluck the thorns out of his side and plunge them into yours. But even in the beginning, even though the jokes were bad, you could tell he had something. Stage presence, is the phrase.

People only called him Little J because he was very tall. That made it funny, I guess, a lanky guy being called little. It was as simple as that, sometimes. People liked being misdirected. They liked being in on the joke.

I, too, had personas. I had a teaching persona, and a book club persona, and a daughter persona, and surely there were others.

I thought I knew Reid's on-air persona well. At one point in my life, I listened to him on the radio every day. But that was in the before-time, when so many things were different.

"Just calling to make sure we're still on for tomorrow," Reid said. "For our first date." We hadn't had a date planned, but I felt like I'd rather jump in front of a car than say so.

"Can't wait," I said, surprised at having said something so true.

October was coming. I could taste the tang of autumn under the air. I disagreed with what so many people said about the weather in LA, that it was monotonous and unchanging. Even that night, I could feel all the haunted October possibilities in the wind, in the bonfire smell of the city.

"I'll pick you up tomorrow," Reid was saying on the phone. Inside the bar, Otis Redding begged for a little tenderness.

"From my apartment?" I asked. What I meant was, from Van Nuys?

"Where else?" He laughed. It was the same laugh I'd heard so many times on the radio. It was shock to hear it directed at me (at me!).

"And anyway, I won't be driving."

I thought for a second that he had a self-driving car, some invention I'd never heard of. But no, of course, he had a driver.

Another adjunct ambled out of the bar and pointed to the phone at my ear and mouthed "Important?" and I nodded.

I'd slept with this man a few weeks ago, a man called Christopher (not Chris), in his small studio apartment that looked almost identical to mine except for the paintings hung up everywhere, so many in so many different shapes and sizes I could barely see any wall.

He taught art history and studio art. Now he mimed plugging his ears in an exaggerated way, like I was afraid he might try to listen.

When we slept together, I hadn't been with anyone for what felt like a long time and everything I did seemed to make him grateful, amazed.

"Geez," he'd said, when I put my mouth on him, "Lord, geez." Afterward, he said I'd made him grow a hundred feet tall.

I'd gone about the sex voraciously, like an athlete, a little feral even, moving with the intensity of a woman being chased. On top, I could see my own reflection in the iPad on his bedside table, and I'll just say this: I didn't love what I saw. In the reflection, I was grimacing.

Still, I'd just been happy not to be at my own apartment, with no art and no framed photographs, just one wallet-sized photo of my brother I kept in a drawer: when he was a toddler, clutching a gigantic prawn in his hand, a buffet stretched long behind him.

After Chris and I had finished, he wanted to talk about the people we worked with, our boss, our students. He wanted to tell me the story of his life.

"I'm not—" I'd begun. "I'm not looking for anything serious."

"Someone important?" Chris asked now, after I hung up.

"Nobody good," I lied. "Just my mom calling."

Chris often talked about his three sisters, his parents too, told breezy stories about them all. They went on cruises and had weddings in which he was his sister's maid of honor.

"Even though you're a boy," I'd said, the night we slept together.

"Yes," he said. "Even though I'm a boy." We lay beneath the ceiling fan, which continued its steady whirring as though we weren't even there.

"You can't be a maid of honor if you're a boy." I'd said it a little meanly— I knew I had.

"I can and I was," he said, though he still sounded cheerful. "The bride can have whatever she wants."

"She can say she wants something," I said, "but you still weren't a maid of honor." He'd been spooning me from behind and now he uncurled himself and lay flat on his back. I'd wanted to be difficult, maybe even injurious, but instead I'd come off as weirdly close-minded, like I was addicted to fringe talk radio.

"I guess you can call it whatever you want," I said.

"We're just close," he said. "So she wanted me up there with her." His sister was a speech pathologist who taught babies the correct way to hold their little tongues when it didn't come naturally to them. He talked about her—about his whole family—the way people did when there had been few tragedies. He was very proud of his mother, a doctor, and brought her up often, right out of thin air. "She'd love this bar," he'd said, only moments ago.

He'd unturned a kernel of meanness in me, like there was some bubble inside of him I longed to burst, with his dopey paintings all over the walls, and his sister's destination wedding in Tulum.

Everything about me seemed to make him work harder—every mean thing I said made him more determined to win me over.

So your family isn't so perfect, is what I had thought. Someone made you like this: made you reach for a hand in mid-recoil.

Now he offered to walk me to my car. At another time in my life, he would've been the right kind of person for me. Or rather, in a different life, if I had a different life to live. I could picture a different life, like a tiny photograph held in a locket around my neck: I would be with someone soothing, easy.

I would be with someone who took care of me in a way I never took care of myself. Sometimes I missed out on basic survival necessities. Drinking water, for instance. I was always in varying stages of dehydration, forever lightheaded. Why had my parents not instilled these in me? And when would I stop blaming them?!

"My car's so close," I told Chris, "you'll be able to see me get in from here."

8.

If I'd inherited a quarter of my father's difficultness, my brother had inherited the other three-fourths. Jack hated everything my father loved, or so he pretended. (My father loved bacon, and so my brother only ate pork in secret, like our Jewish grandparents.)

I didn't know then what I know now: your personality is a direct result of your parents, whether you're copying them or opposing them, it's all on the same demented bell curve.

I was fifteen when my brother left Reno—not for college, but for Las Vegas, though the plan had always been for that to be a brief stopover before he made it to Los Angeles or New York, the shining beacons of show business. He'd wanted to be a comedian before he'd known it was an occupation (there were other photos of him at five years old, standing on tables, speaking into a flashlight or a banana) and he was sure he needed to leave Reno to do it, out from under the long shadow of our father, the hugeness of his personality, the volume of his fits.

Everyone in town knew our father, had a nickname for him also: Joe Man, the Joe Joe, that kind of thing. My grandparents had also grown up there, outside of Reno, and so my dad was a fixture in the town—its residents felt possessive of him. The fact that my father could inspire such intimacy in everyone he met was one of his best qualities. The thin and flimsy dime on which his mood could suddenly turn: that was by far the worst.

*   *   *

My father loved playing sports and therefore, my brother refused. He liked watching, he said, but he wouldn't play.

I played sports to appease them both.

I remember being at a Little League baseball game, when I was up to bat, turning to my father on the sidelines, and pretending to use the bat as a cane, to make my father laugh, like a tiny baseball-playing Charlie Chaplin. The Problem had been in a bad mood that morning, having agreed to coach, only to find out that he'd be coaching with two other men, who were already holding clipboards. My father was to be the assistant coach, an unthinkable demotion.

Our father had always been easily intimidated by other men, and much preferred the company of women. Other men made him feel threatened, nervous. Was it because he'd had no father? No practice talking to other men? Maybe. Whatever his reticence around men was, it had something to do with my brother's problems—the way my brother grew quickly angry when he felt he wasn't being heard, the way he talked over men he felt were trying to demonstrate a version of machismo with which he didn't agree. He just wanted our father to understand him. He just wanted our father to listen!

"Face the ball," another coach yelled to me that day, getting more and more frustrated. "Goddamn it," the coach said, "stop acting stupid." Weirdly, I remembered thinking: Wasn't this anger normally reserved for boys?

My brother was in the stands, and he rushed to the field then. "Stop," he shouted. "Fucking stop." At that moment, I thought he was jealous of me: jealous of making our father laugh, of my Charlie Chaplin impression. I imagined we had the same, small pettiness. I did not realize he was coming to my defense.

"Fuck you," he said, to the coaches. "Fuck you. Never talk to her like that. Never." He overturned the hot dog machine. He swiped the sodas off the table with one long arm. It didn't matter that his anger was so out of proportion with the stimulus. His anger was righteous. Even my father agreed.

That night, it was easier between them, warmer: my father read the book of *Guinness World Records* out loud and my brother didn't leave the room as usual, but instead hovered by the door, saying, "Just how many gumballs?" They talked about what records they might be able to beat. It had been one of their few, shared dreams. I never played softball again.

For a long time after my brother left home, I thought I was the only person who knew the truth of his life, his stormy insides. Yes, I was naive, and yes, what I did know of the world, I knew only from books, which I didn't read exactly, but consumed in stacks, like a boa constrictor, but still, I felt my brother could trust me. I assumed he did.

I assumed he was telling me everything.

In those early years, his successes—as meager as they were—he saved for our father, and for our mother, he saved only the statistics of his existence: what he ate for breakfast, what time he went to sleep, if he was wearing sunscreen at the hotel pool where he worked as a lifeguard, watching people drink their cheap beers and tall frosted margaritas glittering with salt and shots of whiskey—Cheers! Cheers again!—where they would kiss and vomit and kiss some more. Though our mother probably didn't know about the last part.

I thought I knew the way his life wore him down—the myriad of failures and indignities, did Jack even tell his friends? Did he even have friends? Real friends? Or only peers, other stand-up comedians, whom he admired and hated in equal measure. His envy, it seemed to me, must seep out of his pores. He hated the booker who'd ignored him the night before, and another comic who was a hack but somehow got spots in every club in Vegas, and the audience who didn't laugh, and this stupid city and this stupid life in which he'd somehow found himself. Sometimes he'd call once a month, if things were going well, and if they weren't, he'd call every day, when he knew I was walking home from school, before I arrived at our parents' door. He'd call when he had me all to himself.

The quickest way to hate something is to dedicate your life to it, he'd said, though he'd often say the opposite, that most men led lives of quiet desperation, and to ignore the small voice inside of you that whispered your purest desire—to let it go unanswered—was a fate worse than death. It was a fate of two snot-nosed kids and an impatient wife at home tapping her foot on the linoleum floor and a beer gut and a mortgage and an all-day, everyday existential crisis; though would I have known what "existential crisis" meant at the time? Maybe I'd read it in a book. It didn't matter; I always let him ramble as if that was my job: to be a container for the frothy anger, which was also exciting, to hear of everything that existed only hours away from the one-story ranch house where we'd grown up (in which I was still growing up), only a mile away from the Haunted House, even if what was out there "sucked shit half the time."

Unless.

Unless of course he had a good set in front of a booker he wanted to impress, at the Laugh Factory inside of the Tropicana let's say, or opening for someone famous, like the doofy brother from a sitcom on CBS who'd stopped in Vegas during a tour. Then suddenly Jack's talent was an ever-expanding balloon, the city not large enough to hold it. He might not even be large enough to hold it, on the verge of exploding, his talent explosive, scary even—"it was scary how funny I was"—how everything out of his mouth had been flammable, the crowd's laughter the match.

You should've seen me, he'd tell me on the phone, and though I couldn't see him imitating the audience, I could picture it, their mouths open like corn-husk dolls, shaking in hysterics, gasping for breath, as though the laughter was being pried from them without their control.

As it turned out, I didn't know all that much about his life. I knew a little. Maybe I knew more than most. But he had a brother persona, too—he was telling me a brotherly version.

Now, I still keep one of his baseball caps he always wore onstage in my car's glove compartment. Sometimes, I still reach for it at a stoplight to sniff the inside, see if I can find a trace of the familiar doughy smell of his sweat. It doesn't smell like anything anymore, only like old hat, but it still calms me down. What can I say: I've always been susceptible to placebos.

9.

It was the night of my date with Reid Steinman and still, I hadn't spoken to The Problem. I was sure he would've called me by now. Instead, pacing my one room in Van Nuys, I called my mother.

Raj, my mother's boyfriend, answered her cell phone on the first ring. My mother still had a landline, though I never called it. "It's so the telemarketers know I haven't died," she said.

Raj had a thick accent and gave the impression of always having just finished laughing about something that happened in another room. I liked Raj. When he spoke of his childhood in Pune, India, he talked only about the food his mother cooked and the trees he and his many cousins climbed, where they could see so much of the city below, linty and opaque beneath the smog. For him, all his childhood memories were fond. At least those were the memories he shared.

"Raj has been through things," my mother said. "He has been through things and survived." Now, he told me I sounded well and immediately handed the phone off to my mother. The best thing about him: he never spoke when he had nothing to say. "Not true of most men," my mother said.

"Have you called your father?" she said, by way of greeting. "He says you haven't."

"Then why did you ask?"

"He loves you," she said, as though this was ever up for debate.

Now, when the doorbell rang, I knew my mother wouldn't believe me when I said, "I have to go, I have a date," but I said it anyway.

"Hear that?" my mother said, probably to an empty room. "She's the busiest girl in Los Angeles."

At the front door, stood a small, smiling woman wearing a hooded sweatshirt and incongruous diamond earrings, long enough to reach just above her shoulders.

"Allison?" the woman said.

"That's me," I said.

The woman gestured toward the car, but not to a seat exactly.

"Do I sit in the front?" I said.

"That's okay," she said, like I'd offered it as a favor. "You can sit in the back."

I wanted to say: Tell me how this works.

Her name was Kelly, and she'd been Reid's longtime driver. I knew he'd mentioned her on the show before—my driver, Kelly!—though I realize now I'd been picturing someone else, someone more glamorous-looking.

"Allison's a pretty name," the driver said. "I used to date an Allison."

"Oh yeah? I hope she didn't sour you on all Allisons altogether."

"Quite the opposite. We're still in touch." She turned the music up, a classical station. "Beethoven," she said, before the DJ did. "You know what else? That Allison married another Allison. Imagine saying your own name for the rest of your life."

Surely, I thought, they used private nicknames, shreds of unguessable intimacy. Wasn't that the point of love: to develop a secret language—a set of passwords only the two of you understood?

"Have you heard the Elvis Costello song?" the driver asked. She searched for it on her phone, and I prayed for my life while she swerved. I clutched the door handle until my knuckles turned pale. And then, turning it up, she sang along, ALLISSOOOON. "I love this song," she said. "It still gets up and goes to work."

Of course I'd heard the song.

More family lore: I was named after the song. It had been my father's choice. When my mother was red-faced and panting, having just given birth, she nodded along to her husband's wishes, or maybe to the song itself, which my father had been singing in a low voice as my mother pushed me out of herself and into the world. Did my dad have some relationship to the song before then, or to Elvis Costello? Was it his favorite song? Did he always plan to name a daughter after it?

No, he'd said, laughing, when I was old enough to ask. It just happened to be on the radio that day in the truck. But now, I wondered, how could that be true, when he only ever listened to Reid. A commercial break, maybe. Or perhaps the song Reid himself had chosen as he got up to use the restroom during the show, which he sometimes did. Maybe it was Reid all along—it was he who had named me.

The drive was quick, by LA standards, meaning it was under twenty minutes. We smoothed up to a curb in a suburban neighborhood I'd never seen before. I'd never even bothered to ask where we were going, a thought that would horrify me, if this was the story of someone else's life.

You didn't even ask?! I would've shouted playfully at a student.

Often, the younger students told me elaborate stories about their wild weekends to get a rise out of me, to make me react. I gave them what they wanted. Please be careful! I said. You're important! I said. You have exactly one life to live! Maybe all that lecturing was just me talking to myself.

Reid was standing in front of an indistinct-looking apartment building, already waiting for me.

"Does he live here?" I asked the driver.

"No, no," Kelly said. "Of course not! His place is beautiful. This is just where he wanted to meet." I got out, and she pulled away before I could ask any more questions. Seeing Reid, I realized I'd overdressed. I was in heels, a tight jacket. I looked like I might be on my way to a job interview, or to ask a panel of scientists a series of complicated questions. Meanwhile he dressed for a jog or a stroll, wearing those large white sneakers, the kind that professional basketball players wear. They looked new and very shiny, which might have been dorky and embarrassing on another middle-aged white guy, but not on him. He looked—not overly cautious, but like someone who moved through the world with intention.

"Welcome to beautiful Studio City," he said. Evening was settling over the neighborhood—all that harmless, diffuse streetlight softening the world.

"I didn't know—" I began. "I didn't know what we were doing." I gestured down at my shoes, and then at the sidewalk, the neighborhood—the strangeness of it all.

"Well," he said, "I remembered you lived in Van Nuys. And it turns out my favorite ice cream shop in the whole greater Los Angeles area is located in Studio City, and I thought..." He trailed off here. What had he thought?

"Okay," I said. "Is it a long walk?"

"Not too long," he said, but he looked unsure.

The attraction I felt for him at the moment surprised me. I'd said "I love you" to one and a half men (one I only started: "I love" but never finished the sentence; had never said "you") and I was definitely attracted to them, but not like this. Anyone I'd been with before: they were my peers, my equals—around my age. Some were better-looking than me and others much worse. But before now, I'd never felt like I'd *won* something.

Plus, I was moved by his uncertainty, this man who has made a living evaluating women's breasts on the radio, telling them who would benefit from "big fake knockers," and who lucked out in the genetic lottery—the arbiter of all things titillating and disgusting and taboo. He was a shock jock, yes, but the most shocking part was this: the softness of his palm as he took my hand, the gentleness of his tug in the direction he wanted me to go.

"Okay," I said, "okay," and I began the tottering high-heeled walk beside him.

"Tell me about your apartment," he said, "is your neighborhood like this?"

"No," I said. "It isn't like this at all." My apartment building was in a constant state of disrepair. The whole neighborhood looked like it was run by fraternity brothers who had no access to their parents' money.

Here were tidy family homes, modest-looking, but probably upward of a million dollars. (I didn't know a lot, but I knew what I would never in my life afford.) The people who lived in this neighborhood were probably movie execs and lawyers, doctors and accountants. When was the last time Reid had even been in a grocery store, bought a gallon of milk? Probably he had no idea what anything cost, how normal people lived. And before he became rich and famous, he had a wife, a woman about whom it was difficult to find nearly any information online. I only knew he met her his freshman year, at the University of Washington, when he worked at the college radio station and it was her job to sort and shelve the records. I knew this woman was by his side as he built his career one dirty joke at a time, like filthy logs in a disgusting cabin that horrified Christian mothers everywhere. I knew Reid and his ex-wife divorced quietly nearly fifteen years ago. Apparently, he paid this woman exorbitant amounts of money.

"My neighborhood's a lot crappier than this," I said, "but there is a pool at my complex." I could picture it now: dirtied with leaves and sticks and a few red plastic cups from some long-ago party. I'd never seen anyone use it.

"I lived in a shitty apartment once," Reid said. "When my ex-wife and I were first married. It's not far from here actually." We were walking at a brisk rate; I was almost breathless. I thought about wiping my damp palms against my pant legs. Instead, I kind of wiggled them around in the air, like someone signaling the phrase "so-so." "I kind of want to show you my old apartment," he said.

So that was why the driver brought me to this neighborhood. That's why I was here.

"I think the place must be condemned by now," he said. "Black mold. Roaches. Even then." When he looked at my face to see his comment land, I was reminded of just how much taller I was. I figured he must be about five foot seven, though when you looked him up online, the internet claimed he was five foot nine. Had he lied about his height or simply been misrepresented?

The world is filled with people who have the wrong impression of you, was my father's favorite line. Or maybe that was from Reid's book—a thing he said about himself—something my father stole.

You don't have to do this, I wanted to tell Reid. You don't have to convince me you once lived like me. How could I explain it to him: I did not want to be reminded of my own life. I wanted to be in someone else's life. I wanted to be the kind of woman I sometimes saw in LA from afar, through a coffee shop window or in a passing car, laughing with a friend or into a phone, carefree.

We were walking down a steeper sidewalk now, and I had to lean against him to keep my balance. He slowed down, matching my pace. I was trotting a little, like an idiotic horse.

"There," he said. "There it is." And so we'd arrived: a condemned two-story apartment building, decrepit and crumbling behind its yellow tape. It looked like an old shoe, peeling at the sole, unwearable. How many women had he taken to view the before image of his life? I was not impressed by the shorn-off poverty. Show me the money, I thought. Show me the money!!!!

"I took my daughter to see it too," he said. "She couldn't believe I once lived like this."

I knew even less about his daughter than I knew about his ex-wife. Online, I'd learned she also went to the University of Washington, where she rowed crew. Also, I knew her name: Emma. Reid suddenly placed a hand on my shoulder.

"Hear that?" he said.

"What?"

"A sparrow." He pointed to a treetop in front of a rickety-looking Victorian house. "Sorry," he said. "I like that kind of thing. Nature."

I thought of my father, who also liked that kind of thing, animals moving at their own paces and rhythms and internal rules, uncaring of what the mess of humanity was up to. He'd sometimes pull his truck over to take a blurry photo of the stars, send it to me after I hadn't heard from him in weeks. "Are you seeing this?" he'd write.

"Kids sound stressful," I said, trying to nudge the conversation toward him, toward the facts of his life I wouldn't know from the radio.

"Do you have any?" he asked. "Kids."

"Oh," I said, surprised. "I'm only twenty-eight," as though that explained it. But I knew plenty of people had kids at my age. Some of my students. And of course, my parents had had my brother. Jack was already a fully upright human then, captured on videos I no longer watch, performing into Coke cans and half-peeled bananas.

"Twenty-eight," Reid repeated. Hearing my age spoken aloud seemed to quicken his pace. What did twenty-eight mean to him?

"A good age," he said, as though hearing my thoughts. "You're still at the beginning of things." Then, "Ah-hah!" He gestured to where he'd been leading me—to a local ice cream place. "They have the best cones in the city," he said. "Or at least in the Valley." The smell of waffle cones was, in fact, drifting through the air.

It was dark—quiet, suburban dark—and we sat quietly beside each other on a bench and ate our ice cream: chocolate for us both. At the table next to us, a small child explained an animated movie to his mother in great detail.

I hadn't wanted a cone, just a cup, which seemed to disappoint him. I understood immediately: he was not the kind of man who people liked disappointing. I was not immune to men like that. What women were?

My father was a man like that—I hated to disappoint him. On my eighteenth birthday, my best friend, Marcella, and I decided we'd go to Mexico, where we could drink margaritas at a bar with other eighteen-year-olds and buy tiny wooden turtles with bobbing heads. We had our backpacks on that morning, we'd saved up for months, when The Problem appeared at the door, saying he had other plans for us. He'd rented a small motorboat—he wanted to zoom around Lake Tahoe with his daughter beside him, the wind in our hair, a seam of ocean zipping open behind us.

I got terribly seasick; I'd always had. He didn't remember that, or maybe he'd never bothered to learn. Maybe he didn't care—though I don't think that's quite right. At least, he thought he cared. He wanted to care.

"Aren't we having fun?" my father said, having to shout over the wind.

I was nauseous and pale and trembling the entire time.

"We are," I said, "we are."

For a long time after, he said it was one of the best days of his life, before my brother was no longer alive and even the best days were difficult to remember.

* * *

"What?" Reid said now.

"What?" I repeated.

"Oh," he said. "Your mouth was moving. I thought you were saying something."

He was looking at me curiously and I said, "I wasn't. Saying anything." I didn't like being watched unexpectedly. Lately I kept seeing my reflection in the mirror and being surprised by what I saw.

I thought I'd like to tell him something about my father or brother just then, or even my mother, or Marcella, or the town outside of Reno where I'd been put together, but instead, I looked back down at the ice cream, cold in my palms, and said, "I don't even like chocolate."

He laughed. "Why did you order it?"

"Because *you* did," I said. "I was trying to make it easier on the girl behind the counter." The girl behind the counter could have been my student—looked like one, wore the same kind of thing, stared at her phone as she waited for us to decide what to order, looking preoccupied in the same kind of way. The girl obviously didn't recognize who Reid was, didn't know he was anyone other than a middle-aged bald man with a woman who was young enough to be his daughter, who maybe was his daughter, and I wondered if younger people were a gift to Reid for that reason: they rarely recognized him. His fans were an older generation. Even I was a bit too young, having inherited the fandom.

"What flavor do you like then?" he asked.

"I'm not really an ice cream person." I felt too tired to lie. Maybe it wasn't bravery, my being honest with Reid, but exhaustion.

"Well why didn't you say something?"

"I didn't—" I began. I hadn't known I'd had a choice. "It's good though," I said.

There was a small slot of space between us and occasionally our elbows knocked together while we ate. He finished his ice cream very quickly and made a small, satisfied noise.

"Sorry," he said. "I always eat very fast. I have ever since I was a kid."

I wanted to ask something specific about his childhood, but I worried I'd sound like I was interviewing him—like I was a journalist, or a student doing a project. I had not been a student that long ago. After all, that was the only source of power I had, the only way I could one-up him: my youth.

"Do you have siblings?" I decided on.

"One," he said. "A brother." I knew this of course. The brother had even called in a few times to the radio show. They seemed oddly formal with each other. Maybe that was what fame did: made you unfamiliar to people who once knew you best.

He didn't offer more so I didn't press.

"He's a good guy," he said finally. "Works in finance. A confusing job I can never understand." He was looking for something in the night sky a little beyond me. A friend of mine, who works very high up in a company that makes exercise clothes, once told me that all powerful men have one thing in common: they are always a little distracted. "He lives in Boca Raton," Reid said finally. And then, "There it is. Venus."

He pointed toward a glowing pinpoint in the night sky and I scooted a little closer, so I could follow his eyeline. I could feel the heat of his breath on my cheek. I set down the cup of melting ice cream.

"Do you?" he said very softly.

"Do I what?"

"Do you have any siblings?"

"No," I said. "I'm an only child." I felt surprised, how quickly I said it.

When he turned toward me then the gap between our lips was almost nonexistent—as slim as the stack of papers at home I still needed to grade. I refused to use the online portal the junior college begged me to adopt, and I almost said that aloud: I don't understand the portal. I like doing it by hand.

He kissed me softly, politely at first. Then he kissed me again, still politely, and then again, less politely, and again and again, so that it was a kiss with no middle, just a very long beginning, and then suddenly, when we parted, a very distinct end. I'd forgotten that when you first kissed a person there was a kind of shock, an unlocking that never happened again. With him, I felt more shocked than usual.

"I wonder what you do like," he said, afterward. "If you don't like ice cream."

10.

At night, in my studio apartment, I tugged at the thread that ended with my brother's last day and started with— What? That was the problem; I could never find the beginning. Maybe there was no beginning.

I thrashed against the sheets, which had become suddenly coarse-feeling. Outside, all the nighttime neighborhood noises: screeching tires, signaling someone's escape. A teenager's skateboard banging repeatedly against the curb—an attempt to master a trick. I loved this noise best, the optimistic sound of someone's repeated trying.

Often, I'll start with the summer I first kissed a boy, the summer after seventh grade, which was also the summer Jack turned sixteen. Now, I'd call it the Summer My Brother Paced the House Like It Were a Cage, but that is just what loss does: It makes you give past summers a name.

Yes, in retrospect, I believe my brother was extra restless, though every teenager in my town was restless, waiting. What was there for teenagers to do in a town like that other than to wait: to wait for school to get out, for your shift at the casino to end, for your sneakers to wear out so you could buy new ones, for the weather to turn a little bit cooler, a little bit less hostile, for your parents to divorce, for your parents to get back together, for your parents to recognize the unhappiness in you and do something about it!

So much of my brother's time waiting was spent on a motor scooter he had purchased off a meth head in the parking lot of Walmart. He liked to zip around town with a gang of boys who all had given themselves non-sense nicknames: Charlie-Horse (real name: Derek), and Slide-Rule, and Lance, and Cougar. Probably, this was when everyone started calling Jack Little J, though he hadn't liked it at first. Once my father said it was a stupid name, demeaning somehow, then yes, yes, my brother liked it.

He was staying out of the house for longer and longer stretches of time, which wasn't that unusual in our town—or any town—for a sixteen-year-old boy: to want to be out of the house. Still, this coincided with my father's "projects," which had become more frequent.

The Projects:

At the start of the weekend, my father would gather us all into the wood-paneled living room for what he called "a family meeting" and then he'd offer us some options for what we might do. It usually went something like this:

A. Should we go over our finances?

This meant searching every crack in the couch and the easy chair and the space under the oven and fridge to find any loose change we might've dropped. Or, it might mean going through the cupboards and finding every boxed food item our mother had spent too much money on and eating it that night. Or it might mean upping our allowances, because weren't we great kids, his pride and joy, new chips off the old block?

B. Should we landscape the front yard?

This meant pulling the ugliest weeds up from the ground. Not all weeds, but some. Or, it meant leaving every weed and trying to plant more of them.

C. Should we just have fun?

This could mean anything from watching the movie *Casino* again, to buying an old piano wholesale and rigging up a pulley to get it inside, to hiking Mount Rose, to going in the backyard with a flashlight and telling ghost stories we made up on the spot.

Here's the thing: sometimes it *was* fun. But other times, especially when our answers upset him (we didn't want to search for loose change or watch *Casino* or get a piano from a man aptly called PianoMan) he became downright depressed. I have never known a man to cry more than my father, not then or since, and at that time, I hadn't known it was unusual—I thought all men were constantly on the verge of tears. I thought all men were innately delicate.

My father often accused me of being "prone to worry"—a phrase he used to describe my constant vigilance, a vigilance he claimed came from nowhere, sprouted up from the ground as though it were a mysterious stalk of corn, not born from the family unit itself, from The Problem specifically, whose emotional storms required someone to forecast what the weather looked like that day.

This restless summer, my brother was mostly gone, and my mother was at work, so I attended the family meetings alone. I often did what my father wanted. I felt I had no other choice.

This was also the summer my brother began to make jokes. I remember thinking he was funnier when he wasn't *trying* to be, but still, he had bits I liked, that I begged him to do, like when he pretended to be a weatherman forecasting the temperature that week. (Every day was the same and every week was the same: horrendously hot. But he said it all in a deadpan, pinched voice, and even my father laughed, even my father couldn't help himself.)

It was then Jack started talking about moving. He didn't want to be here anymore, in this town. He wanted to *do* something—do anything! No, not anything. He wanted to be funny on purpose. He wanted to be famous. And he knew he couldn't do it here. But where? Los Angeles? New York? Those were expensive, unimaginable. What about Vegas?

And I understood. Sometimes I wanted to *do* something—do anything!—and the heat in that town could confuse you, could spoil your intentions like tomatoes too long on the vine.

Hadn't I, only one year prior, etched *Mr. Constantellis Is a Gaylord* on the history teacher's desk with a boy's penknife when Mr. Constantellis was in the bathroom? I'd only done it because I'd been dared. I could've refused, but I wanted to seem brave, and I wanted to break up the monotonous chain of days. When Mr. Constantellis saw it, he'd simply said, "Great job stating the obvious," and then gave a quick lecture about destroying school property. I felt acutely ashamed. I wanted him to yell at me and tell me I was a little shit. So I stayed after class and apologized and he said, "Oh forget it, it's probably not your fault." Now I understand what he meant: It wasn't my fault, it was probably the town's. Or at the very least, my parents.

So I, too, had wanted out, into a life I created for myself, that would be livable for me and only me, but I still had more patience than my brother. And I had books: a creator of patience, an expander of time.

That summer, the summer after seventh grade, I'd fallen in with a group of evangelical Christian girls who had never paid any attention to me before. Suddenly, in the hallway between classes, one of these girls pulled from the depths of her locker a long, gaudy pink pen with a fur bonbon attached and offered it to me.

"Here," she said. "If that pen bleeds." She was pointing to the flimsy pen in my hand, which happened to be one of the pens that collected haphazardly on every surface in our house, with the words *Peppermill Casino* etched into the cheap plastic.

It was true, the pen did bleed.

And just like that, this girl (The main one? The leader?) seemed to signal to the others that they should approach, that I had passed some inscrutable test. How mysterious those years were! Girlhood! When it seemed as though even the wind could change the course of a friendship, start it or end it, cause its brushfire destruction.

The girls' names were biblical: Eve, Rachel, Rebecca, and though they had different interests (soccer, crafts, boys), they had one thing in common: their lord and savior Jesus Christ. Still, one had a trampoline and the others had a chicken coop and an aboveground pool—plenty to do in the high heat of a Nevada summer, in which heat seeped into everything. My own parents were rarely home during the week, and when they were, the house was crowded and stuffy and loud, and occasionally, frightening.

I think these girls viewed me—my lack of religion, my half-hearted bat mitzvah—with a mix of curiosity and pity. But what about Easter? And Santa? And, they seemed to be thinking, though it was never said aloud, What about hell?

They even took me to church. It was the largest in the area—forty minutes away, and had a kind of celebrity pastor, who wore his hair slicked back and sported several gold chains. I'd pictured a pastor at a pulpit, but instead, he was on a stage, speaking into a small microphone clipped to the lapel of his leather jacket. We sat so far away, we could only see his tiny face magnified on one of the church's giant screens.

"I invite Jesus into the boat of my life," he said. "I invite Jesus into my dilemmas, my decisions, my choices."

Later, I'd told this to my mother.

"Jesus seems pretty nosy," she said.

It was through these girls, with whom I played handball against Rachel's garage every day after school, that I learned my older brother had a reputation.

"What for?" I'd asked.

"For being crazy," Rachel had said, or maybe it was Rebecca—hard to know. Then, crazy could mean a lot of things: funny, outlandish, somebody who frequently got detention for talking too much, someone who loved to pull pranks as a teacher's back was turned. And he was funny. I'd thought that was his reputation. Of course, funny could mean something else too. But the word "crazy" fell plinking inside me like a coin at the bottom of a well.

"Crazy how?" I'd asked.

Rebecca, or maybe it was Rachel, looked regretfully at the other two, like she'd already said too much. "You know what," she said. "Never mind."

That night, I impersonated his weatherman bit, and they did laugh. Of course they did. I felt smug about that. Church couldn't save them from the long arm of comedy, of laughter. Probably it couldn't save them from anything at all.

Jack said as soon as he graduated he was moving to Las Vegas. I knew I wouldn't get much more time with him, so I watched him even more closely. I watched Jack and his friends on their motorbikes, sitting on the hoods of their broken-down cars, grappling like puppies do, cheerfully, stepping on the backs of each other's sneakers, or twisting each other's nipples through their shirts until they cried out in pain. I watched them elbow each other hard in the ribs when a woman walked by—attractive women always made them go silent.

Mostly, I watched my brother make his friends laugh. Yes, everyone laughed. His friends rolled theatrically off the hoods of their cars, laughing.

I watched him pilfer red Gatorades from the 7-Eleven after riding ATVs, charming the elderly woman behind the counter, asking after her granddaughter, did the baby still need the helmet to reshape her head? And it was kind of a cute helmet anyway, wasn't it? He might like a helmet to reshape *his* head.

I watched him when he thought no one was watching: slinking out after midnight to meet a girl at the Haunted House where the adult son had murdered his parents. Then, back at our door, as my brother and the girl had parted—said their prolonged goodbye—I'd turned away quickly, having seen more than I'd wanted. (Oh, how some things could never be unseen. And now, even those scenes had to be saved in one's mind, if not treasured.)

He was so often normal that summer. Or reasonable? Whatever word people used to distinguish that kind of thing. Now, I know those distinguishments mean little.

Regardless, when we were both home at the same time, and it was late enough that the heat turned flat, we played long hours of chess (he was much better than me), and watched baseball (which he liked to watch when my father wasn't around), and looked at celebrities in magazines. (He would sometimes say, "What if I met her in real life. Do you think she'd dig me?")

Yes, he'd punched a hole in the flimsy wall of our garage when his beloved Diamondbacks lost, but he apologized profusely, promised to buy drywall at the Home Depot and cover the hole himself. The fact that he never got around to it didn't mean he hadn't intended to, or that he wouldn't eventually. That was a core principle in my family: a good apology could save you. And, intention was most important. If you hadn't *meant* what you'd said, or what you'd done, well that's what mattered. Then you were forgiven. My family had come from a long line of apologizers, a long line of people with good intentions who sometimes didn't act quite *right*. We should've been Catholics, we were so into forgiveness. My father was a very good apologizer.

So yes, Jack had punched a hole in the wall of the garage (but that was perfectly normal for a boy sometimes!) and then, there was the business with the girl from the Haunted House. The girl's boyfriend coming to look for Jack (Jack hadn't known she'd had a boyfriend), threatening to do things to Jack that would prevent him from ever being with a woman again, if you were catching his drift, and Jack punching him once, very hard, square in the nose and making him concussed, a word I'd never heard until that moment. I hadn't even read it in a book.

The guy still has trouble with the order of the months.

A few other instances, too: a tire thrown through a 24 Hour Fitness window, an overturned breakfast table in the local café, syrup pooling on the floor. But he always had his reasons. *The awful thing about life is this, everyone has their reasons*—a line from a movie I've always liked.

I'm sorry, he would say. I'm sorry that happened.

Our parents yelled at him and threatened him and complained to him as though he were just the guard at the door of his own psyche, helpless.

"Ask yourself why you do these things," my mother often said. She and my father shouted at him and he apologized. They shouted at each other and he apologized again.

"I'm sorry," he said to me one night after a string of chess games in which I'd played particularly badly. "I'm sorry I'm fucked up."

"You're not," I said.

If I had asked my father if my brother seemed like he had a hair trigger, let's say, or an anger problem, or some other murky and unspecified issue, my father would've said, "Of course not." You can't see in other people what you can't see in yourself.

"He can be a pain in the ass," my father said. "But so was I."

And anyway, so much of this is in retrospect! In the thick grip of that summer, I know I thought mostly about myself. The days crawled by, and I had a new obsession to turn relentlessly over in my mind: kissing. I created imaginary scenarios in which boys in school were forced to confess whom they were in love with, and the answer was always me. (Me?! I'd picture myself saying, dainty hand pressed against my chest. Me?!?! Yes, they'd say, we can't help it. There's just something about you!) They'd tell me this in tree houses and in the backs of classrooms. They'd say it over the school's PA system. They'd even tell my brother, though they were always a little scared of his reaction.

At that time, the only people who ever told me I was attractive were friends of my mother, and that was mostly because I looked like her.

The culmination of my obsession came one week before school began, when I was expelled from the group of evangelical Christian girls, who'd referred to themselves all summer as The Chicks—some forgotten, inside joke about the girls chasing Rachel's chickens in and out of their coops.

I hadn't known I'd been banished until Monday at school when none of the girls would speak to me, or even glance in my direction.

The reason: I'd let one of the girls' cousins kiss me on the mouth at Rebecca's family barbecue—or Rachel's! Or Eve's! Who could say which girl!—the verdict delivered in a curtly written note dropped inside my locker.

It had been my first kiss: I'd let the cousin move his hand tenderly below the waistband of my shorts, only to rest it there, pulsing with fear, beneath the elastic. I'd wondered where the strange noise came from when we kissed. It turned out to be the sound of his jaw clicking—he must have ground his teeth at night. I'd love to ask him about that now. Now, I wear a night guard.

I'd felt unusually comfortable around him, this hunched boy with crooked teeth, probably because he'd been so reticent—he'd wanted me to take the lead. Even then, I knew that was a quality I should look for in a man: a little bit of fear. And anyway, this is how I knew a man liked you, because you made him a little bit scared.

Yes, the girls had found out I'd sullied the cousin, or been sullied, or we'd sullied each other. Or maybe that was only a ruse, and they'd actually decided there was just something about me that didn't sit quite *right*. I'd accepted that this was the girls' way—they were missionary types, finding a hapless, lonely-seeming girl in the hallway where they might set up friendship camp for a while before moving on to the next one. After me, they chose a foreign exchange student named Yvonne, which suited them perfectly—next semester, she'd be returning home.

(How worried I'd been about those girls, about wandering the hallways alone. And, how worried I'd been about making out! When I could do it next, and with whom.

This, one of my students once said, is the gist of all classic literature— Shakespeare and *The Great Gatsby* and *The Catcher in the Rye*. It was all about someone who was really, really horny.)

A year later, Jack's reputation had already morphed into something new: a kind of mythic popularity. He was a senior, and mostly kind to everyone, unless they deserved unkindness. He had a firm sense of justice, and enough social generosity that it cost him nothing to spend. The fact that I was related to him—that he was my brother—moved me up a rung on the ladder of coolness without me even trying, or having to prove anything at all.

I chose my own friends then. I kissed more people.

11.

Back in my barren office at the Glendale Community College, my student Julie apologized for canceling our meeting. I might've said: I can't thank you enough. I might've said: If you had shown up, I would've never gone to that bar on a whim, choosing it only because there was a metered parking spot directly in front of the door, a miracle in Silverlake. And, I'd only chosen Silverlake because it was on my list of places in LA I hadn't yet been and needed to visit. I planned to have a drink in every region of Los Angeles.

I had never before been a keeper of to-do lists, but I'd been trying to turn over a new leaf—I'd been perpetually trying to turn one over. If it hadn't been for you, I might've said to the eighteen-year-old sitting across from me, I never would've met *him*. He was always in italics now, the word like a shudder moving through me.

"Why are you telling me this?" Julie might've said. Or, "Good for you, I guess."

But I didn't tell her any of this, and Julie said, "Family shit came up," and waved a manicured hand through the air. Her nails were long and painted black, filed to sharp points at the ends, like talons. I knew only the basics about her: she took care of her younger siblings, she loved to read, and she had a nerdy-looking boyfriend who waited for her outside of class every day, kissing her tenderly and deeply every time, as though she'd just returned from war.

She was already a writer. She had what all writers required: a funny, strange way of seeing the world.

(Then, I was sure I knew what made some people successful and others not. The fact that I'd had no success was only proof: I hadn't worked hard enough. I'd gotten distracted. I'd been led astray.)

Julie was impatient with her life, where it was now. She just wanted to arrive wherever she was meant to go. She longed to have already arrived there. So many of my students were like this: like cars in rush hour, hurrying to get somewhere better than wherever they'd just been.

At least, that's what I took from the short story she turned in, which we were meeting to discuss. She could barely meet my gaze when I told her as plainly as possible: "You're a writer. The story—it's good. It's better than good."

The story was about a family of mice, grown large, towering over the neighborhood. But the story wasn't about the mice, it was about a girl across the street, watching the mice grow. "Nobody will believe this," the girl in the story thought to herself. "Nobody will believe what they haven't seen for themselves."

"Do you have a boyfriend?" Julie suddenly asked. The students often asked questions like this. While some weren't interested in books, they were all interested in me—in what my life looked like outside of the classroom, away from their purview. It was because I looked young, I thought. I was young! And because I did not act like a "professor." I was only adjunct, after all; I only acted like myself. When the students said something funny, I laughed, and when they said something rude, I yelled. I did not make myself immune to them. It is one of my assets.

Now I answered in the faux-cheeky way I always answered, "Wouldn't you like to know," but Julie said, "I have a brother. That's why I ask. He's cute. Or other people say he is. I wouldn't know, obviously. He's my brother. But he has his shit together. I know that."

"I didn't know you had a brother," I said. Did I seem that lonely to her? That incapable of attracting someone my own age? I should buy a new, more flattering bra, I thought. I should've put on mascara.

"Yeah," Julie said. "He just moved back home. To help with everything."

I cleared my throat in the way I imagined more professional, tenure-track professors might. "I'll keep that in mind," I said. "But for now, let's talk about revisions."

＊   ＊   ＊

By the time we finished, I felt flushed, as though I'd exerted myself—had run a long distance, let's say, or had sex up against a wall, quickly, in the way I imagined Reid and I might. I felt energized—euphoric even—from discussing writing with someone talented, someone still at the start. Trying to fix the story felt like attempting to build a raft together, plank by plank, while the boat floated down a rushing river, Julie even grabbing my wrist at one point, saying, Yes, yes that's exactly right, after I said, I think the story is about longing. (Aren't they all?)

Walking across the abandoned parking lot to my car, I felt so distracted by the remaining glow that I didn't check the caller ID when I answered my phone, surprised to hear The Problem on the other line.

"Whose daughter is this?" he said. "Surely it can't be mine. Surely."

"Don't call me Shirley," I said—his favorite joke. He liked to hear his favorite jokes repeated. I knew his moods by his voice; now it sounded strained, thin, like fabric coming apart—his feelings were hurt.

"You never call me," he said.

"You could call me," I said, though that wasn't the point; it never had been. Then I said, "I've wanted to call." This wasn't untrue, though who can say if he believed me.

"Liar," he said, and then laughed, like it was a private joke between us.

Once, after I'd lied about my grandfather being in the space program, a teacher suggested I see a child psychologist, though we didn't have the money for that, so it would've just been the public school guidance counselor, a weed-like middle-aged man named Steve we all called Straw on account of his whispery features. And anyway, our mother didn't like other people knowing our business, especially if you were sure to see that person again, walking the school hallways you also walked, or buying groceries at the Ralphs where you also shopped. Plus, my father didn't think there was anything wrong with me. She's creative, he'd said. So what if she lies. Who's it hurting.

My father had a different set of ethics, strongly held, and very specific. For instance, it was okay to steal if you needed (or wanted) something badly and the owner wouldn't miss it. This was especially true if the person you were stealing from was rich, or maybe not even a person at all, but a business or a corporation. And it was okay to lie if the lie was entertaining, made someone laugh, or both. It was also okay to tell the truth to an authority figure—a boss or a teacher, let's say—if you felt they needed to hear it.

"But what if I get in trouble?" I'd asked.

"Well you wouldn't be in trouble by me."

Ironic, then, that my father had so much trouble hearing the truth. That had been the last conversation we'd had—I'd been trying to tell him the truth about my brother, Jack, and he'd said over and over again, "I don't agree."

"With what I'm saying?" I'd asked.

"That it's the truth."

Now I said, "How are you?"

"Oh," he said, and his voice took on a different tone, a kind of singsong quality, "here and there, good and bad." In other words, he was hanging by a thread. "I've got a route through LA, so I'll stop and see you," he said, like I'd invited him.

My father had worked two jobs for as long as I could remember: he dealt cards at the Peppermill Casino and when he wasn't doing that, he drove a truck.

"Your mother says you've been feeling lonely," he said. My father does not wear a backward baseball cap. He wears a cowboy hat. He looks like a man who eats ribs with confidence. He would never ask for help.

"When are you coming?" I asked.

"Soon," he said.

"You can't give me a day?"

"Why?" he said. "You too busy?"

Again, I heard the reedy hurt in his voice and said, "I just want to set up a bed for you."

"Don't go to any trouble," he said. "You know me—I can sleep anywhere."

* * *

When I was growing up, he'd taken me on a long haul a handful of times. I remembered one trip specifically. It was only to Colorado, two states over, and I'd begged my mother to let me go.

I was ten. Eventually, she relented, but only because I had begged in the way my father always begged—relentlessly. In other words, I made it nearly impossible for my mother to say no.

We'd listened to Reid fill the car with opinions and interviews and women. Sometimes my father would smile crookedly when Reid featured a guest who'd done sex work, or had an affair with the governor of New York. These aren't girls like you, my father said.

We'd listened to the Beatles sing about heartbreak, and we drank milkshakes—thick and slow through the straw. We parked at the picturesque rest stops and watched nature move through the windows, all of it on its own time.

At night, in motels, my dad seemed to have a magical ability to find something on television I'd like, cartoons and kids' shows he'd never watch with me at home. That, alone, moved me in a particularly ten-year-old way. Watching the Rockies through the window, I'd known then that when I returned home, everything—my own town, my own life—would seem small.

And it had.

"So I'll see you next week?" I said, attempting to confirm.

"Can't say," he said. "Maybe." He might've meant that it depended on his route, but he also might've meant that it depended on his mood; regardless, it could not depend on me—on my schedule, on what I wanted. His only daughter, now his only kid; he needed me like a sailor needed a lighthouse: stationary. I was a beacon of safety, a symbol of home; even if once he reached me, he was baffled by what was inside.

12.

The third date was at a bowling alley, if you counted the bar where I met Reid as the first date, which I did. This time, I had the wherewithal to ask him how I should dress, and he said, "Sneakers are fine." Before I asked, I'd assumed we'd go somewhere fancy—velvet ropes and dark-suited security guards with gigantic arms—somewhere I wouldn't have access to without him. Now I wondered if a bowling alley was actually a good sign: he was trying to make me feel comfortable, to prove he was a man of the people.

I'd been surprised when there was nobody else in the entire alley, the entire place. Three times I said how strange that was—a Wednesday night and nobody else wanted to bowl!—until I realized he'd arranged it that way.

I was much better at bowling than he was. It was something my father loved to do—and I was good at most things my father loved.

It's called being enmeshed, my brother had said, after he moved away. "Making your needs everybody else's." (We rarely had conversations about my father, but when we did, my brother would adopt an aloof, ironic tone, like a doctor.)

When I threw a strike, Reid cheered for me and when I threw a gutter ball, he booed. At the end of the first game, he wore a bashful expression and said, "I'm terrible."

How few men are willing to admit they are terrible at things! On-air, he only talked about being bad at sex—he said his favorite position was fetal, that he just lay there the entire time, afraid. He said he let the woman do all the work. I assumed the opposite must be true: Wasn't that the whole point of a persona? You could pretend to be someone else? After all, his audience was mostly men, and men didn't want to hear about other men being great in bed. Instead, Reid disarmed them with vulnerability. I'm just like you, he seemed to be saying, afraid of my own incompetence—afraid that I am not good enough to make a woman come.

I was surprised at how easy the time passed, as though it had been compressed into something small and shiny, a ball bearing shot through the air.

"So," I said, during our third game, "when was your last serious relationship?" I said it offhandedly, at the same time as I tossed the bowling ball, so that he had to say, "What?" And I had to repeat it again, this time louder.

"Hmm," he said, "depends on what you consider serious."

"I guess the last person you gave a house key." Though did his house even require a key? Probably not; probably there was just a very high-tech keypad. Or maybe there was an armed guard standing outside of a very tall gate, like the rich women in Beverly Hills whose book clubs I dreaded facilitating. Or maybe he gave keys out freely. Maybe there was an array of women walking around with keys. Maybe he had a locksmith on the payroll whom he always called, maybe his name was Ray, and maybe Ray said something like, "So another one bit the dust?" every time Reid needed a new key made.

Maybe Reid or his security had already background checked me, already knew things about me I could hardly articulate to myself. Surely there were safeguards in place for a man like him.

"One girlfriend," he said. "Since my wife."

"One girlfriend," I repeated.

"I've..." I could tell he was trying to put it delicately. "I've been with people."

"You've fucked people," I said, trying to shock him.

"Sure," he said. What would it take to shock him?

"Why did the relationship end?"

"Oh," he said. "The usual reasons."

I thought of a book I liked, in which a woman explains her exes: "Our timing was bad, the light was ugly, things didn't work out." I said this aloud and he said, "All of the above. And we both had kids, so that was tricky. My daughter was a lot younger then."

"What's she like?" I said. "Your daughter."

"You'll like her," he said, though that hardly answered the question. And does a father ever really know his daughter—know her the way other women do, the way her mother does? Daughters are so often distorted in their fathers' eyes.

"And you," he said. "When was your last relationship?"

"Oh," I said. "I had a boyfriend in college. And then after that, a different guy." A chemistry graduate student with a soft voice and a face that looked easy to draw: startlingly straightforward. "But it got complicated."

I was grieving—I'd been difficult to be around; I made myself difficult. But I didn't know how to say that aloud. I'd cheated on the graduate student boyfriend, let a man I'd just met at a party bend me over in the coat closet. And that hadn't been the only time. The grief had made my need impossible, an ever-deepening pit. What had I wanted? To prove I was alive? Still lovable? And I needed multiple men to prove it? I needed them to fuck the grief right out of me, until there was no room for pain, only penis. Penis not pain, I'd said to a friend at the time, laughing in a miserable way.

On those nights, when I picked someone up from a bar, let's say, I'd orgasm and feel distraught, like I was watching myself from a different room. Or worse, I wouldn't orgasm, and then I was not in a different room, but on top of the house altogether.

Instead of all that, I said, "I didn't treat my last boyfriend all that well."

"I'm sure a lot of us can say that," he said. "How so?"

I looked around the bowling alley as though the words might be there. "I was in a weird place in my life."

"You're very private," he said, and I almost laughed aloud. Me? Private? I felt like I moved through the world like an open wound. But I knew what he meant. The word came to me with a suddenness: it was shame. Not secrecy as much as shame. To reveal myself would be to reveal what I'd lost, and what I did to speed the loss up. Or didn't do.

"Come here," he said, putting down the shiny, iridescent bowling ball—which might as well have been a planet, so significant did every object seem in that moment—and pulled me close. "It's been a while since I've felt like this."

"Like what?"

"Excited."

For some reason, I thought about a disturbingly filthy game from his radio show, in which the fathers of porn stars had to pick out their daughters' vaginas from a lineup. I remembered a father who, laughing, said, "I'll be ashamed if I win."

"Me too," I said now. "I'm excited too."

13.

Growing up, I was not allowed in the center for girls with eating disorders where my mother worked. It was against a privacy law, something medical and official-sounding. I thought it was something else: the girls wouldn't want an outsider, a "normal girl" so close in age, seeing them like that—skeletal and sick and terrified. At school and at home, I was unused to anyone caring if I looked at them—what I thought of them—the idea of someone wanting to hide themselves from me felt flattering.

But one January day, when I was twelve, too fluish to stay home by myself, and with no one else to watch me, my mother was forced to bring me to what she only referred to as "the office."

"Stay here," my mother had said, leaving me in a small, cream-colored room that didn't look all that different from the nursing station at school. I had been surprised to see so many photos of me and Jack on my mother's desk—we had very few family photos at home, only a few trinkets my mother said reminded her of us: a small marble pyramid for me, a cactus in a bright, blue bowl for my brother. Pictures are just for other people, my mother said. And who needed other people. "I already know what you look like," she said. "I want to be reminded of your essence."

My mother had left me on a vinyl sofa with a blanket, a Pedialyte, and a coloring book. The coloring book was filled with the outlines of exotic animals: zebras and kangaroos and stingrays and crocodiles. On every page a cartoon version of a human man loomed: a cowboy type from the Outback named Steve Irwin, the Crocodile Hunter. Mostly, I remember being surprised by the childlike doodling on the first few pages—weren't these girls older than me? Adolescents: fourteen to seventeen, some as old as twenty-two.

But the girls *were* childlike, or at least, they appeared that way: small and birdlike and weirdly energized. I stood shyly at the doorway of their "living room," wrapped in my blanket, watching them bent over their arts and crafts and jigsaw puzzles. (In reality, I had not been able to avert my eyes.)

"Who are you?" a girl asked. She was very small, like a kid, but her voice was unusually deep. She wore a polo shirt buttoned up at the collar, like it was her job to be there.

"I'm Carrie's daughter," I said.

"She has a daughter?" she asked.

I assumed they'd all be sullen, quiet types. Maybe with goth makeup. I assumed they might even look like models, these girls, like Kate Moss at her thinnest. But they didn't look like models at all, and they certainly weren't demure. In fact, many of the girls wouldn't stop talking! So much chatter, incessant and nervous.

"You can sit," polo shirt girl said. "You can do a puzzle if you want."

But when I sat, I could barely hear myself think. They had so many complaints! They didn't like the crackers they were forced to eat; they wanted more water (my mother said they always wanted more water); they wanted to pace; they wanted their phones; they wanted out of here; they wanted freedom; they wanted wanted wanted. Even the therapy dog, Rufus, seemed overwhelmed by the girls' manic complaints, his golden retriever head bowed, his movements oddly slow.

I had thought these girls would be mysterious in a more adult way than I was: their adult problems turned inward, eating them alive. Instead, they seem stalled in some hellish in-between—on the border of girlhood and adulthood where nothing fit right.

Finding out who my mother was made me a minor celebrity among them. She was their favorite, they said. She was the nicest. She was the only one who understood, or who tried to understand.

When my mother saw me, she lunged for me, and for a second I felt scared. I was not used to feeling scared of my mother. It was my father whose arrival at home so often caused a sinking feeling in my chest. My mother was usually the leavening agent—she made the whole feeling in the house rise. She lightened everything up.

After she dragged me back into her office, she said, "They don't have normal immune systems. Being around you could really hurt them. They could get really sick."

Later, on our way home, I'd asked why the girls came there—to this town in the middle of nowhere. I knew it was expensive to send them, that they often came from wealthy families—wouldn't they prefer to be in Malibu or upstate New York, or even Dallas, Texas?

"Does it help them to be in the middle of nowhere?" I pressed. Maybe it was good to be surrounded by nothing. The girls didn't have to see the native thinness in their own cities everywhere they went, squeezing grapefruit in the grocery store or stepping on the subway. Surely that wouldn't happen here, I thought, where even the buildings were squat, and chain restaurants abounded.

"It doesn't really matter where they are," my mother said. "They can't escape themselves—the thing inside them that they hate."

"Don't their mothers feel guilty for sending them here, so someone else's mother can take care of them?" I said.

"Oh honey," my mother said, "all mothers are guilty of something."

At that time, I felt envious of the girls, their painful-looking bodies, how much of my mother they were allowed. Later, it would be my mother who became frustrated that I told her so little about my life. It had switched, somehow, somewhere along the line, not all at once, but gradually, so that neither of us was quite sure how it happened.

Now, I let my mother tell me the same story again and again—I give her that kindness. She hasn't worked at the center for girls with eating disorders for a long time now. She could no longer handle the issues of other people's children.

Now, she works at a car dealership, doing the bookkeeping. Occasionally, something exciting happens—a man once tried to steal a Volkswagen Passat on a test drive. Or she'll discover a minor mystery in the books: Did someone make a calculation error, or is a salesman carefully draining an account? But even that stresses her out, she tells me.

"I'm not looking for problems," she says now. "I've seen enough in my lifetime."

14.

One month after I met Reid (and two years and one month after my brother died): I was facilitating a book club in Beverly Hills at a palatial estate. It was a room full of middle-aged women, many of whom have been "worked on" in one way or another, as my mother would say. Halloween was around the corner—fake, gauzy spiderwebs glittered tastefully from every windowsill. The owner of the house wore a headband with cat ears and served cookies shaped like tiny skulls. Her husband was on a respirator in some room in the depths of the house, though this woman rarely mentioned him.

For this month, they were supposed to have read a long book about a nuanced marriage, intricate and devastating.

"Who read the book she assigned us?" a woman said, gesturing toward me. The woman had long, dark hair blown very straight, like Cher. "I know I didn't."

"I never do," another one said. And then, pulling a goofy face, "Don't fail us!"

Sometimes a stray husband would attend, and either speak over the women the entire time or not utter a single word. Husband roulette, I called it.

In the novel we were supposed to be discussing, the protagonist's marriage was neither good nor bad, just complex. I thought it would hinder the discussion to have a husband lurking nearby. The women might've been easily shut down by his soupy cough or too-loud laugh. No husbands appeared, thank God.

"Wise and deeply felt," a woman read from the back cover.

"Who can trust the critics," another one said. Her eyebrows were in a different place than typically seen on a face. A little higher. But it wasn't unattractive—it signaled a kind of trying, a position toward the future, that impressed me. I didn't think I'd have that determination to remain young-looking. I assumed I'd cower in the face of aging. I'd completely crumble. I felt that way already—I was losing ground fast.

"I'm more interested in how you liked the book," I said.

"I'll tell you this," said a woman with an ornate brooch on her sweater in the shape of a bumblebee, "that lady *hated* her husband." She quoted a line, in which the women said she could never outrun the thought: You should leave him.

"See!" the woman said. "She hates him!" She read more aloud: a complicated metaphor comparing marriage to a paper plate. "What's that supposed to mean?"

Metaphors scared them, and so did poetry and abstraction. They read so literally! It always startled me. Subtext flew by their heads, whipping up their dyed hair like wind in a convertible. Sometimes it felt like speaking a different language, trying to talk to them about books. I might as well have been barking like a dog.

I felt myself sinking into the woman's finely upholstered chair. I couldn't tell how my face looked. Was I frowning? I tried not to show my displeasure. Did they not have complicated relationships? Did they not look at their own husbands or children or fathers and think, what would it be like to be free? Love was a tether, after all. It tied you down—it obligated you to something other than your own happiness. Whoever said love set you free never had parents, never had children.

"Any other feelings we might add," I asked, "what else did the protagonist feel for her husband?" I was using a voice I referred to in my mind as "even-keeled customer service representative." I could've been piloting an airplane or renting them a car—efficient and unshakable.

"Annoyance," a woman next to Cher said. "But who doesn't. I'd love if Frank would take out the trash more." And here all the women laughed, because they must have known Frank, and they, too, had husbands who rarely took out the trash.

"I like the part where she imagines her husband with someone else after she's gone," another woman said. I liked her; I'd been surprised when I found out the woman's job—finance or corporate law, something like that. I assumed maybe she was a therapist, some occupation that required thoughtfulness. "I liked this idea that you could want someone happy and away from you at the same time," the woman continued.

An ally. I nodded, moving my hand in a way I hoped would be encouraging.

"What can I say," the woman said. "I have an ex-husband." And the others laughed at this too, because so many of them also had ex-husbands, or knew ex-husbands, or married someone else's ex-husband. "I still think of mine a lot," the woman said, "even though we divorced many years ago."

"That's sweet," I said, "Does he know that?"

"Well he's dead," the woman said. "But that hasn't changed anything. He was a great father, too. A much better father than a husband."

"Was the divorce difficult?" I asked, even though this really had nothing to do with the book, and I'd been given explicit instructions by my boss not to pry into the women's personal lives. Some of them really didn't like that, I'd been told. Rich people were very private. I'd once been inside a gated community that was inside another gated community—like a Russian nesting doll of gated communities. I didn't know how the women got rich, but I would guess mostly through their husbands. It seemed like the kind of extreme wealth that did not require an education, like real estate or inheritance. Maybe most extreme wealth does not require an education. How could I know if nobody told me!

"I remember it was the worst leading up to the divorce," the woman said. Everything the other one said or did seemed like an attack. "He made me crazy at the end. I couldn't remember what I ever liked about him. And the things I did like I now hated."

I thought of the Lorrie Moore line: *This is what happened in love. One of you cried a lot and then both of you grew sarcastic.*

"You wanna know something strange?" the woman went on. "Before he died, I thought maybe we could try to rekindle. By then we'd been divorced, for what, like...?" She looked around at the other women as though they might know. "Nine years, at least?"

I liked the way she spoke, her voice like butter melting in a pan. I thought she should've been able to get the ex-husband back. Wouldn't their old troubles seem ridiculous in the face of death?

"How did he pass?" I asked.

"Cancer." And here the woman laughed. "He knew he was dying, and still he wouldn't take me back."

"These men," Cher said. "Even when they're on the verge of death, they still think something better is about to come along!"

"I liked the book," the thoughtful woman said. "It made me think about my own life."

"See," another woman said, "that's exactly why I hated it."

15.

Saturday, October twenty-seventh: I had a date with Reid Steinman written in capital letters on a calendar I kept on my desk. Sometimes if I waited too long to get out of bed the whole day was ruined, shunted off into a hole I couldn't climb out of, and I'd spend all day in bed, watching high-stakes poker on YouTube. It reminded me of my brother, I guess, the intensity of these men, trying to outsmart each other. Or I'd watch pointless clips: a raccoon eating cotton candy, a baker's disembodied hands kneading mounds of dough. Once I even joined a message board for women whose husbands had gone off to war. I never participated, but I liked to read their complaints, their secrets. One woman was having an affair. She asked the chat room how best to cover up a hickey. "Are you 16????" a user named Fyte4Lyfe wrote. "Your husband is serving his country and your sucking face??!!!" I posted a heart next to every single comment. I agreed with everyone.

But today, the anticipation of the date was gently tugging me through the hours.

Again, the same driver, Kelly, in the same tired but tidy Prius.

This time I knew where we were going: to his house. To Reid Steinman's house!

"Have you worked for him a long time?" I asked.

"Oh, I've known Reid forever," she said. "I've known him since I was young. In some ways he saved my life." I wondered how old she was—in her mid- to late forties, maybe. She hung sentimental Christmas ornaments from her rearview mirror. When we went through a McDonald's drive-through, she said, "Come to Mama" when the guy handed her a Diet Coke. At stoplights, she sometimes let her eyes drift shut. "Reid loves this one too," she said, about a song I didn't recognize.

The car pulled up to a tasteful but expensive-looking home, modern with two stories, tucked into the trees in a place called Laurel Canyon. I thought the house was beautiful, yes, but still a little disappointing. What had I been expecting? Maybe a house like one of the women in my book clubs owned: something grandiose and less sophisticated. Where were the fountains? Or the lions made of marble? Or the koi pond under a Thomas Kinkade–like bridge? I wanted to see the money spelled out on the roof: M-O-N-E-Y. It should be lying out in bundles, sunning itself under the palm trees.

There was a very long driveway, and Kelly said, "If I pull all the way in, it's a pain to get out."

"I can walk," I said.

"I don't mind though," she said. "If you're wearing heels or something."

"No, no," I said, "only sneakers," and opened the door. Walking down the very long driveway, I felt a little like a character in a book, not a fairy tale exactly, but an allegory nevertheless, in which a character crosses a threshold over which she cannot return.

That's how I defined "the short story" to my students just last week—a character moves through a door they cannot return through.

This felt especially true when I watched Kelly pull away—that last shred of familiarity, gone. Maybe all relationships follow this same plotline: stranger in a strange land, and the strange land is always another person.

I rang the doorbell and waited outside for what felt like a long time. The doubt began to creep in: somehow, I'd gotten something wrong. Eventually, Reid opened the door, his bald head shining with sweat, a pale blue dish towel over his shoulder.

"I'm cooking," he said. "I hope you like pasta."

I hugged him and felt surprised that I'd already grown accustomed to his smell—and not cologne, but his skin smell, the feel of his faint beard against my cheek.

"I'm so glad you're here," he said.

"So am I." He had a way of tilting his head back when I spoke as though he were trying to absorb every word. I wouldn't have assumed he was a good listener. He talked over everyone on the radio—he made his listeners laugh by cutting callers off and saying, "Nobody cares what you have to say." But here, in person, he made everything I said seem important.

He led me into the house, which was decorated so expertly and so expensively it seemed specific to his tastes while still—somehow—universally stylish. Even the bathroom impressed me: the toilet water was a bright, effervescent blue. Yes, I thought, the house was much nicer on the inside.

Two upright arcade games sat in the corner of the living room, which reminded me of my brother, as so many things did. (There was a Pac-Man machine in a pizza place where he worked in high school.) Reid caught me looking from the doorway of the kitchen.

"You can play," he said, "if you want. Those machines have every game: Tetris, Asteroids, you name it. I bought those for my daughter. God, when she was a kid, I guess. But now, no one ever plays them." I had questions about the daughter, but I wouldn't ask them now. I was trying to play it cool. I already regretted how much I'd revealed—that I'd listened to him before, that my father did too. It put me at a disadvantage, I thought, seeming like a fan.

"Also, feel free to put on a record," he said. One of the walls of his living room was covered in shelving from floor to ceiling, and those shelves were filled with records, without even a single notch of space in between, like a page out of *Architectural Digest*.

"There's a ladder," he said, pointing to the corner of the room. After the college radio station, he'd started out playing music at a small rock and roll radio station in Washington, but I wouldn't admit to knowing this out loud.

"Hard for me to choose," I said. I was only looking at what was directly in my eyeline. I couldn't fathom climbing up the ladder just yet, making myself at home in that way. "And your place is beautiful." This seemed so obvious I felt embarrassed I hadn't said it earlier. Blueish hills filled the expansive windows. The sky was the pink of candy necklaces, the kind from childhood or parties where people took drugs and sweated all over each other.

"Thanks," he said. "I had help. Kelly. My daughter. All the women around me," he said, and laughed. "I'm helpless."

I saw an Elvis Costello record and reached for the Beatles instead. I heard my father's voice, "You never go wrong with the Beatles." Then, I changed my mind, and chose Sinatra. I was tired of my father's voice in my head—I didn't need it now, of all times.

"I've never used a record player before," I said. Would this remind him of the gap between our ages, between our lives? Let it, I thought, because surely that must be some of my appeal—how unlike him I was. How utterly unfamiliar. That was some of his appeal for me.

"Don't worry," he said, "they're hard to break," which I thought couldn't be true. He came up behind me, trailing steam from the kitchen. I could smell onions on him, and garlic. But it didn't repel me. Quite the opposite.

He took the record gently from me and placed it on the record player. It was, in fact, simple. Or at least he made it look that way. What I wanted to say was, I've never been around such expensive things. And also, this was everything my brother had wanted: to be famous, to have your kind of life.

When he gently turned me to face him, his hands on my hips, I felt a lick of arousal run through me. We kissed just as the music kicked in, long-held brass notes, Sinatra saying he doesn't want to dance, and that you can't make him. Yes, even you, lovely as you are.

Eventually a timer in the kitchen rang, high-pitched and jarring. When we pulled away from each other, the lights seemed too bright. I laughed, a little embarrassed. He'd been kissing me deeply, as though he wanted something from me, and I'd been kissing him back, as though I'd wanted it returned.

I wiped my mouth with the back of my hand and then wished I hadn't. I needed to save any trace. At least I'd have a story to tell.

When he disappeared into the kitchen I felt like a little kid in this beautiful home, like someone's mother might walk in at any moment and ask me to remove my shoes.

"I'll turn off the sauce," Reid shouted, "and we can continue. The pasta's already made, so it won't take long to cook."

"You made fresh pasta," I said. I'd never seen someone do it in person—only on TV.

"Yes," he said, "I sure did." He returned and laid me down on the floor of the living room. I let him lay me down—more than that. I wasn't just acquiescing. When his mouth began at the bottom of me, at the very tips of my toes, I thought of my first real boyfriend, in college, who'd been squeamish about this kind of thing, about putting your mouth where a mouth didn't normally belong. (When he did it, I could feel him mouthing words into me. I was sure he'd spelled out H-E-L-P.)

When Reid pulled off his boxers and T-shirt, I was shocked to see a body in its sixties: a sparse patch of gray hair on his chest, gravity tugging at his pecs, his belly. (Despite what his money allowed—the personal trainers and nutritionists, I assumed—he had not outrun age. And if he couldn't, I thought, nobody could.)

I'll say this: He was very good in bed. Did I think he wouldn't be? He continued to do something with his tongue I couldn't even picture in my mind. I wanted to laugh, it felt so good. The oddest thing about being with an older man, I decided then, was the knowledge that they'd been with—if not a lot of different women, then at least with a few women for a very long time. He'd had years on me, and on every man I'd been with prior. He'd been studying; he'd been practicing.

And, I thought, every joke he told on the radio about being bad in bed was untrue, just as I knew it would be.

When we finished, he wrapped me up in a blanket and brought me a bowl of pasta. The bowl had a bright red rim, probably belonging to a set purchased from a very expensive home decor store, probably by a professional interior designer who'd been paid a handsome fee. Or, his daughter. Or, his driver! One of the women he claimed to keep his life afloat. In my studio apartment, I had only mismatched plates and bowls I'd purchased on Craigslist. I tried to picture him in my apartment, eating scrambled eggs from a plastic plate meant for a child.

Now he sat cross-legged in his boxer shorts—patterned with miniature
Scottie dogs—and watched me eat what he made. He'd shaved a small pile
of Parmesan curls onto the top, and this, if nothing else, felt like enough to
undo me. How lonely I'd been before this! That a pile of Parmesan cheese
was enough to undo me? His carpeting was the softest I'd ever felt in my life.
I hadn't even known carpeting like this existed.

"You're not hungry?" I asked, lips slick with oil.

"Not at the moment."

This gesture—making me food and watching me eat it—seemed
fatherly to me, except for the fact that my own father would never do it. He
didn't cook, and had no patience for watching someone else eat when he
wasn't hungry. Maybe this is romance, I thought, what I was now confusing
with fatherliness. Maybe those things could be easily confused.

"What do you think?" Reid said, watching my mouth as I chewed.

I swallowed hard, and smiled. I wondered if I had a tiny speck of oregano
wedged between my teeth. "I love it," I said. "You're a good cook."

"I'm so glad," he said.

"Did your mother teach you to make pasta?" I knew she had. I'd read it
somewhere.

"She did," he said. His face changed: not forlorn, but blank-looking.
Wiped clean. To pretend I didn't know anything about his relationship with
his mother would be dishonest, of course, because I'd listened to the show
(at one point, every day) and not just with my father, but after I'd left home
and gone away to college in a town near San Francisco and missed my parents terribly, missed their fights and their shouting and the space they took
up. I'd always assumed that once I was rid of them, it would be easier to
breathe. They'd chiseled me down to a manageable size. Without them, I'd
become larger, more expansive.

Instead, alone in a new city, I felt I took up no space at all. I could turn to
the side and disappear. I missed my father then, especially, when I was writing every day, thinking of myself as a writer. I'd call my dad on the phone
on my way to the coffee shop where I worked, and he'd tell me what he saw
through the window as he drove: cow, cow, cow, bull! And I'd listen, and
then I'd interrupt eventually to say, I wrote something for a magazine and
he'd say, What's the name?, and I'd tell him, something academic-sounding

like the *New Bostonian Review* and he'd say, What kind of magazine is that? A good one, Dad, don't worry about it.

Now, I said to Reid, "I know your mother passed away recently." This was the opposite of playing it cool, I knew, and maybe shifted me into the realm of "knowing too much," but at that moment, I only wanted to say: I, too, know loss.

Instead, he looked surprised, maybe even a little put off. Then suddenly he seemed to realize: he was famous and so the events of his life were widely known. Not only that, but he often revealed details of his personal life on the radio—or at least, a version of his personal life—there were a hundred different portals into the cabin of his ship.

Then again, maybe he didn't always remember what he said on the radio. He was performing, after all. This is what my brother had said when he got offstage: when it's going well, I have no idea what I just said. Same with when it's going badly.

"I'm sorry you lost her," I said. Sometimes I said this about my brother: I'd lost him. I liked pretending he'd been misplaced. A little joke I told myself.

"It wasn't unexpected," Reid said.

This was the tricky thing about dating him: the public and private blurred, so that there seemed no way I wouldn't mistake some new intimacy for something I'd heard him say long ago on the radio, to everyone. I wanted to say: tell me things nobody else knows.

"Are you close with your parents?" he asked.

"Do you have a pool?" I asked. I figured he must. And then, "Yes, we're very close." We were close like a foot is close with a bunion—I felt their presence with every step. We were close in the way three polar bears on the same lone iceberg are close. There might not be enough to go around.

"I do have a pool," he said and led me outside. The sky was now dark—close and touchable—and his pool was a neat, prim square, lit from beneath like a gem.

I was standing in the blanket he'd given me, something that probably costs twelve hundred dollars, made of cashmere mixed with llama wool or something, which made me feel very precious, to be wrapped in a blanket like that. I slipped it off and moved nude, into the pool, step by step, until my feet and then my ankles and then my thighs went underwater, turned bluish and spooky. He stood in his T-shirt and boxer shorts and watched me. I felt very powerful just then. It was hard to remember the last time I felt like that. I wondered what I looked like—the back of me. I had an idea of myself in my mind, but don't you always? And isn't it so often wrong? The one thing we never truly know: what we look like to other people.

16.

"Here's something that'll surprise you," my mother said.

"What?" I was in the car on my way to a book club, to a neighborhood of monstrous houses perched on a man-made lake.

"Guess?"

"No," I said, "I won't."

"I'm friends with a pigeon on the internet."

"Congratulations."

"Raj thinks I'm on my phone too much," she said. "He says I'm always scrolling." My mother impersonated Raj's accent—"scrooling"—and I said, "Please stop. That's offensive." My mother went quiet, chastised, and I said, "What's the pigeon's name?"

"José," my mother said. "He does all sorts of tricks."

How humiliating for someone to watch you scroll—and worse, watch your stupid fucking thumb tap its way over the stuff you liked or hated or loved or were attracted to or secretly pined for. It was not that different from reading a diary.

Lately, my mother had become very into being "online."

After we lost my brother (ha!), my mother joined a grief group online, which led to other groups, and other passions, all of which seemed to help her. Now she takes public speaking classes on Zoom and has many internet friends she calls "my onliners."

She often suggested I do the same—join a group!—which sounded terrible to me, to try to explain my brother to a room of strangers while they sobbed about someone else. But my mother is a joiner—she likes being a part of something larger than herself.

"You and your father don't talk to anyone about it but each other," she said. The conversation had led here again—to The Problem—as so many of them did.

I didn't have the heart to tell my mother that we didn't speak of my brother very often. When we'd tried, it hadn't gone well.

"I heard he got ahold of you," my mother said, "your father." This is how it always went: my mother became my father's mouthpiece, even after all this time, even after Raj, even after following pigeons, even after watching their tricks.

"Yes," I said, "he wants to visit soon."

"Good," my mother said, "you know how he is."

Her problem, even after all these years.

Before I got off the phone, my mother said the same thing she always said, after I love you and before I'm worried about you: "Call your father."

If it matters: My mother's father had passed away long ago, and her parents had disapproved of the marriage from the start. My mother had grown up religious, some type of Christian I couldn't distinguish from the rest, from a hole in the wall, and my mother refused to explain it. I only knew it was *not* the kind of religion that spoke in tongues and palled around with snakes, but it was the kind of religion that disapproved of sex before marriage and gay people "shoving it down your throat." Most of all, they disapproved of my father, who seemed to think he was some kind of "Jewish cowboy," as my grandfather put it.

Maybe her parents' opposition had been part of my father's appeal: his denim jacket, his domineering mother, his constant panic over whatever new crisis tomorrow would deliver. Trust in God? My father couldn't trust in the sun coming up. The sun could change its mind. The sun could go apeshit on you for no reason.

※   ※   ※

My mother had met my father between men. That's how she said it, "I was in the lonesome ditch between men." My mother was twenty-six, working as a veterinary tech. The Problem brought in a dog he'd found behind a Krispy Kreme Doughnuts, where he'd pulled over his rig to urinate. "I was taking out my schlong," was how my father told the story, "and my pal was just sitting there staring."

The dog was too thin and had pointy, alert ears, like a Doberman. "I've been calling him Chuck," he told my mother, cradling the dog in his arms under the fluorescent lights. "I figured all animals need a name."

Something about the look in my father's eyes (the watery concern) coupled with his manliness (his height and cowboy hat and broad shoulders) made all the broader-seeming in his worn Levi's jacket—moved something inside her that felt like it couldn't be unmoved.

On their first date, he'd opened the door of his car and a truck drove by and took the door clean off. They'd watched the door fly into someone's front lawn. My mother shrugged and asked if he'd still like to go to dinner, maybe somewhere closer, where they could walk. He was charmed, I'm sure, by the way my mother had carried on as though nothing could surprise her.

This—still—is what I find scariest about long-term relationships: that you are often working off a very early impression of someone that has lodged itself in your brain and colors every impression that comes after.

What I realize now is that my mother's father was also a problem. He was stoic, yes, and probably spoke fewer than twenty words to his family every day, but a single glare could drive you from the room. When he said "no" in a certain tone of voice, my mother's whole posture changed. She only started working as a veterinary tech because he told her it would be a good idea. "You like animals," he'd said, and that was true.

"But did you want to work there?" I asked.

"I'm not actually sure," she'd said.

So, problems abounded for my mother. So many problems they must have started to appear like solutions in the right light. Make the men happy and you would be happy, too. Soothe the man and you will soothe yourself. Solve the problem and so, too, you shall be solved. Though she wouldn't have put it that way.

Now, as I walked toward another book club—this gigantic house!—one of the women began to wave. This woman was climbing out of a car, which looked like it was built from leftover robot parts.

"Book girl!" the woman said, and gestured at my hair. "Is it windy?"

"No," I said, and followed her inside.

17.

Halloween. I brought Reid to a costume party in Culver City for the adjuncts at the Glendale Community College. I could feel that spooky expectancy in the air. I thought Reid would wear a mask, completely disguise himself. Instead, he wore a top hat, a monocle, and an ill-fitting suit—too long in the sleeves.

"Mr. Peanut?" I said, as we stood on the porch waiting to be let in.

"The Monopoly man. I wear it every year. When I wasn't married and I wasn't dating, I would go to Halloween parties with Kelly and she'd be Mrs. Monopoly."

"I hadn't known there was such a thing," I said.

"There isn't."

Inside, the host has changed the lightbulbs from white to red so that when I first walked in, I felt like I'd entered a different time. The twenties maybe. A man wearing suspenders was playing the piano, a ragtime number that seemed to grow faster and faster. Someone had propped two skeletons against the makeshift wooden bar, as though in conversation.

"We're in hell!" one of the poets yelled. She was dressed as a hippie, flower-crowned and pleasant-looking.

The party was loud and crowded, with people pressed against each other. Outside, a siren blared. A group of boys were kicking a soccer ball in the street, and it kept hitting the side of the apartment building. After every goal there came an explosion of noise.

This was my boss's house, a woman around whom I felt myself immediately relax. A long time ago, she'd published a very successful novel and had written nothing since then. She seemed very much at peace with the shape her life had taken. I wished for that: to wake up one day and decide the life I lived was something I'd wanted.

"I like teaching junior college," she'd said, "the students are far less annoying than at the big universities."

She appeared now, dressed like a zombie librarian. "I'm on theme," she said. If she recognized Reid, she didn't show it on her face. She clasped both of his hands in hers and shook them slowly.

"I love her," she said, meaning me. "You're lucky."

My heart quickened. What could he say to that?

"She's the best," he said, which was general enough that it could mean anything from "I also love her" to "She's not too bad to be around." But in this case, I knew he was leaning more toward the former.

Just that morning, he'd called me on his way to the studio and said, "I'm like a dog with a bone. I'm obsessed with you." At first I'd been confused: Was I the bone or the dog?

"I'm the dog," he'd said. "You're my bone."

In a sense, time with him was passing in some form of dog years: every day seemed like seven months. Maybe this wasn't dog years, maybe it was dating-an-older-man years. I already knew the medication he took (blood pressure), and how many times he peed in the night (several). In the evening, we each ate one of the sugar-free Popsicles that always reappeared like magic in his fridge while we watched the tangerine sun sink leisurely into his pool. Sometimes I told him about my day, my students, and other times we'd say very little, just observe what we noticed in the backyard: a red spider, a darting raccoon. My mother said grief did strange things to time, but so did sex—so did love. Time had become a demented accordion, compressing and expanding the days. Time flew, was how I felt. What other way is there to measure time than how it is felt?

At the Halloween party, Reid was friendly—asking everyone what they teach, how they liked it. Would he ever introduce me to his friends (Are they famous?! Are they old?!) or was he embarrassed—not of me, necessarily, but to be dating someone so young?

You're not that young, I thought to myself. Not anymore.

Or maybe that was my father's voice. Or my mother's! Talkers, both of them.

"Did you get her writing again?" my boss asked Reid. She'd painted black around her eyes so they looked sunken.

"Oh," Reid said, "I hadn't known she'd stopped."

I shrugged, as though I might pick it up again, simple as that, like it was a purse I'd dropped on the ground.

"Something's in the works," I lied.

The man I'd slept with, Chris, milled around the kitchen, arguing jovially with a woman in the visual arts department about a painter. I couldn't figure out either of their costumes: something intellectual, or a reference I didn't understand.

The woman thought the artist they were discussing was overrated; Chris thought this was just a trick of the mind. Artists were inherently envious, and they wanted so badly to be famous—which was almost impossible!—that when someone actually achieved that fame, they were automatically deemed a sellout. Now all artists who ranked beneath them in success and popularity called them overrated, like it was the law.

"Like physics," he said. "Like the law of gravity."

"That's not it," the woman said, newly defensive. "I just think his paintings aren't that good. You don't have to agree."

Chris was still smiling. "I don't agree," he said. "I think he had a huge influence on me. He had a huge influence on a lot of people. Probably even you." He gently knocked his plastic cup against the woman's, cheersing her, though she didn't look like she wanted to be cheersed.

I thought maybe he was sticking up for the man because he still hoped to one day be famous, hoped his former friends wouldn't say *he* was overrated, wouldn't deem him a sellout. Probably the woman worried she would never be famous, and therefore, she could forever say, "I never sold out." She would be an artist's artist, poor in money but rich in integrity. They were arguing for the same reason, or at least, on two sides of the same coin. Maybe they will go home together tonight, I thought. Maybe they will fuck angrily, gratefully. Maybe afterward they will talk about art.

Reid had been listening to them closely. He'd set his soda water down on the kitchen island so he could better pay attention.

"You can join in," I whispered, but he hung back. The two were so invested in their conversation they didn't seem to notice anyone was watching.

Eventually Reid looked at me and said, "They're onto something. People used to like me more before I got famous." He said it casually, like it didn't bother him either way. Still, there was something in the casualness that threw me—it was too adamant.

I wasn't sure if he meant people didn't like him anymore because of the fame, or if he was just less famous now. In general, I knew his listeners were declining. They'd jumped ship—to podcasts and younger voices. More shocking voices. Newer voices. Who listened to the radio anymore? Reid was the old guard. He was hanging on by his carefully buffed fingernails.

"You still mean a lot to a lot of people," I said, but it sounded sad, like I was trying too hard to reassure him. It sounded like something someone says at a retirement party.

"Allison!" Chris noticed me just as I was searching for the host, getting ready to say my goodbyes. His adjunct counterpart was long gone. When he noticed Reid, his whole face seemed to blink with excitement.

"I can't believe you're here," he said, after Reid introduced himself pointlessly. "I know who you are," Chris said.

"A relief," Reid said, and I wasn't sure if he was joking.

Chris was looking at me with new and naked awe. "I can't believe you know him," he said, as though Reid wasn't there.

"Trust me," Reid said. "Getting to know me is a huge disappointment."

He'd said this to me too, after that first night together. That can't be true, I'd said.

He'd grimaced playfully. "I'm boring."

"There are worse things to be."

But I knew boring wasn't quite what he meant.

18.

When I was a freshman in high school, I met my first and only best friend, Marcella Jones-Hernandez. This was after the trio of evangelical Christian girls, and after I'd made out with four more boys, but before I lost my virginity. Her last name, Jones-Hernandez, was a product of her parents' long-ago compromise. Her parents both felt they'd given up too much in the negotiation, and they eventually divorced. Marcella spent the majority of freshman year at my house, and then the following summer, when we went to the public pool every day, and wore each other's swimsuits interchangeably, bikini bottoms forever hanging damp across the backs of chairs.

How many times had I seen Marcella wiggle into my own faded red bikini? At that time, I'd only ever seen my mother's breasts and my own. Marcella's nipples were different from mine: larger, flatter. There was porn, sure, but I didn't watch it. I thought it would scare me. I didn't think of myself as a brave child, a brave teenager. I thought of myself as someone who was attracted to braveness in other people. I had the makings of a great sidekick: loyal, agreeable, quick to improvise a solution when cornered into trouble.

Marcella slept so often in my bed she even left her own pillow, an especially flat and tattered one that we referred to as Flattie. We liked to give inanimate objects proper names. Marcella had two older sisters, and they taught us all of the secret, encoded girl skills I'd never learned from my own mother (who was too busy taking care of other people's daughters) like how to apply eyeliner or put your hair up in one of those effortless kinds of buns.

And Marcella was privy to so much of my house's underbelly: the see-saw of my father (his exaltation and despair), Jack's magnetism, my mother's fatigue. Whatever embarrassment I'd felt at first was quickly washed away by so many days spent in each other's presence. Of course, I thought my family loud and bizarre and humiliating, but Marcella found them funny and welcoming and warm. Wasn't it so much easier to accept other people's families? And easier to forgive other people's parents, too.

She especially loved my father. She found The Problem to be a generous laugher and an elaborate storyteller, and she watched his moods with interest, rather than dread. My father called her Marcy, which she liked, though she would've hated the nickname if it had come from one of her own relatives. Marcella said mine was one of the few dads who, when you told him something he'd never heard before, said "Well, I'll be—" instead of immediately googling it to see if it was true, or hounding you about where you'd heard it first. He never cared much about citing sources. He found that kind of thing boring.

Being with Marcella was like taking off a coat I hadn't realized was so heavy and uncomfortable. I was constantly falling asleep next to her in the middle of conversations, like a narcoleptic, my head on her shoulder, or resting in her lap. I was that relaxed, maybe for the first time. I hadn't known before how often I thought something through before saying it aloud—feeling the texture of the thought in my mind, in my mouth, before letting it loose in the world. With Marcella, I said a thought without thinking it through first, so that talking to her became its own form of thinking.

Yes, it was my house where we spent most of our time, partly because Marcella liked to be around Jack, liked just knowing he was in the room next door, doing his unimaginable boy activities (she had no brothers), and then seeing him the next day in the hallway in only his boxer shorts, her whole face reddening, even down her neck.

Once, during a weekday sleepover in the long daisy chain of our sleepovers, she asked what kind of cologne he wore.

"I don't think he wears any," I said, "unless he shoplifted some from CVS. Why?"

"No reason," she'd said. "He just smells good is all."

In the darkness of my bedroom, there was a prickly energy between us that might've led somewhere else, had Marcella's imagination not been mired in the room next door. And anyway, Marcella didn't seem to have the kind of imagination I had—elastic with potential.

Through high school, her crush only deepened. She'd find reasons to visit him in detention, or hang around with his friends after school—ask for a ride on the handlebars of someone's bicycle, trying to get his attention. At our house, it was worse. Every time he entered a room, she'd sit up straighter, unfurling her spine. Or she'd stand catlike, in the doorway of the kitchen, pawing at the ground, as he rifled through the refrigerator.

"What's eating you?" he'd ask, and she'd say, "Nothing."

"Just wondering if you're coming to the casino," she'd ask, "if you have nothing better to do." But he was older, and popular, and he so often had better things to do.

On summer days when we so often had nothing better to do, we liked to hang around the Peppermill Casino where my father worked, where we could drink free Sprites in the sportsbook and indulge in the industrial-strength air-conditioning. The men and women who worked in the sportsbook cages had known me my entire life, and they let us make fake bets with real printed tickets, stuff like whether my father would want pastrami sandwiches or hot dogs after work; would he be in a good mood or a sour one; or who would score higher on the SATs, me or Marcella? The odds would change depending on how many hours we claimed we'd studied, or if we'd had pastrami sandwiches just yesterday, or if my father had been in a good mood all week (and therefore was due for a downswing).

It was on one of these summer days that Jack dropped by the sportsbook unexpectedly, hoping to beg a little spending money off our father.

"Where's Big Joe?" Jack asked, meaning The Problem.

That night, my dad was dealing poker in the high rollers' room, which you'd think would be filled with businessmen and trust fund heirs, but was actually just filled with gambling addicts and electricians.

"I can walk you," Marcella said. Jack and I looked at each other, confused.
"Why? he said. "I have legs."

"Fine," she said, "never mind," and then she didn't speak for the rest of the night, not even to me, not until bedtime, as she fluffed Flattie, when she said, "Sometimes I can hardly breathe around your brother." How strange— that I knew exactly what she meant. He took up all the air in the room.

"Is Marcella mad at me or something?" Jack had asked me later. The smell of casino was still in my hair.

"Sort of," I'd said. Because how else could I explain it? Love drove people crazy, didn't it? It made them angry and sick and insane. It made people poison themselves! (I'd just read Shakespeare.)

Much later, at Jack's funeral, Marcella stood beside me, crying quietly into a soft, black scarf. She'd slipped a card into my backpack, which had begun *I can't imagine how you're feeling—*

That was the new distance between us, the margin of the unimaginable.

By then, Marcella had a curly-haired boyfriend named Patrick who stood dutifully next to her through the service, and at the burial, like a bodyguard or a soldier. We'd called ourselves best friends through high school and college, though after we both graduated on opposite coasts (Marcella had moved to New York), it had gotten harder to keep up with each other. We no longer knew what the other's day looked like. We each promised to call more, like one does with a relative.

Now, Marcella had a baby. She had a whole other life.

So cute, I had written, under a photo of the new baby squeezing the pulp of an orange in her tiny palm.

👍, Marcella replied.

19.

Mostly, I was a good teacher, when I didn't find the students tiresome or annoying, like when they hassled me about a grade, or held their phones up in class, right in front of my face, as though I didn't exist. Sometimes I'd shout at them—shout passionately about a book!—and they'd look at each other and then away, embarrassed for me. When the bell rang, they'd file out, smiling sadly as though they were viewing me through glass, a patient at the ward.

"What's in her head?" they must have been thinking. Things! Things I couldn't articulate, but I wanted to try.

When I was a bad teacher, it was only because of my ego: how much I needed the students to reassure me I was giving them something worthwhile, something they could use. When I was a good teacher, it was because I forgot about my ego and only thought about them. I wanted to be good—good at ushering young people into adulthood, or else, letting adults rest in my classroom, away from the world.

Most of my students had only just left adolescence, were in its tail end, acne-prone faces still soft and undetermined, personalities alternatingly shy and arrogant. They were not yet sure who they'd become. One day, I'd be a faint, whisper of a memory in their minds: their junior college writing class.

Maybe they'd think of me fondly. Maybe they'd say, she wasn't bad-looking either.

That was all I had in terms of legacy—the hope that I would be a figment in a former student's mind. I worried about how that figment would appear: Disheveled? Lethargic? Like I was a bumper on a car about to fall off? Maybe they'd remember something I'd said: that they were allowed to make their papers interesting. They were allowed to entertain me.

In my first semester teaching, a student wrote a story about "fucking his teacher" in great detail. The teacher in the story had very few distinguishing qualities except for a houndstooth blazer, which the student had called "an ugly brown plaid." This was especially upsetting because of how long I had stared at the blazer in the Gap before I'd bought it, thinking, this will make the students take me seriously. This will earn their respect.

When the student read the story aloud, the class laughed behind their hands, and when he finished, I, trying to control the heat crawling up my neck, resolved to be still. (I didn't feel still, my hands shook so badly I was sure even the students in the back row noticed.) I stared at the student until his face fell into something else. Still, I thought, be still. I'd taken one acting class in college, in which a professor wearing those round John Lennon glasses would shout, Be still! My God, be still! You're like a shaking Chihuahua!

I waited until the pressure in the room felt too great, like someone had asked me a question and was tired of waiting for the answer. Finally, I said to the student, "Do you value your own time that little that you'd waste it on something like that?" I'd spoken so softly, the class had to go silent to hear me.

After the class, at the tiki bar where all the adjuncts hung out, I told the story as though it was hilarious, as though I'd been in control the entire time, that I'd even wanted to laugh (to laugh!) when he read it aloud. I was channeling my brother then, telling the story like a comedian, pausing at the right moments, going loud, then soft, and then loud again. The adjuncts clapped their hands. They laughed, they gasped. This wasn't that hard after all.

"He said he wanted to fuck you! The nerve!" they said.

"But wasn't it also sort of a compliment?" I asked. At this, they laughed even harder. I kept the apology the student gave me after class a secret.

* * *

This was the strange thing about time, or maybe it was perspective: you could slant drama into comedy, or the other way around. I'm sure my brother had taught me that. Also, two things could be true at once: something could be funny and sad. I'm sure novels had taught me that.

Today, I taught an Intro to Creative Writing class. It was November, and the trees near the college were bare. The air smelled like charcoal and wet matches.

"Every sentence can't be perfect," I told them. "And it doesn't need to be." Two guys in tank tops with the junior college's football team emblazoned on the front laughed about something on their phones.

"This is what I'm like when I'm teaching," I thought, as though Reid were watching me right then. The imagined awareness made me want to be funnier, speak slower. I needed to project my voice!

"You two," I said to the football players. But when they trained their beady eyes on me, I couldn't think of anything pithy to say. I imagined Reid disappointed. "Pay attention," I said.

But the students were distracted that day, or I was. Sometimes I wished I could shake them, scream in their faces, Listen to me!!!

Today I was bombing—a phrase borrowed from my brother when he did poorly onstage.

The audience just stares at you, he'd said. They just watch helplessly as you sweat and panic and stutter and feel your heartbeat in all the wrong places. Places you didn't know a heart could beat.

But this wasn't an audience; it was only a classroom filled with students. During a creative writing exercise, I asked the class to describe the room they grew up in, where they might have experienced pain or joy or both.

"What do you remember?" I said. "Describe as many details as you can."

A student put her pen down, and said, "Vahz or vase. Vahz or vase. I think my boyfriend would kick my ass if I started saying vahz."

"It doesn't matter," I said.

"You said every word matters."

"I don't always know what I'm talking about," I said. Sometimes living my life felt like pulling on a glove I found on the sidewalk, like it belonged to a stranger.

Forty-four days after my brother was no longer alive, I decided to see a doctor. The doctor happened to be a gynecologist.

After my forty-fourth day of being unable to get out of bed, I simply called the first doctor I could find in my phone. As it turned out, she'd been the doctor to examine my vagina and said, after closing the metal stirrups, "It all looks hunky dory." I remembered she had a matter-of-fact, nonjudgmental way of asking after my sexual activities: "how often, with what gender" and that's also probably why I'd called her. I liked her ease with difficult subject matter.

That day, as she was gently opening my paper gown, I told her I'd come for something else, I'd come just to talk.

"How many sexual partners have you had since your last visit?" she asked.

"No," I said, "not that kind of talk." Instead, I told her about my brother— I told her about my life. Mostly I'd been eating chow mein from my bedside table and watching reruns of a plastic surgery show where bodies had gone terribly wrong and now were about to be fixed.

She still examined me. "It sounds like you're depressed," she said, from in between my legs, as though that wasn't obvious! Just the sound of the word "depressed" made me cry again. Maybe the sadness was even visible on other parts of my body—it was even visible down there. (Was it newly sagging somehow?) "A psychiatrist could prescribe something for grief," the doctor said. I might've imagined it, but I felt the doctor look away just then, as though this loss might be contagious.

I had clocked the photos on her desk: two twin daughters, an older woman who had the same reddish hair and ruddy complexion as the doctor.

It can happen to you, I had wanted to say.

For a while, I took the pills a psychiatrist prescribed when I remembered to take them, strays that fell out of the container and into the bottom of my bag. But soon, I didn't bother. They made me cotton-mouthed, and turned the world hazy and dreamlike and lavender-tinged.

I was outside of my life then, watching it from a building across the street, and now I thought, I was ready to be back inside of it. My life was a bus, and now I had to tear the steering wheel away from some exhausted, elderly driver. "I've got it from here, buddy," I'd say. "It's time for me to take control." I had an older, famous boyfriend. I had a whole life to write about.

Now there was a new kind of loss: I thought of my brother slightly less. Still every day, every hour, but not every moment. He was not always lingering at the surface of my mind, trying to break through the membrane of my memories into the world at large. He was not the shadow of every thought. Most thoughts, but not every single thought. Now, too, I thought of Reid.

"Starting is the hardest part," I tried again, to the class, "probably because we're afraid." I went out of my way to make eye contact with each student in the front row, one by one, in a way I hoped was intense but not frightening. Another girl yawned, stretched her arms out, showed me the fillings in the back of her teeth.

"I know you're afraid that whatever you're writing won't turn out perfect," I said. "Or it won't even turn out good."

"Vahz or vase," the girl said again.

Through the window, the November sky was shockingly blue, as though it had been shucked from a duller sky. I wanted to tell them something important about fearlessness, about honesty, about how that's all you need when you're writing, that you can't control if the writing is good but you can control if it is true, and not true in the literal sense—I wanted them to make up the events, the plot—but true in its essence, unearthed from somewhere inside of them where truth resides. A story about giants can be true. Or a story about a talking potato. On the contrary, a story about a dead brother could be very untrue, could be filled with lies. Things the family told them-selves, let's say, about the brother or about each other.

When I looked at the clock on the wall, I saw that we were, blessedly, out of time. Before I'd even dismissed them, the students began to gather their belongings and zip up their backpacks.

"Wait, so what's the homework again?" a student wearing a high and buoyant ponytail said. "If you don't mind repeating." She was the kind of student who was very good at making sustained eye contact, and often acted overly agreeable until she didn't like a grade or found an assignment too time-consuming. She didn't enjoy the class all that much, or didn't enjoy writing, or didn't enjoy me, though she tried her best to conceal this information.

"Just keep working on your stories," I said. Ponytail girl shrugged, as though the jury was still out on me, on whether I could be trusted.

"Keep doing your best," I said.

Oh, but it was a relief to get into my car and think of Reid and only Reid, undistracted. I was on my way to his place, watching palm trees tick by in their cement.

Just this morning he'd called me and his voice had filled the car as though I was listening to him on the radio. In fact, I'd been careful to not listen to him on the radio since I'd met him at the bar—since the beginning of things.

This morning when he'd called, he'd been trying to make plans.

"I can't wait to see you again," he'd said. "Every day I can't wait to see you." He was silent on the other end and I realized he was waiting for me to respond. He was doing what an *Atlantic* article I'd read referred to as "active listening."

"Me too," I said. "I think about you too."

*　　*　　*

Now, on the way home from the junior college, I turned his show on using an app on my phone—a subscription I paid for, though couldn't afford—and it was a shock: his voice, surrounding me, filling my Honda Civic once again.

"Allison," he said. Or I thought I heard him say. I turned the radio up. A liquidy panic moved through me. I thought about my father somewhere, listening. Would Reid talk about what I was like in bed? What he'd said into my ear? What I'd said? The filthy things I'd whispered during sex, in the midnight-colored, spasmy throes of it.

But no, it was just a famous actress with the same first name: Allison. Now Reid was listing her many popular films. This was merely an interview that had been scheduled long ago. Idiot, I said aloud. Idiot!

He was marveling at the length of this Allison's legs, how tall she was! He joked that he was as tall as her vagina, that's where he would line up, face-to-face, er, no, lips to her—er, lips. Famous Allison laughed in that way famous women laughed when they wanted to make it clear they could take a joke.

I wasn't offended: this was Reid's spiel, his persona. But he was no longer just Reid the shock jock. Now he was also the man I was seeing, and it felt surreal, to hear the man I was seeing talk about what it would be like to see a different Allison naked—to see both sets of her lips.

I could picture this Allison in the studio, separated from him by a flimsy piece of plexiglass. I knew the chair she was sitting in—I'd seen photos of it many times. She was one of these actresses who knew when she was most attractive, knew just what to do. I'd watched her on talk shows, crossing and recrossing her gleaming shins, smiling warmly. In fact, I liked many of her movies. One I'd watched at least six times: a romantic comedy in which famous Allison falls in love with her work rival, her worst enemy.

Last night, in Reid's bed so large I'd felt marooned, we'd eaten takeout from a steakhouse I hadn't even known you could order takeout from.

I knew of the restaurant, though, from tabloids I sometimes flipped through in the grocery store checkout line. Famous people often went there to eat a storied Cobb salad and be photographed together. This, they said, is where the Cobb salad had been invented. (Could that be true? If so, who could prove it? Might anyone claim to have invented the Cobb salad? Maybe this was the whole point of Los Angeles: you just had to claim something with confidence.)

On sheets the color of eggshells, I balanced the takeout container in my lap. The steak was so tender, I cut through it with a fork, watched blood pool in the corners of the plastic tray.

We were watching a reality television show in which people agreed to get married without ever laying eyes on each other. One of the contestants was a software salesman by day and a comedian by night and I said, "My brother was one too."

"A software salesman?" Reid asked.

"A comedian," I said.

"Would I know his name?"

"Maybe," I said, though I really didn't want to say his name aloud. I thought it would push me over some edge, like I was an egg balanced on a spoon.

"I thought you were an only child," he said.

"Well I am now," I said.

"Oh," he said, and I set the plastic container of bloodied steak aside and got up to use the bathroom, where I stood looking at myself in the mirror and wondering if I might be sick. I started concentrating on the size of my pores, and that seemed to help. How did they get so big? Was there a way I could minimize them?

When I returned, I could see on Reid's face that however I looked at that moment was frightening him.

He patted the spot next to him and so that's where I sat. It was that simple: he patted and I sat. Sometimes it felt good being told what to do.

"Come here," he said, but he was the one who moved closer. He laid a hand on the nape of my neck, didn't move it, just laid it there, on the soft baby hairs that had escaped my ponytail. I rubbed my eyes as though it were only allergies, something in the air that bothered me.

When he asked if I was okay, I made a small, odd noise—it could have meant anything, and so he turned the volume up on his very fancy remote that looked like a computer in itself and moved closer to me, so that we were pressed against each other, like two blocks getting ready to build.

He had a funny way of mimicking the contestants on the show, making them weirder and goofier and yet, somehow, sweeter too. He gave them intricate backstories. He pretended to be their Jewish mothers, calling to say, "I could've set you up! Don't you trust your mother? Don't you? *Don't you?*"

He said it all into my ear, conspiratorially. I wished someone were there to witness it: witness how special I was. When I thought about the Halloween party, surrounded by all those people, I felt amazed that I'd managed to keep his attention so thoroughly on me, without even trying.

"I'm so happy to be with you," he said, his face in my neck. "I'm so happy you're here."

"Where else would I be?" I wanted to say, as though no previous life had existed until he'd arrived in it. Instead I said, "What are you doing for Thanksgiving?" and he said, "I was hoping to spend it with you."

I thought of that all now in the car, as I listened to him use the same conspiratorial voice on this very famous actress. Maybe it was just the voice he used when he wanted a woman to trust him. Somehow, that didn't make me feel less special. Quite the opposite: It made me feel very desirable. I now belonged in a rarefied group of very important women—the kind of women whose trust powerful men wanted to earn.

Also the night before: He'd given me the code to the keypad that unlocked his door, 5902. I didn't ask the number's significance. Sure, I wondered if he'd given this code out to many women before. And yes, I wondered if it had to be changed, and changed again, once things soured, went south, however the saying went. And okay, I imagined the technician who would have to go to the trouble to reprogram the code: maybe a pudgy bald guy, maybe even a woman. But I didn't ask.

"Meet me there," he'd said that morning.

How strange it felt to be walking up to Reid's house in the middle of the day, when he wasn't home, like I was interrupting the house during its private routine.

At the high-tech keypad, I pressed each button extra hard, with significance—with poignancy!—as though I were the protagonist of a story that was published in a prestigious magazine. I typed it in wrong, cursed, typed it in again. I was wearing an unflattering striped sweater; I was behind on laundry. I guess I'd reached a new level of comfort with Reid: I no longer felt the need to show myself only at my most attractive—to trick him into something. Life was getting away from me, in that pleasurable way life sometimes lags behind the things you'd rather do when you've met someone: fuck, talk all night, eat steak in bed.

I was already picturing myself inside—using his beautiful bathroom, all of the amenities! His shampoo had a gentle, wintery scent. Every shower-head was the size of a sunflower. The keypad blinked its approval, and I prepared to go in, tugging the stupid sweater down, though I didn't think anyone would be inside.

20.

Reid's house had the mild, citrus smell I'd gotten used to (a cleaning crew came twice a week) and the rows and rows of records, solemn, against the wall.

Just as I was thinking maybe I'd get into his large bed and wait for him, get completely naked and lie like something out of a Renaissance painting, I noticed a glint off the pool. Then, a splash. It was a girl swimming. No—a woman. Someone from the in-between.

The day was still, breezeless. Palm fronds drooped against the blue dream of sky. I had a weird feeling in my stomach, like I'd forgotten something I was meant to bring. The patio doors had been thrown open. I knocked politely on the doorframe.

The girl hauled herself out of the pool, and did so clumsily, getting on all fours like a dog. Her legs looked strong, muscular. She wore a blue one-piece Speedo, the kind you might use for a race. Her hair was the straw-like blond caused by too much chlorine—a lifetime spent swimming laps. She stood at the edge of the pool, backlit by the white globe of sun.

"Where is he," the girl said, by way of greeting. She didn't say it unkindly, just curiously. I knew who she was right away. The daughter. Emma.

"I guess he's not here yet," I said, and then I introduced myself—"I'm Allison," I said—and she nodded, as though my name didn't surprise her at all. I hadn't expected to meet her, and now I felt I'd needed more time to prepare. For one, I wouldn't have worn this unflattering sweater. I didn't know if I should hug her, but luckily, she was too wet for me to attempt. She draped herself over one of Reid's Adirondack chairs, moving like a kid, like someone who didn't think at all about her body. I admired women like that—who made their body a home. I was a vacationer in my body, a person who'd purchased a hotel room on one of those discount websites and didn't like what they found when they arrived, looked around and couldn't wait to leave.

"You know when he'll be home?" Emma asked. She had a face I wanted to look twice at, then one more time—compelling, as though the top half and bottom half had been fit together arbitrarily.

"I'm not sure," I said. "He just told me to meet him."

"Of course," she said. "My dad loves to keep people waiting. I'm Emma," she said, which I pretended I didn't already know. She thrust her hand out, and I took it. Our hands were the same size, and I was surprised; I'd always thought of my hands as being unusually large.

Man hands, my brother used to joke, quoting some long-ago episode of television. This is what it meant to have siblings: every joke was an inside joke, from the inside of your childhood. Then, I remembered Emma was an only child. Then again, so was I. She was dripping all over the chair, a little shivery.

"You want a towel?" I asked. "I know where they are."

She barked out a laugh so loud I flinched. "So do I," she said. "I know where everything is." And then, "Let's go in. I can make us drinks."

She dripped all over the wood floor while she moved around the kitchen, finding old, almost empty bottles of gin and rum in odd places: below the sink, above the cabinet.

"I'm the only one who drinks around here," she said. "But you probably knew that."

Just then, a floppy-eared hound bounded in, his haunches shifting like machinery as he sniffed around the place.

"You like dogs?" Emma asked, and I said, "Of course." I did like dogs, but it also seemed important I said yes.

"Kelly!" Emma said. "We're in here!"

Kelly walked in looking sweaty, panting a bit just like the dog. She had a plastic-covered stack of dry cleaning over one arm.

She wore the same dangly earrings, and a new baseball cap. This time, the St. Louis Cardinals. "He did well at the vet," Kelly said. She looked genuinely surprised to see me. (I now drove myself to Reid's. And when we went somewhere together, I drove him. He liked my car, he said, the "old humble Civic" is what he called it.) I felt a little hurt he hadn't told her about how serious it had gotten between us—I spent two or three nights out of the week here. She seemed to have made herself scarce since I came around. Maybe that was its own kind of acknowledgment.

"Allliisoooon," Kelly sang, Elvis Costello style. "What a surprise!"

Had she not expected me to make it this long, or this far?

Emma was rubbing her nose against the dog's nose, whispering intensely into his ear. "A very, very, very big man," she whispered. "My big, good man." She looked up at me, noticed I was staring at her, and said, "This is Bones."

"Hi Bones," I said.

"A stupid name, but I didn't want to change it. He's had a traumatic life so far. I didn't want to make things any harder on him."

Bones looked like he'd had a traumatic life. Sad, expressive eyes, though I had always liked that in a dog, when his eyes seemed to convey some pain he couldn't, on account of being a dog. I thought of my parents' poodle, Peter, the way my father carried him around like a baby. He knows what I'm thinking, my father would say. We have a very deep connection. But everyone knew what my father was thinking: he couldn't help but tell you aloud.

"I didn't know Reid had a dog," I said.

"Bones is my mom's dog," Emma said. "But she's not great at taking care of him. So he's more like my dog."

At the kitchen table, Emma put a glass of something clear in front of me. She was still towel-less, still dripping. She had the wiry, urgent muscles of someone who had always been very good at sports.

I'd always played them, but I was never good. I turned away then, worried that I'd been staring at her too long, that I'd been obvious about it.

"I'm gonna go pick up your dad," Kelly said, at the counter, straightening up what Emma had moved.

Meanwhile, I wasn't sure where to put my hands. I felt in the way all of the sudden. I wasn't sure how to arrange myself. Am I looking normal in this chair? I thought. How do people normally sit in chairs? How at ease Emma seemed, play-fighting with the dog, pawing at his head. Of course, this was her house—or her dad's house—why wouldn't she feel at ease?

"Did you grow up here?" I asked.

"Nah," she said. "My dad got this place like five years ago. I've stayed here off and on." She took a big swig of the drink, wincing at the taste. "We could swim, if you want, I bet I have a suit that fits you. The Jacuzzi's heated." Why had I not left a swimsuit here!

Kelly told Bones it was time to go, and Emma hugged first the dog, then Kelly for what seemed like an unusually long time. We watched Kelly climb into the Prius and drive away, Bones hanging his head from the open window, flapping his long ears in joy.

Emma turned to me and said, "Well now it's just you and me."

I had not been led to another girl's room this way, through their parents' house, since I was in high school. Since Marcella.

Emma's room looked like a guest room in a bed-and-breakfast, another page out of *Architectural Digest*, with a modern Danish-looking bed and built-in bookshelves (something I had always wanted). The only trace of her childhood was on a shelf above the desk: stuffed animals and swim trophies.

Emma caught me looking. "Oh yeah. My dad refuses to get rid of that stuff. And this too." She dragged a gigantic stuffed bear, larger than a five-year-old, from the closet. "A few years ago we had a screaming match about this bear." She dug through a drawer.

"Here," she said, pulling out another one-piece bathing suit. "Sorry I don't have anything flattering."

"That's fine," I said. How did I look in that moment? Like I needed something to flatter me? Did she think that was the reason her father was dating me, because I always went to the trouble to make myself look attractive? But I don't, I wanted to say. I'm not *that* attractive—not attractive enough for that to be the sole reason I was chosen. I'm interesting. I'm more interesting than I appear!

I changed in the bathroom, where it felt like the volume had been turned up on every maneuver: unzipping the fly on my jeans, the whoosh of my ugly striped sweater over my head. It felt painfully intimate, all the private sounds. I changed quickly and then knocked on the bathroom door. I didn't want to catch Emma unaware.

She laughed. "I've never seen someone knock from *inside* the bathroom."

When I opened the door, she blinked and said, "That color's good on you."

A square of purple-blue night shone through the kitchen window. Emma was mixing another drink in her swimsuit. Reid had one of those rich-people kitchens I had only ever seen on reality TV shows, where all of the cooking equipment was hidden—even the fridge blended right into the wall. Why would blankness be preferable to the evidence of appliances? But maybe it wasn't blankness people wanted, it was the implication of magic. The everyday minutia of life got done here unseen. Probably, Reid had nothing to do with the construction of this kitchen. Surely someone else picked it out.

"I'm making it a strong one," Emma said.

Submerged in the Jacuzzi, ice shifting in our glasses, I said, "Sometimes I like a hangover because it's something to *do*." I had forgotten how much I liked drinking, the oblivion it offered. The world looked softer—felt softer, like I was in an oil painting.

"So," Emma said, "how did you guys meet? You and my dad."

"At a bar," I said, and held up my glass.

"Let me guess," Emma said, "in Silverlake?"

"Uh-oh," I said, "are you a psychic?"

"He was looking for me." When she laughed, she threw her head back like it was a door opening. "Don't worry, I was fine. But I wasn't answering my phone. I was chasing a girl," she said.

"Did you find her?"

Emma waved me away. "Yes, I found her, but it didn't end well. My dad worries I have bad judgment."

What would that be like to have a father worry about you, and not be the one to worry about your father. "Do you?" I asked. "Have bad judgment?"

"Who knows," Emma said, "I date guys too, but I don't get as hung up on them." She looked up at the sky, then back at me. "You're not who I pictured," she said. "For my dad. I don't mean that in a bad way."

"I'm not taking it bad." I only felt curious—who did he normally date? Was there a canyon of difference between me and his usual type, or just a gully, just a ditch?

My father had only dated one woman seriously since my mother, and I'd never met her. I knew she was very unlike my mother because she worked at a tanning salon and didn't like food "she'd never heard of before," which was a surprising number of foods. The relationship had lasted less than a year and when I asked him what went wrong, he couldn't say. He couldn't explain. Maybe it simply ended in the way so many relationships do, without fanfare: a familiar body moving slowly through a doorway, becoming less familiar every second of the day.

"She had a terrible laugh," my dad said. "It sounded like machine-gun fire."

As good a reason as any other.

"The girls!" Reid said, when he arrived.

The code to the door, it turned out, was Emma's birthday.

He kissed me deeply, right in front of Emma, both of us still in our swimsuits, which didn't feel that different from underwear, at least when you're being kissed.

"Will you stay for dinner?" Reid asked Emma. "We'll order in."

"Yeah," she said, "things aren't great on the home front." Then, as if the thought had just occurred to her, she said to me, "That is, if you don't mind I stay."

"Of course not," I said. I was surprised to be asked—it still felt like it was her house, that I was the visitor.

"What about your mother?" Reid asked.

"What about her?" Emma looked at me now. "I'm staying with my mom," she said.

"Congrats on graduating college," I said.

"I didn't graduate," Emma said. Why had I assumed? "I just came home."

Over Thai food, Emma wanted to know what I did for a living. We were inside, but I could still see the pool through the window, which looked like a cough drop, like a perfect blue lozenge I could pop in my mouth.

"I mostly teach," I said. And then, maybe wanting to impress her, I said, "But I'm a writer too."

"What have you written?" Emma asked.

"Not a lot lately."

"Why not?" She'd pulled a hooded sweatshirt over her swimsuit, and I could see the wet outline through the material. I was back in my unflattering striped sweater. She had a way of asking questions that didn't seem intrusive, only curious.

"Life got in the way," I said. Sometimes clichés are necessary. What else could I say? I'd been busy smashing myself against my brother's absence, and probably would be, for the rest of my life?

Plus the logistics: every morning I had to take care of myself! I had to eat, shower, brush my hair, become presentable to the world. Then, I was supposed to get up the next day and do it all over again? Life was so long!

"Time management," I added.

The clichés were good enough for Emma, and now she turned to her father and said, "I like the Thai place on Beverly better." He agreed. They talked about a waiter they liked there, who worked a Rubik's Cube while he waited for customers to decide on their entrées. Reid seemed very relaxed around Emma. They seemed relaxed around each other, father and daughter. I found their relaxation stunning. Around my own father, I could crawl out of my skin with anxiety.

"Ya know, Emma," he said. "Allison teaches at a college."

"A junior college," I said. "And I knew someone. They got me the job. I'd dropped out of graduate school." It was true: a woman in one of my book clubs knew someone in charge. This was another thing about rich people: they had connections in all kinds of places—sheer, gauzy webs of influence.

(I'd found out that my brother died during my first semester of a graduate degree, which I was pursuing at a red-bricked, towering Ivy League. Now when I see the mascot—a red bear with a sinister jack-o'-lantern smile—I'm still filled with inexplicable rage.)

"But still," Reid said. "A junior college is still a big deal."

It made me uncomfortable the way Reid was bragging about me like I was his daughter and Emma was the guest. I didn't want her to see me as competition for her father's attention. I wanted to feel like we were on the same side. And it was a surprise to hear Reid talk about me this way. It reminded me of my own father, who loved to tell people about my accomplishments—what few there were—though he always got the details wrong. "You're going to Harvard?!" someone would say in the grocery store. No, I'd say, not quite.

"Maybe I should enroll where you teach," Emma said now.

"Maybe," I said. "What was your major?"

"Well I'm a comedian. But I majored in theater. I guess this time I'd major in something useful. Like accounting?"

"She's trying to be a comedian," Reid said. For the first time, Emma regarded him over the tom yum soup with something like coldness.

"It's really difficult," he continued, and now he was only talking to her, continuing a conversation that seemed like it had been going on long before I came into the picture. "It takes so long to get a career going. And even if you do everything right, the chances of it happening for you—"

"You think I don't know that?" she said. They stared at each other and I wondered if they'd forgotten I was in the room. "You think I don't know it's hard?" She scooted out her chair and left the kitchen, left us there with our cooling soups.

Reid said nothing. My dad, I thought, might have gone after me. He might've apologized.

21.

That night, in Reid's massive bed, he said, "I'd like to read something you've written."

"Is your daughter funny?" I asked. I was trying to change the subject.

"I'm not sure," he said. "I mean, *I* think she's funny. But it's different onstage. As a career. The Business is very hard," he said. I thought he sounded old just then, calling it the Business. He sounded like my father! But he was old. I was staring at his gray thatch of chest hair, thinking I'd like to see a photo of what he looked like at my age.

"I'm writing something new," I said. So far, my writing had been—not exactly a secret, but something I was keeping to myself. I'd been waking up early, while the city was still enshrouded in fog, letting the words pour out of me. I didn't know if the words made any sense. I figured I'd worry about that later. I thought it had something to do with Reid maybe, his presence in my life. He'd opened a valve. Or I'd opened one, and he'd made it easier.

"Did you always know you'd be successful?" I asked. He was watching a football game beyond my head. "One second," he said. A running back was tearing down the field, the football tucked under his arm like something precious.

I was sure he'd say yes. I thought I'd heard him say that on the radio: that he'd had a deep and abiding belief in himself since childhood. That he always knew he'd "make it." When he started at the radio station, he made ninety-six dollars a week. He'd said this many times on his show, but when he said it now, I made my eyes go wide as though it were new information.

"By the time I became successful," he said, "it was no longer a lucky break. It was no longer even a break—forget the word 'lucky'—it just felt like my due. That's what I'd worked so long and hard for. I don't think there's a person on earth that feels like the break is lucky, that he hadn't earned it through talent and hard work. It always feels like his due."

"Or her due," I said.

"Of course," he said. "And then all you do is complain about it."

"What do you complain about?" I asked.

"You're either too famous or not famous enough."

"I haven't heard you complain."

"I've been trying not to," he said. "Not around you." I felt very moved by that. I was not used to the men in my life shielding me from their complaints.

Even if I'd never had a dream come true, I knew how it went: a dream, once realized, always turned mundane. Time, too, could render anything stale and problematic—careers, relationships. I wanted to say something about Emma, about her own relationship to her father's fame, or her own. I wondered if she had that same gnawing sort of ambition, the kind with teeth. My brother had had it—the double *had*'s of the deceased—he'd had the teeth.

Instead, I said, "I've always wanted to write a book." I had it too, I guess, the teeth. They hadn't gnawed for a few years.

"You will," Reid said. "I have no doubt you will." But he had a far-off look in his eyes, and I got the feeling he was still thinking of himself—his own long and treacherous journey into the wilderness of success.

When he began to kiss my neck, the ridge of my collarbone, I said, "But Emma's here."

"So?" he said.

It was true: she'd stormed off to her own room after dinner, on the other side of the house, and the house *was* large, much larger than the house I grew up in. Didn't my parents have sex when I was at home? Didn't my brother? Yes. Yes, they did. I'd heard it all.

That's how I'd always defined a close family: you had to hear it all.

And so, the sex Reid and I had was quieter and gentler than usual. I

covered my own mouth to keep from crying out, to keep from saying something insane—something dirty, or worse, like I love you.

Afterward, I slid carefully from the bed. I wanted a glass of fancy, sparkling
water from the kitchen where a special tap had been installed.

There, at the table, Emma sat, eating leftover pad thai and scrolling on
her phone.

"You scared me," I said, more as a formality than a feeling.

"You don't look scared. You want noodles?"

"Sure," I said, because suddenly I did.

She was wearing a baggy, loose T-shirt, which I assumed she'd reserved
especially for sleeping. Later, I'd find out this was how Emma dressed all
the time: in shirts that seemed like they'd been shot from a cannon in a
sports arena. In reality, each shirt had been carefully chosen—this one from
a hardware shop in Montana, another one from a hockey team in Alberta,
Canada.

Now I know: People who liked to look like they weren't trying were
often trying very hard.

We sat quietly in the dark kitchen, slurping cold noodles, me still trying to eat them daintily, when finally I said, "My brother was a stand-up
comedian."

"Was?" Emma said.

"He's gone," I said.

"I'm sorry," she said. "Was he funny?"

"Yes," I said, "he was."

"What was he like?"

I could only think of odds and ends: as a kid, he'd had a turtle named
Alyssa, after a babysitter he'd had a crush on, one of my mother's former
patients who'd found herself at a normal weight. The only food he didn't
like was beans (he didn't like the texture). Once at a Diamondbacks game, a
fly ball hit him in the face and he'd needed his jaw wired shut for six weeks.

"He was sort of difficult," I said. I said it like a question.

"Were you close?"

"Yes," I said. "Surprisingly." And it did feel surprising, in our family, with our parents. We both longed for my father's difficult and erratic approval, though my brother spent so much time pretending he didn't. And we both longed for my mother's scarce attention, though, again, my brother spent so much time pretending he didn't. All of this should have made us rivals, or enemies, but instead it made us allies. At least, that's how I would've described us: partners—comrades in the battlefield of our family.

"God," Emma said. "I always wanted a sister. It's hard to go into battle alone."

It was a relief to talk about Jack in this beautiful kitchen. This could have been his kitchen, I wanted to say. He was that funny, that good. He could've earned a kitchen like this.

22.

Jack left for Vegas after he graduated, the day after, actually. He'd left his cap and gown pooled on the floor of his bedroom.

My mother and I stood on the front lawn, waving as he drove away. My father wouldn't come out to see him off—he was too emotional.

"I don't want my only son to see me cry," he'd said, though my brother had seen him burst into unexpected tears many times before. But there was something about the formality of this type of crying that my father didn't like.

"He's not going very far," I'd said.

"He might as well be," said my father.

People said Jack and I looked alike, that we could've been twins. Jack's lips were unusually red and feminine, cherubic even. We were both tall, and we had a similar way of standing, with bad posture, as though we were always beginning to droop in the sun. When we went into Reno, strangers sometimes thought we were dating. Humiliating, I'd say, disgusting! Though I found it less humiliating than he did.

At school, everyone knew me as his little sister, a buoy bobbing along behind, and also as Marcella's friend, who was prettier than me, and had her own brand of charisma, warmer than my brother's.

The first day of every class, the teacher would say, "Jack's little sister," and they'd never say it like a question. It didn't matter if they'd hated him or found him charming, impish—I had a backboard against which to bounce.

* * *

Jack's last year at home, he'd saved for Vegas by painting houses. The week before he left, he had accidentally painted the wrong house. The owners of the house returned home and were terribly confused. That morning, they'd had a dark blue house with gray trim. That evening, they had a gray house with dark blue trim. The owner of the house thought he was having a nervous breakdown.

"A little excitement," our father said, "will be good for that family."

Jack's friends had decided to have a party that night in celebration, not just for Jack leaving, but for his wonderful, hilarious failure. The Gray House Party, they called it, to be held on land owned by some kid's uncle, where there'd been a rumored orgy that included a guy from the Blue Man Group. By that time, there were more than just three Blue Men—there were many. (People said there was tape of it, though I had never seen it.)

I was late to the Gray House Party, my father had insisted I help with a project—he wanted to make kimchi. He'd just learned about it from a Korean dealer at the Peppermill.

"We can jar it and sell it," he said. "It's a miracle cabbage." Or so he was told.

When I'd finally made it to the empty plot of land, now lit up with floodlights someone had stolen from the high school gym, a boy in the grade above me, trying to ingratiate himself, said he'd been partying earlier that night with my brother.

"He's hilarious," he said. "What are we gonna do without him?"

I'd been distracted, searching around for Marcella, wondering if my hands still smelled like fermented cabbage, though I was sure my father had gotten the directions wrong.

"He's absolutely insane," the boy said. "Your brother is nuts." He said it like a compliment. "We were all taking shots," the boy continued. "A bunch of us gathered around. And your brother drank it, and afterward, he bit down, and tried to eat the glass."

I was horrified. "No," I said. "Really?"

"Yup," the boy said. "Blood was dripping down his chin."

"He ate the glass?"

"Well no, he just kind of bit down on it. I don't think he, like, swallowed the shards."

"What?" I said, and turned away from him, before he might try to explain again.

"No," he said to my back, realizing he'd said the wrong thing. "It was funny," he said. "Everybody was laughing. Everybody was amazed."

I saw Jack just then, pumping the keg, filling somebody else's cup. He was eighteen and made people laugh so hard they couldn't catch their breath.

When he looked at me and smiled, his mouth looked like he'd been eating a plum, pulpy with blood.

23.

Another creative writing class at the Glendale Community College. The discussion today: clichés and metaphors.

First, I'd tried to define a cliché: something you'd heard many times before.

"It is often used as a shortcut to something that would be too complicated or painful or difficult to explain," I said. "Or maybe just something you're too lazy to explain."

"Sounds good to me," a student had said.

"I want you to try and explain the thing."

"Damn," he said. "Who wants that."

"You have to try and grab the bull by the horns."

"What?" he said.

"See," I said. "That's a cliché."

"I've never heard that," he said. "Did you just make that up?"

Next up: metaphors. I'd passed out a list of examples.

"I don't get these," another student said. "Why not just say, 'her eyes were blue' instead of 'her eyes were like a pool or a Clorox tablet or whatever.'"

"A metaphor," I said, "is for when explaining something outright just won't do it justice."

"Or," Julie said from the back, "it's for explaining something unspeakable."

"That's right," I said. "Exactly."

The class filed out, and Julie hung back.

"How's the writing going?" I said.

"It's going good. I haven't shown it to anyone. It would totally freak out my family."

"That's how you know it's going well," I said, "if the thought of your mother reading it humiliates you."

"Well my mother's not around," she said. "But I get what you're saying."

In the car, I decided to call my own mother, who was very much around.

"Two things," my mother said. "Number one, have you heard of semen retention?"

"Mom," I said.

"I read about it online. Some men have stopped masturbating. They say retaining their semen makes their voice lower and their attention spans better. It makes them more attractive to women too. Don't research it," she said. "I did, but you shouldn't. You won't like what you find."

"Mom! I don't have that long to talk." I was going to Reid's again for dinner. We were in a relationship, though we hadn't formally discussed it. Maybe this was what adults did, I thought. They got into relationships without needing to explain the rules to each other. It hadn't been like this for me in a while: seeing someone naked and then wanting to see them again, the next day, clothed. And then the day after that. And so on and so on.

"I don't want to hear about semen," I said.

"Why are you yelling?" my mother said. "It sounds like you're shouting at me from a roof."

"I'm not!" I shouted. "I'm not yelling! Now what's the second thing."

"Well, Raj and I are fighting."

"What about?"

"Two things," my mother said.

"Mom!"

"Fine," she said, "I'll just tell you one." She must have been outside—I could hear the low hum of a mower.

"He's having trouble sleeping in a bed with me," she said. "I wake up and he's on the couch."

"Why?" I said. I drove by a group of teenagers lined up in front of a sneaker shop, jostling each other, thumbing at their phones. Everyone looked so young to me lately.

"He said the TV's too loud at night. He can't sleep. And when he finally does go to sleep, it wakes him up." My mother watched true crime shows to relax. She preferred when the wives killed the husbands, and not the other way around.

"Are you listening," my mother said.

"I'm here," I said. "I'm listening."

"Anyway, I feel like we need to reconnect. Me and Raj. I might plan a vacation."

"Where to?" I said.

"*Not* Niagara Falls," my mother said, which is where she went on her honeymoon with The Problem. "Maybe we'll visit you," she said. And then when I didn't respond, she said, "Or maybe Hawaii."

There's a photo of my parents on their honeymoon. I still have it actually. They're standing in front of the monstrous, rushing water. Even the photo looks loud. They're wearing yellow rain slickers and my mother's hand is clutching my father's arm so tightly you can see the tendons doing their hard, gripping work. Her face is washed out from the sun, but you can see that she is smiling very wide. You can tell she thinks she's won something.

When she tells the story of their honeymoon now, my mom says they went to Niagara Falls because The Problem had never been and always wanted to go. My mother, in contrast, had been several times before—she'd been going since childhood.

Most things they did in their marriage were because my father wanted to.

The first night in their bed-and-breakfast, a pipe burst and flooded the carpeted room. I can picture them: staying in bed, watching the water seep in, turning the flowers on the carpet from pale pink to a sinister brown.

They must have felt they were an island unto themselves. My father, his moods—they must have still seemed interesting to my mother then, a unique challenge, the way everything about the person you love is interesting in the beginning. Love felt like being introduced to a new country, its customs and cuisines. (How had you not traveled here before?!)

This was before they had a house and a joint bank account. Before they found themselves in a small town outside of Reno, Nevada. Before the clinic for girls who did not know how to eat normally, before truck driving and dealing cards, before my brother and me.

"But I have Peter now," my mom said. "So I'm stuck watching him for a while." My parents' standard poodle. "Your father dropped him off. Which means he's probably on his way to you."

"Good lord," I said. "Thanks for the warning."

"Don't shoot the messenger."

"Goddamn it," I said. And then, "Sorry, I love you."

Marcella had always told me I was lucky I was able to yell at my mom. "I always have to be polite to mine," she'd said. "I don't have any other choice."

Closeness allowed for anger, meanness. My mother and I knew the contours of each other's grievances. I had never been meaner to anyone than my mother, especially after my brother was gone.

"Don't you work with fucked-up people," I'd screamed. "People who can't even eat! Couldn't you pay attention to your own son?"

Was there a person in the world who did not feel injured by their childhood? I felt maimed in some elemental way. But I knew this from teaching, and from reading books: so did everybody.

*   *   *

"How did that date go?" my mother said now. I'd been seeing Reid for almost two months. Dog months, I thought, stretched long on the sofa.

"The date went good," I said. "I like him." I didn't want to say too much. Maybe I had some superstitious belief that talking about him would make him disappear, make my old life come rushing back—"jinxing it" is what we called it as kids.

"Well thank God," my mother said. "You like *someone*."

She knew not to press for more, so she ended with her usual refrain: "I love you, call your father, don't worry me."

24.

We had dinner in Reid's beautiful kitchen. This time, Emma cooked. I hadn't known she would be there, though seeing her swimming her expert, soundless laps in the pool was less of a surprise this time. Her strokes were so even, they looked mechanical, like she'd been built in a factory for this very thing: swimming.

When she hauled herself out, on all fours again, she said, "Take a picture, why don't you?"

I looked away, embarrassed.

"I'm kidding," she said, "but can you get me a towel?"

Emma and I were in the kitchen alone together while Reid picked out a record to play.

"Nothing sad," Emma yelled, poking her head out of the cool fluorescence of the fridge.

"Did he make you pasta?" she asked. She was piling vegetables on the counter. "That's the only thing he cooks."

"It was delicious," I said. I felt defensive of him. Did she know how few fathers could make fresh pasta? How many even wanted to? People with normal fathers always assumed you had one too.

"I make it better," she said. "But I won't show him up tonight."

A bluesy song began, sung by a woman with a deep, scratchy voice. The song drifted around the room and started doing its job on me, raking at my insides.

"Who's this by?" I asked, and Emma said a name I'd never heard.

"Good, right? God, I wish I was a musician. Being a comedian is so embarrassing, people talking over you while you're trying to do your job. Getting pepper ground on their grilled chicken. At least with music, it can be background noise. It sets a tone."

"I'd like to see you perform." I'd meant it to be polite, but as soon as I'd said it, I decided it was true. I wouldn't ask a stupid question my brother had so hated, like, Where do you perform (everywhere!), or What kind of jokes do you tell (lots!). Or the worst: Tell me a joke right now.

"I'm off the clock," he'd say.

"I'd love you to come," Emma said. "My dad's never watched me." I couldn't tell if this hurt her, or if it was a decision they'd made together. Reid came to the doorway now, asking after dinner.

"Hold your horses," she said, and he neighed.

After we ate, Emma wanted to swim again.

She was bobbing up and down in the water, pretending to be a seal. I felt like someone's nanny, standing over her like that.

"How tall are you?" I asked, which might've been a rude question. People often asked about my height and I couldn't tell you if it was rude or not. I guess it depended on the person. It depended on their motives.

"Five two," she said. "Do I look taller?"

"Yes," I said, because I knew that's what she wanted to hear.

"I was always the smallest one on the swim team," she said.

She was very tan, and had a funny way of moving her mouth when she talked. Not a twitch exactly, but an affect I'd never seen before. She looked like a woman I'd seen on Instagram who made a lot of money advertising tea that supposedly drained your lymph nodes of a fluid they weren't supposed to have. (My mother had sent me her photo, saying "Is this something I should buy?") I also wondered if Emma had her lips injected with something—they were very full—and I thought to myself, Maybe I should get mine done too. There was no other way to say it: her face was hard to look away from.

Reid made a joke about how you shouldn't swim with a full stomach, about how we might need to jump in and save Emma, which made me think of my father, who'd rescued a pregnant woman on vacation in Long Island, her stomach bobbing in the water like a beach ball.

"She was heavy, too," he said. "Don't think she wasn't."

The Problem had so many stories in which he saved someone's life. He was forever pulling people from cliffs or out of banged-up cars. Where did all this calamity happen? Or rather, why was he always around for it? Did he attract it somehow? Did he follow it around?

"I could've been a doctor," he'd said. "I bet I've saved more people than doctors have."

Jack had even witnessed a rescue, when our father saved a small boy from choking at the casino (there were always little boys at the casinos, waiting for their fathers to finish up losing).

My father had been about to go on break, and the boy had been waving his arms outside the gift shop, something stuck in his throat. I imagine he looked like he was alone in an ocean trying to signal a boat. The Problem tried everything—the usual backslapping and squeezing (he squeezed so hard, he broke one of the boy's ribs). In the end, my father needed to force a hole in the boy's throat with a key. It was a key my father still used, his lucky key, though I don't know what it opened. I thought about saying all that now, telling them about my father, the casino where he still worked part-time, but instead I said, "Do you play poker?"

Emma was wringing her wet hair out with both hands, twisting it.

"I don't," she said, "but I'd like to learn."

Reid said he knew a little but didn't remember all the rules. I thought he was just being kind then—he wanted to offer me an opportunity to teach them something.

I dealt cards and told them about growing up near a casino, all the time I spent there: the famous deli by the sportsbook where tourists dislocated their jaws on the thickest sandwiches you've ever seen. How my brother and I would escape to the gift shop whenever my parents fought, play with the slot machine key chains, the chocolate poker chips. (Once, my mother tried to heave an aquarium at my dad. It was too heavy, she'd only ended up sloshing the water around, unhousing our few lone fish.)

I told them about the time a single roll of a craps game lasted over five hours, until the shooter threw the dice too hard and it hopped off the table and landed on the huge belly of a man called Jumbo, a longtime regular.

"It's a seven I'm afraid," he'd said, looking down at his stomach.

They were laughing, Reid and Emma both, and it was a pleasure to make them laugh, to tell the stories of my childhood like they were little anecdotes, and not outsized tales about ghosts. There, in that kitchen, I felt witty and expansive.

I was telling them about another regular, a limo driver who sat at the poker table and talked on the phone to his wife the entire time, asking if she felt lucky. He'd look down at his cards and then say into the phone, "How do you feel about pocket nines?" Then "How do you feel about kings?"

Emma grabbed my shoulder and shook it.

"You're funny," she said. She looked at her father, "Who knew."

I think what she meant by "funny" was actually "observant," but I knew those two things were often the same. And anyway, she was a flirt, I could tell, one of those people who do it constantly, skillfully—forever leaning too close and placing a hand on your arm. I knew the type. Maybe I'd even been the type, in the before-time. When someone flirts consistently with everyone, they can also argue that they're flirting with no one. That's how it works.

Emma was wearing another big, long-sleeved shirt that she claimed had once belonged to her father, advertising a radio station I had never heard of. Later I'd find out she wore a lot of shirts that were once his.

"It doesn't exist anymore," Emma said, adjusting the sleeves, and I noticed a small tattoo on the inside of her arm: a tiny lemon wedge, a single drop of water sliding off the rind. It was one of those delicate line-drawn tattoos I now recognize as a fad. At the time, Emma must not have known, and neither did I, that hers—as artful as it looked—would age her eventually, pinpoint her to be in her twenties at a very particular time. Those tattoos would become like tribal bands. Like Chinese characters. (My brother had both.) Of course, it was hard to recognize a fad when you were in the midst of one, swimming in the current with the other oblivious fish.

"I like the lemon," I said now.

"It's an orange slice," Emma said. "Don't ask what it means."

"Something private?"

"No," Emma said. "Nothing. It doesn't mean anything."

I could've said: there's meaning right there, to go out of your way to get a tattoo you claim signifies nothing. To permanently mark yourself for what—Rebellion? Freedom? To convey nonchalance? But it was not my job to close-read another person's body.

"I like it," I said finally. And I did. Or maybe I just admired the impulse.

"Me too," Reid said patting his daughter's hand. "I didn't like it when she got it, but I'm used to it now."

"See," Emma said, "parents can get used to anything."

25.

My own father hated tattoos, and hated gambling—two things my brother loved. "I wouldn't bet on my own mother's love," he'd said.

A dealer who gambled was the biggest idiot of all—it would be like working at a sawmill only to get chopped up by the machines. He also didn't trust casinos: They were always making him work holidays, or cutting his hours for no reason at all. The pit bosses don't respect me, my father always said. That was a big thing with him: respect.

(It didn't matter what industry you were in, people always thought they were not getting the respect they deserved. Even Reid felt that way! Maybe that was why Rodney Dangerfield was so popular, it didn't matter what you were—a CEO, or a school custodian. You didn't get no respect.)

My brother liked poker most of all, in casinos or small home games, it didn't matter.

"It relaxes me," he said, "to think about numbers. To think about something other than myself."

And, he said, he didn't always play. Sometimes he'd sit in the bathtub and listen to people lose money in the other room. Sometimes that alone soothed him.

26.

At another book club, we were discussing a novel about a mother who abandons her family (her only child!) to live the life of an artist, the life she'd always pictured for herself.

This decision made the women furious. Being a good mother was very important to them. They said things like, I am a mother above anything else! It is the best job in the world! And by far the most important! But, I wondered, how many jobs had they actually *had*?

"I was a better mother before I had children," my own mother always said. Parenting was like holding a block of ice—forever melting, and you had nowhere to set it down. After I became an adult, my own parents often accused me of having amnesia: I never remembered the way I'd been loved.

I tried some of my own mother's lines on the women: "People are hardest on mothers, right? Mothers are always guilty of something."

"True," they said. "True, true." Then the talk turned to their own children, who were mostly adults. The women loved talking about their children!

Their own children didn't realize how hard parenting was. Unless their children had their own children—grandchildren!—in which case they thought it was much harder than it needed to be. (These newer generations, they so often got it wrong!)

"I would rather die than abandon my kids," a woman said. She'd just returned home from a vacation to India and now wore a silk purple sari draped around her shoulders. She'd been divorced three times, the last of which she referred to as "the Godfather—the divorce to end all divorces."

The other women agreed with her. They'd die for their kids. Nobody had ever said anything truer in their lives!

"I love my kids so much," another woman said. But this talk turned, too: what they wanted from their kids (more grandchildren!), what they wished for them, and would those wishes ever be granted?

Yes, yes—how they adored their children. Yes, yes—how their children disappointed them.

Was there anything harder for a parent to do than let their child be themselves? How could something so easy require so much effort? But I understood: It can be like separating the marrow from the bone, freeing someone from your expectations.

That was what made things so difficult with The Problem. I expected him to be normal, and he was committed to being himself.

27.

Reid asked if I would go to drinks with his daughter. "I gave her your email address," he said. "I hope that's okay."

"My email address?" I said.

He'd emailed me exactly once before: an article about a British man who'd secretly lived in his local library for two months without being caught. *YOUR DREAM!!!* he wrote in the subject line. He was impressed by my constant reading, he referred to it as "doing my homework."

We were getting ready in the morning—me, to teach, and Reid to go to some mysterious collection of meetings. Kelly was waiting for him downstairs. I could hear her singing along to something breathy, like Joni Mitchell.

He stood next to me in the bathroom mirror, dabbing on expensive face cream from a small glass jar. He was still barefoot and I was wearing shoes— I seemed to tower over him. He kissed my ear, my forehead. He had to reach up and pull my face down to him.

"Can I see you again tonight?" he said.

I thought maybe I should make a big thing about taking things a little slower, doing it all gradually. I was still waiting for some other shoe to drop, to come out of the sky and crush me. But suddenly I didn't have the effort. Who was *I* to push *him* away?

Sometimes I'd wake up in his bed and forget where I was, whom I was with. It came as a shock to see it was him! I'd gently remove his heavy arm draped over me, and then I'd sit up in bed and stare at the shape of him in

the dark. I thought, If he wakes up right now, I'll look insane. I'll look homi-
cidal. But still, I needed to stare.

Reid said he thought I'd be a good influence on Emma, this daughter who,
as he put it, was clearly in need of some direction. A comedian?! As if she
didn't know how impossible that was.

I could hear Kelly opening and closing drawers downstairs. I didn't
want her to see me. With her there, I felt I was intruding somehow. Without
me there, they had their own private jokes and daily rhythms.

"Reid," she called from downstairs. "Time's a' tickin'."

Over email, Emma and I agreed to meet at the same bar where I'd met
Reid. My regular place, Emma called it.

I was already waiting at the bar when she sat down. The smell of her
hair reminded me of childhood—the smell of suburbia, of my ranch house,
of neighboring towns that were nicer than mine, like that of the Christian
girls, who had whole drawers devoted to swimsuits. The smell of Emma's
hair reminded me of walking through one of those nicer neighborhoods on
a breezeless March afternoon, someone's father washing his Mustang in the
driveway, another organizing boxes in the depths of his open garage. (So different than my garage, which was constantly spitting up our family's debris,
as though it had tried to swallow and couldn't manage to keep it down.) Yes,
I thought, it must be Emma's hair, or her very essence, that smelled like a
fresh-cut lawn in spring.

"Your hair smells good," I said.

"It's drugstore stuff," Emma said. "Garnier Fructis." But I'd already
guessed that.

Now, Emma told the bartender, "I'll take a vodka tonic."

"Put it on my tab," I said. I had the dregs of a Diet Coke in front of me.

"You have to drink with me," Emma said. "You can't buy a lady more
alcohol than you're having. Or else you're taking advantage."

"We're both ladies," I said. "So I don't think that rule counts." But she was already looking past me, deeper into the bar.

"Sorry," she said, "I thought that was someone I knew." When she turned her attention back to me, I felt a click of satisfaction. It reminded me of her dad, of his roving eyes, his scattered attention—watching birds beyond my head. When Emma squared up to me on her barstool, I felt like I'd earned her back.

"I guess it depends on who invites who to drinks," she said. "So technically the drinks should be on my dad. Because he set this up."

"I'll have one," I said, "but let me pay. I'm older."

"Not by that much."

"But still," I said. "I'll have the same as her," I told the bartender. When he walked away, Emma said, "He and I went to high school near each other." She leaned close to me, whispered in my ear, "We had a threesome once."

I wished I'd paid more attention to what the bartender looked like, how he carried himself. I wanted to know who she'd been attracted to, who she *was* attracted to right now.

"Is it weird when you see him?" I asked.

"Not at all," Emma said. "He could be a distant cousin, or an old friend."

"I've never had a threesome," I said, though she didn't ask. "I've never even considered it."

"You should," she said. "You might enjoy it." Just then I didn't know where to look. I'd wished we'd gone to a dimmer bar, with a TV in the corner, or a pool table. There was nowhere else for my eyes to rest other than her.

The bartender returned with the drinks and Emma said, "Hello Josh," and he said, "What do you want?" with a little playful eye roll, like they were gearing up to do a vaudeville act they'd done many times before. How much Emma reminded me of Reid right then, with his expert flirting, the teasing way he drew you out. Not Reid in person, but Reid on the radio.

"Do you think it's weird between us?" she asked the bartender. He had sleeves of colorful tattoos.

"Why would it be weird between us?" he said.

"See," Emma said, turning to me. "We're like cousins. We're like friends."

"You know your dad was in here a while ago," the bartender said.

"I know," Emma said. "With her." She pointed toward me and he scanned my face with no recollection.

"Right," he said. "He was worried about you."

"Not that worried," she said. "Not so worried he wouldn't get distracted by a good-looking girl."

I took in the words "good-looking" as the bartender moved away. "Have you talked to the girl you were chasing?"

"No," she said. "And I probably never will again."

"Was she a comedian?"

"Not really. She makes videos online."

"What kind?"

"I don't know how to explain it. Just random stuff. She builds weird little Rube Goldberg machines. She pulls pranks. Does weird performance art in public places. She's very unique. Of course people are copying her now, but she was the first. She's very popular."

I thought about how people had been doing that kind of thing for many years now—probably since the beginning of time—making strange inventions for their friends, doing jumping jacks in the grocery store and laughing at the people who stared. But thirty years ago, they did not become celebrities. The most they could hope for was a feature on *America's Funniest Home Videos* and the treasured VHS that would result, to be passed around to friends, to be whipped out at every holiday. They were just people like my uncle Bobby, who came to Thanksgiving with a potato invention he created that could mash and peel simultaneously. It never occurred to anyone that Uncle Bobby could be famous for that type of thing, that he could be rich. Now, the internet would fawn over Uncle Bobby. He could build a following. He could make a promotional post partnering with Starburst. Instead, my aunt Gena—my mother's sister—insisted she had no idea why she ever married him, why she ever thought he was funny. He's a loon, she would say now.

"What are you thinking?" Emma said.

"About my uncle Bobby," I said.

Emma ordered another drink and so I did too. "Make it a double," she said to Josh.

"Bossy," I said. I wondered if she had a best friend, if she had a sidekick. I could see how easy it would be to follow her around a school lunchroom— around a whole town.

"Why did you drop out of school?" I asked her.

"Oh," Emma said offhandedly. "I hated it." She had a way of leaning into you when she spoke. Even her conversations were athletic.

"I was extremely lonely," Emma said.

"Say more," I said, which is what I said to my students, or the women in my book clubs, when I was afraid they'd get too shy, that they'd withdraw something interesting I might actually want to hear.

"I was in love with my roommate and nobody knew. I was miserable." She was holding my gaze now, like she'd fixed me beneath a pin.

"I can't imagine you lonely," I said.

"We're the loneliest!" Emma said. "People who seem like they're friends with everyone." Now she was looking at me very intensely, as though she were trying to see beneath my skin. Probably the intensity would've looked ridiculous on someone else, if she wasn't so empirically good-looking. I realized then that if I hadn't felt attracted to her, I would've felt embarrassed for her, looking at me like that. Attractive people can get away with a lot—they can take big swings. I was surprised to find the attraction I felt for her was not something I needed to talk myself into or out of. It simply existed. Emma had the same turned-up nose as her father, but it looked better on her. The small nose, the full mouth: she could've modeled for a magazine that sold well-priced jeans to the middle of America.

"That makes sense," I said. "I mean, when I think about my students. There's one in particular. Everything he says comes out like a joke. Meanwhile, I know that isn't true. He takes everything seriously. He takes everything to heart."

"How do you know?"

"I see his writing!"

I was thinking of a football player, always surrounded by an amoeba-like group of rowdy guys. He had the kind of affable, self-deprecating clumsiness that made women his age refer to him as their best friend, when he wanted something else from them. It won't be forever, I wanted to tell him. Eventually, a woman will look at you and think, I could make a house inside this guy. I could make a safe, stable home inside his rib cage. Now, his stories were about dropping women off after buying them pizza. They were about wanting to say one more word before they closed the door on him. I'd told him to carry a notebook around and write everything down. He came up to me after class.

"You were right," he'd said. "I like collecting what everybody says. It feels like money in the bank."

"I like the way you talk," Emma said now. In high school, I'd been told I sounded weird when I talked. Obviously, that hadn't been a compliment. Reading so much had set me apart as someone odd, to be mistrusted.

"What do you mean?" I said.

"I dunno. You really enunciate all your words. Is that a Reno thing?"

"I'm not from Reno," I said.

"My dad said you were."

"I'm from nearby. But no, I don't—I read a lot, growing up. Maybe that's what it is."

"Yes," Emma said. "You talk like you're reading aloud."

"That sounds bad."

"You talk carefully. Like each word matters."

Words were money in the bank, I thought.

Emma's phone vibrated: Reid checking in on her.

"I can't imagine him at this bar," Emma said. Then my phone buzzed. He chose her first, I thought.

"Someone recognized him when he was here," I said.

"Oh I bet he loved that."

"I'm not sure," I said. "He seemed kind of annoyed."

"Trust me. He hates when nobody recognizes him. He won't tell you that, but he's paranoid about not being famous anymore. I tell him, listen: it's unavoidable. Fame, like youth, will always leave you."

I felt a little unsteady, and I worried I'd had too much to drink. "Did you always know you were funny?" I asked. I didn't want to field any questions about myself. I worried I'd say too much, or not enough. I didn't want her to think I was boring, or bland, a woman her father could hang his opinions on, a coatrack with long hair.

"Yes," she said. "I was always funny." She said it like a fact that had always existed, like having brown eyes or a good sense of direction. Had I ever been that confident about anything in my life?

"There was a 'Comedy Night' in college," she said. "And I watched this frat boy perform and I just remember thinking, *That should be me.*" Plus, she said, she remembered seeing her roommate laugh—a weird, horsey laugh—and that had made it worse, or had made her more determined. She had wanted that attention.

"From the girl you liked?" I'd said.

"From everyone," she said. "People think it's because of my dad, but it's the opposite. I wanted to be anything else."

"But you are what you are."

"Exactly," Emma said. Then, "Hey, that guy's looking at you." I sat up straighter, prepared myself to be hit on, right here at this bar. I would act nonchalant, like it happened all the time. I was glad too, that it would happen in front of her. I wanted her to think of me as desirable. Men want me, I thought. Not just your old dad.

But no, a man was waving, like he knew me already. I was not used to running into anyone I knew in Los Angeles. I knew so few people then.

He walked toward us and I felt a flash of dread: It was a boy from my high school, from my brother's grade.

I didn't want to talk about my brother—not now, not here. I was having fun, I thought. I'd forgotten who I was, and where I came from.

His name was Cam. In those years, Cam wore clothes so monochromatically gray and unstylish, it was hard to imagine where he found them. Certainly you didn't go to the mall to buy shirts like that, with wolves and Yoda and monster trucks like little kids wore, but also huge polo shirts with *Anderson Plumbing* stitched into the sleeve. "Goodwill," my mother said, but all gray? All, seemingly, chosen specifically by Cam for whatever reason.

It wasn't just his general weirdness that made people bully him. He had so many other genetic mishaps: a high-pitched voice, his pear shape, his thick glasses. He often came to school carrying some stick or wearing a pirate eye patch, some private, leftover equipment from a game that happened the night before. But with whom did he play? He had no friends. Not that we knew of.

Then Marcella and I returned home one day from school and there he was, with Jack and his buddies.

"Do you know Cam?" Jack said. Of course we knew Cam. He was the butt of every joke in our grade, and he wasn't even *in* our grade.

"Not really," I said.

"He's got great stories," Jack said. "He knows a lot of weird stuff." He didn't say it in a way that was making fun of him, winking over his shoulder at his friends. He was just stating something true. "He has interesting stuff to say." Or "a lot of cool stuff in his head." I forgot now the way he said it. (I hated to forget any turn of phrase he used! If youth was wasted on the young, then memory was wasted on people who don't think they'll need to remember.)

Now, Cam was dressed like any guy in an LA bar—a plain T-shirt, stylishly cut jeans.

"Your brother," he said after we exchanged hellos. "I was sorry to hear what happened to him."

Had Jack invited him to the Gray House Party? Had he been there to see him bite through the glass? Or jump in Lake Tahoe, naked, in the dead of winter? Or kiss the lunch lady right on the mouth? Had he seen any of it?

"He was always really nice to me," he said. And then to Emma, he said, "Not everybody at our high school was."

"Thank you," I said. "That's nice of you to say."

Cam walked away, and Emma said, "That must make you feel good." But it didn't. I didn't like being surprised by a reminiscence. I needed to be prepared, like a catcher with their glove on.

Emma climbed off her barstool. "I have your email address now," she said, with a sly tilt of her head, "and I'm not afraid to use it."

*   *   *

I'd grown accustomed to calling Reid in the car, on my way to and from somewhere. I liked to hear his voice, to tell him something unusual I'd seen or heard.

Tonight, I told him a vending machine at work had spit out two Sprites instead of one.

"What else?" he said. "What about Emma."

"It was good," I said. "She was good." I didn't want to say too much. Especially not the threesome thing, because who wanted to hear that about their own daughter. And he of all people—who had talked about threesomes on-air, that he'd never liked them, that they reminded him of group projects at school (I was always carrying everyone else's weight, and still, everyone got an A. Wouldn't that happen in a threesome? I'd go down on everyone while they forgot about me and still, they'd somehow get As). Would he really want to know that his own daughter had one? And that she might've enjoyed it?

"I like her," I said. "You were right."

28.

That night, I was able to find a clip online of Emma doing stand-up in a sports bar. She went by a different last name. I assumed it was her mother's maiden name. I felt a little guilty pulling it up, like I was betraying Reid in some way.

She was wearing another huge T-shirt, standing on a makeshift stage built of wooden planks, football and basketball jerseys tacked on the wall behind her. I thought maybe the gigantic T-shirts were supposed to distract from her face, from her conventional attractiveness. She had the kind of face that people always said looked familiar, the way in which beautiful people always look familiar—like you've seen them before. I'm sure it had to do with symmetry. In the background, the usual bar din: ice clinking in cheap glasses, the bartender asking, "Another?"

In the video, Emma appeared smaller in person, and somehow—though she was onstage—shier. She had a deadpan way of speaking that wasn't the way I'd heard her talk in regular life. At the bar, she was much more animated, gesturing emphatically with her hands. Was this the more authentic version of her, onstage? Was the version I'd met a persona she'd been putting on? Maybe it was all of those things at the same time: all the versions laid on top of each other.

Either way, the version I met was better, I thought. If not funnier, then looser, and more comfortable. More herself. Though how would I know that, really?

In the clip, Emma told a joke about her divorced parents.

When they were married, she said, my dad couldn't have an affair because he would've needed to ask my mom where to go and what to say.

Of course, Emma didn't say her father's name, didn't say that he was famous.

In the joke, he could be any dorky husband; anybody's clueless dad.

29.

In class, the ponytailed girl who couldn't wait to transfer said, "Why are we always reading stories where someone dies?"

"Loss is an engine," I said. "It can really drive a story forward."

"Oh, God," the girl said. "Here she goes again."

30.

I could sort memories about my brother into different categories: fond memories, awful memories. And then there are the kinds of memories that feel somehow, achingly, like a wound.

The last time I visited my brother in Vegas I hadn't seen him for a year.

At the airport, he'd gotten out of his car to wait for me at the curb, leaving his Jeep with its hazard lights flashing, a clog in the artery of the airport traffic, everyone honking and shouting and flipping him off.

When he saw me, he used a private nickname he'd used for me all my life, before any of my memories existed.

He said he was glad I came on my own, that I hadn't come with our parents. He launched into an impression of The Problem, saying, "I only like to take vacations when we're all together! We shouldn't be split off into groups!" He did the impression with a Long Island accent, though my father had grown up in Nevada. The impression made me laugh, as it always had. Once you lived with someone, the space came alive whenever you saw them.

And my parents had wanted to come. I had convinced them not to. I regret this now—of course I do. Maybe they would've seen something. Maybe they would've *done* something.

✻   ✻   ✻

The sight of Jack made me feel easier inside, even though he looked differ-ent: worse. He was paler, despite the long hours as the lifeguard at the hotel pool. Skinnier too, his clothes baggy, a belt holding his whole life together.

I said the private nickname I'd always used for him: a name similar to Jack but not quite Jack (I couldn't say the "-ck" when I was little).

Normally I didn't say the name aloud in front of anyone other than our immediate family, and Marcella. My dad always felt left out when I said it, like my brother and I had invented a private language only so we could exclude him.

"Come here, you little idiot," Jack said, but I knew he didn't think I was an idiot at all. I knew he thought I was very smart. Had he ever said that? Somehow he never had to. It was not that our family didn't know how to show affection, it was that the affection often came out sideways.

Then he took me to his apartment, though it was actually just someone's guesthouse.

"This is where I've been staying," he'd said, which was different than "This is where I've been living," though I only thought about that later. The place smelled like rotten vegetables and something slightly more metallic.

"Sorry," he said, when he saw me looking around. But what was he apol-ogizing for? There was no mess. The odor was something less visible, like it was coming from the walls.

"You have to pay attention to smells," my father had said. "Odor told the truth when people didn't." Before driving the truck and dealing cards at the Peppermill, my father cleaned out dead people's houses. Much later, the same company asked my brother to clean out the house where the herbal supplement guy had killed his parents. My brother refused. He claimed to believe in ghosts.

✻   ✻   ✻

In my brother's guesthouse, I remembered thinking about the guy from New York whose whole job was to evaluate how the psychological stigma of a property affected its value. If he'd stepped into this place where my brother lived, what would he say? This is worth nothing? *You* should pay a person to take this place off your hands.

Jack had two sagging hiking boots in the corner of the room, caked with mud.

"I've been hiking," he said flatly.

After that, the green room of the comedy club on the top floor of a very famous casino. It had plush red seats, as velvety as the inside of a jewelry box. He'd recently been passed, which meant he could now perform regularly at the club. That's what they called him: a regular. "An honor," he said. "You have no idea."

But I did have some idea. At least I knew the beating he'd taken to get there, or some of it. How often he'd text me at 1:00 a.m., that he'd finally gotten the spot he wanted, in front of the right booker, but it was at a shit time, 12:45 a.m., when the audience was tired. Or guess what, the booker had left right before he'd stepped onstage, had gone outside for a cigarette, or to buy a candy bar. How unfair it was to have his whole life in someone else's hands. (The booker was an imbecile, too, had he told me that? How many times did he have to tell me that!)

But finally, finally, it had happened. He was passed. He was a regular. He'd gotten his due.

"Look," Jack said, pointing out his own framed, signed photo on the green room's wall, in which he was smiling maniacally. His signature was large, scrawled over his chest.

I'd wanted to take a picture of it, so I could show our parents, and I still have it now—Jack standing grimly next to his own face. He refused to smile. That would be too embarrassing. Too earnest.

I remembered finding most of the comedians in the green room intimidating, though I'd liked an older guy who wasn't trying as hard to be funnier than everybody else, to talk over everyone. He had an amused look on his face the whole time, and after anyone told a story, he'd shake his head, as though he was resigned to the strangeness of life. Like existence was pretty funny after all.

I told him an old favorite from my father, about dealing cards for a mob boss and the mob boss telling The Problem he'd hire him as a butler, that's how much he liked his countenance, and his hands.

The reason why this story was particularly interesting is that my father has a dead hand. It was usually the first thing anyone noticed about him, though it was never the first thing I mentioned, not even the second or the third.

If the hand had a medical term, I'd never known it. "My dead hand," was what my father had always called it, and occasionally "my off hand." The hand was smaller than his normal hand, and shriveled, like a spoiled piece of fruit. He'd had it since he was born (he said it made him a better card dealer) and while he never complained about the hand—used it as though it were a perfectly normal hand, gesturing and eating, and doing all the other hand things—he often complained about his unluckiness, in the way other people complained about their height or their hair color. Somehow I had come to associate this unluckiness with Jewishness, the same way people associate Jewishness with mama's boys and oversized noses.

"The hand I was dealt!" he liked to say, a half joke.

"Did your father go work for the mob boss," the older comedian asked.

"No," I said. "He had a baby at home." I pointed to Jack.

"Wild," the comedian said, shaking his head. "What a wild time to be alive." I assumed he meant any time.

Later, I would see this comedian on TV, in a sitcom in which he played the hapless, unemployed brother of a CEO. This comedian was very famous, it turned out.

"Tell her to sit down," a man said, "she's making me nervous." I had been standing up so I could better imitate my father at the craps table, but now I sat down, chastened. I'd been caught taking up too much space, too much air. I wasn't on the lineup. I wasn't even a comedian—I was just someone's little sister.

"This is Tommy," Jack said, about the guy. Tommy wore a cowboy hat and suspenders, though they didn't look like goofy props on him, they looked like the uniform from whatever strange country he hailed. He could've been from Reno, I thought, or outside of Reno. I didn't ask. He had a nose that suggested a history of violent fights.

"This is my sister," Jack said.

"Your boy's good," Tommy said. "I'm thinking of representing him." He had one of those tiny red cocktail straws in his hand and was pointing it at Jack as he spoke. Something about Tommy made me nervous, though I stopped the thought from wholly forming in my mind. How much energy I put into looking away! Now I think: sometimes all the information is there right in the first five minutes, laid out for your inspection.

The talk in the green room turned to other things, exes and overrated comedians and the craziest things they'd done for money. A woman who was friends with Jack said she hated being called a "female comedian" because who wanted to be called a female anything? She told a story about marrying a Russian guy for thirty thousand because he needed a green card.

"Stand-up doesn't pay well," she said.

"How did you meet him?" someone asked.

"I was selling time-shares over the phone," she said. "And we just got to talking. Imagine if we'd fallen in love." She had what looked like a thousand braids, and a great boisterous laugh.

"Are you still married?" the older comedian asked.

"No but we still talk! He has a very cute baby. He married a woman from his Russian Orthodox church." She kept letting her eyes rest on Jack, or not letting—she couldn't help herself. She had to draw her eyes away from him again and again. I liked the woman, and I liked the fact that she seemed to have a crush on Jack, that someone here had her eyes on him, literally. Maybe he was okay, I remember thinking then. Maybe he had people who were paying attention.

"You're a real giver," Tommy said to the woman. People quieted when he spoke. He had some pull over them.

"How about you," Tommy said to me, "are you a giver or a taker?" I looked at Jack, waiting for him to step in, to say, "Hey man, that's my sister," but instead, Jack looked at me expectantly, as though curious about my answer.

"Are those my only options?" I said. From the stage, we heard an occasional line from a comedian's set—"I've certainly had worse!"—followed by scoops of laughter.

"Your brother says you're smart," Tommy continued. "And usually smart girls are takers. It's the dumb ones who are givers."

I shrugged, pretending to look at my phone.

"Answer," he said. The command in his voice startled me.

"I'm neither," I said. "Or I'm both. I'm a giver and a taker." I tried to make my face go blank, thoughtless, like I was playing poker.

Tommy's face changed, puddled into laughter. He was even more unattractive when he laughed. "Great answer," he said. "You're right," he said to Jack. "She's a keeper."

For the rest of the night, his nearness unsettled me. And even more so, his familiarity with Jack, the way Jack seemed to constantly take note of where Tommy was standing in the room, like they were lovers or family members.

Tommy left as abruptly as he came in and I whispered, "Who was that guy?" and Jack said, as quiet as I'd ever heard him, "Someone I need to impress."

That seemed the crux of the problem: the people Jack needed to impress in this place. He'd become a limb bowed under the weight of so many bad apples.

Jack had a great set. There was a wildness to his performance, a lack of self-consciousness that made every audience member lean forward. It was his presence! It was like having a superpower, I thought. As though the shell of him cracked open and his true self was able to burst forth.

I remembered he told a joke about my mother that surprised me. Maybe I even found it a little offensive, though that's hard for me to access now. I just remembered how it started: "My mom loved me, but she didn't like me.

She has a problem with men." It went on from there, though I no longer remembered the punch line.

Before then, I thought we both found my father the more difficult one. My mother could fly off the handle, but it always seemed deserved—my father had been the one to send her careening.

"I found them both difficult," Jack said. "The only one who wasn't difficult was you."

"Tommy wants us to go to his hotel room after the show," he said. We were hanging out in the bar of the comedy club, everyone coming up to Jack so they could tell him things he already knew—how funny he was, how he kind of looked like a famous, white basketball player.

Still, I could tell his set disappointed him. "People are making more eye contact with the guy who went before me," he whispered. People always made eye contact with the person they thought was funniest.

"You were funniest," I said.

"You always say that," he said.

"You want to go with suspenders guy?" I asked now, though I knew the answer. Long gone was the protective older brother, and in his place, not a stranger exactly, but a stranger version of him. He even spoke in a new way, a little jittery, like the edges were cut with the perforated scissors people used for arts and crafts.

"You were a wild man up there," the female comedian said. "Incredible." It was true, at one point he'd ripped off his shirt and banged on his chest like an orangutan. It wasn't as hacky as it sounds. I'd seen him do it before but it never failed to fool the audience: make them think they were witnessing something for the first time. That was part of the magic—making his act appear new again and again.

Jack's shirt was still partially unbuttoned and now he and the female comedian were staring at each other, and it felt like there was some communication happening between them that was just out of my murky reach. "Wild man," she said again.

*   *   *

It was all very disorienting. I felt frustrated, and hurt. He'd begged me to come visit and now that I was there he kept looking at me, surprised, as though he couldn't figure out how I appeared.

"I don't want to go to that guy's hotel room," I said.

"Why?"

"Because he's weird."

"Everyone here is weird," he said, "it's Vegas."

Earlier, when Jack was onstage, I'd had a conversation in the green room with one of his friends, who said, "I think your brother's gonna be famous."

"Really?" I'd said, waiting for whatever compliment would come after.

"You gotta be like him," he said. "You gotta be a little insane to get famous." And then, seeing my face, he said, "And he's really funny."

"Thanks," I'd said.

Later, I'd think about this night so often it was as though the night itself ran under my life like a private river.

But in the hotel room, there was none of the debauchery I pictured: no lines of cocaine or strippers or shattered bottles of champagne. Why did my imagination always run away with me—drag me into some hellish, curdled version of reality? Too many books, I thought. Too many books were maybe a bad thing!

A nerdy-looking guy in a beanie was showing Tommy something on his phone, and Tommy was poking the screen with his tiny red cocktail straw, laughing in a gasping way.

"Show Jack," Tommy said, when he saw us.

Jack left me in the corner of the room by a blue plastic cooler someone had brought (a cooler like we used to bring to the public pool), so I opened it, still angry with Jack, and was surprised to find inside—instead of White Claws and Bud Lights—piles of cash.

An image I will never forget: the cooler filled to the brim with cash.

"Hey!" Tommy said, with hatred in his eyes, or maybe fear—the line at that moment a blurred one. "Shut that," he said. "Who fucking brought that in here?" Jack looked at me with the same expression.

"Ally," he said, a name only our father called me, "don't touch that."

"I thought it had drinks," I said dumbly. Why would a cooler not have drinks?!

By then, girls had arrived, and not the paid-for-girls I'd imagined, but normal girls, maybe girls from the audience—groupies—because they were excited to meet Jack, even excited to meet his sister. He slung his arm around my shoulders in a jovial way, trying to make things up to me. Someone had hauled the cooler out, to wherever it belonged. I was still feeling sore from Tommy yelling at me. I felt tender and on edge. I ducked away from my brother's arm.

The girls started talking only to each other. Probably the party was also much lamer than they'd imagined—no cocaine, no Chris Rock. They were talking about someone they knew from high school who'd had a urinary tract infection for two years straight. They'd known each other forever, they said, since grade school. They French-kissed once, too, if it matters. Hearing them made me miss Marcella—the conversations that felt like they'd been going on for our entire lives, like rope we'd sometimes drop and pick up again whenever.

I kept trying to get Jack alone, to talk to him! But he was holding court, treating me like any other person in this room—just another audience member. Suddenly it seemed to me like his social generosity was more sinister, or else I was seeing it in a more sinister light. Charm was just power he enjoyed holding over people.

I'd taken AP government. I knew this about power: the person holding it didn't have to be reasonable. In fact, wasn't it better when the power was unreasonable? Tyrants, fathers, that's how the power stayed put, grew more powerful.

It was nearly 1:00 a.m. and one of the comedians wanted to go downstairs to the casino's restaurant and eat eggs and play keno and I finally pulled Jack aside and said, "What's wrong with you?" I had so many questions I wasn't sure which to ask first in the long line of them. I'd been doing my best to make small talk with his friends, to chat with the groupie girls about somebody else's bad boyfriend. Mostly I'd been waiting for my brother to notice me, to wonder if I was having a bad time. "Why are you ignoring me?"

I dragged him away from Tommy, where they'd been having some animated discussion about *Saturday Night Live*. It's all losers, Tommy was saying. If you got on it, though—

I'd pulled Jack in the bathroom and under the fluorescent lights. His eyes looked very red, and a little scared.

Alone together, he made his face go soft in apology. "I think the pressure's been getting to me lately," he said.

This was a move I recognized: to be vulnerable in a way that surprised me. He thought that his jarring self-awareness would absolve him. So often, it had. The failures were the worst—and being a comedian was so rife with failure—how could he possibly fail at the one thing he was meant to do with his life? If he didn't have this, he had nothing.

"I'm worried about you," I said.

"Well you don't have to be. You don't have to think about me every moment." I remembered I had trouble grasping the meaning. He'd turned on me so quickly.

"Don't think about you?"

"I don't think about you," he said. "I let you live your life. I don't try to control you."

"You don't think about me?" I repeated, but he'd turned his back to me.

I didn't know why he'd said it, but it seemed crueler than any mean name he might've called me. Wasn't that all I wanted: to be thought about? To be seen? In every family you were lucky if you felt understood by even one other person.

"Fine," I said, "I won't think about you," and booked a flight home that night.

After the trip, I'd called my father. "Something's wrong with Jack," I said.

"What's wrong with him?" He thought I meant the flu, or allergies, something curable. Something simple to explain.

"I don't know," I said.

"There's nothing wrong with him," he said. He, too, seemed annoyed with me. "Moose," he said. "I just saw a moose. Huge guy with gigantic antlers."

"Dad," I said. "Listen."

"I'm listening," he said. "God that sucker was big."

"Well I'm not talking to Jack right now. He was being an asshole." Somehow I was trying to get back at my father, too. I can see that now, though I didn't see it then. My father, the person who I could never manage to yell at, who I could never get out from under.

"I'm sure you're overreacting," he said.

All my brother had to do was apologize. That's what I kept telling myself. I wouldn't be the one to reach out first. I was tired of taking the high road—tired of watching everyone enjoy themselves on the lower road without me.

We hadn't spoken again.

When people asked me about visiting him, I'd lie. I said it was really fun, though yes, maybe Jack had seemed a little stressed, a little drunken. To be honest, I'd say, I couldn't remember all the details.

Not true. I couldn't forget it no matter how hard I tried.

31.

After we had drinks, Emma sent me an email with her miserable little résumé attached. At the time, she was working at a grocery store handing out samples. *I know I need a better job,* she wrote. *If you happen to have any suggestions.*

When I replied, I cc'd Reid, which made me feel responsible—he and I were the adults in the situation, looking out for her.

I'll forward your résumé to the junior college, I wrote. *Maybe they need someone in admin.*

Thanks!!!! Reid wrote.

I don't know what admin is, Emma wrote, *but I can't say I don't like it.*

In the next email she sent, Emma removed Reid altogether.

Would you like to go to the Korean spa, she wrote. *It's very relaxing.*

I agreed, though I'd never heard of the Korean spa. But I had heard of spas in general. I was not a savage; I had not been raised by complete and total wolves.

Inside the Korean spa, there were three different Jacuzzis (warm, hot, and cold) and two different saunas (wet and dry)—and everywhere: women, naked. Everywhere I looked women were laughing, confiding. In the Jacuzzi, a woman with an Afro was telling her friends a story about a man who'd disappointed her. (When was the last time I had laughed with a group of women?) There were women alone, too, eyes closed, heads back in relaxation. In the mirror, a woman studied her eyebrows unhappily.

Emma was already in the sauna—I could see her through the glass door, sitting with her head bowed, like a boxer between matches. I tried not to stare, though it was compelling to watch someone who did not know they were being watched. Her hands looked very pink, as though she'd been applauding. Her abs had those delineated lines, like they'd been molded from clay, quartered and squared.

When I opened the door to the sauna, I coughed, as though I were entering her bedroom again.

She didn't move at all, didn't straighten up, just looked over at me and said, "I can't believe you've never been here."

"I haven't been a lot of places," I said. I delicately draped a towel on the wood and sat next to her, an adult-sized space between us. We sat in sweaty silence. A muted Korean game show played on the television—a heavyset man eating something from a boot. He kept stopping to choke and clap. I hadn't wanted to be the first one who needed to leave, who needed air, but when I couldn't stand the dry heat anymore, I suggested the Jacuzzi.

Inside the hot tub, two women bent their heads toward each other. One laughed, and the other set her hand gently on the laughing woman's back. They might have been friends or lovers or sisters or mother and daughter. That kind of intimacy between women can be very difficult to decipher. I could feel the hot water working on me, loosening me up.

"Do you have many female friends?" Emma asked. She was watching the groups of women too.

"I have a best friend," I said. I wondered if I should be insulted by the question. "Her name's Marcella. Though I'm not great at keeping up with her." I thought of Marcella, who lived in New York now, in a whole different time zone. "How about you?" I said.

"Well I went to an all-girls school for preschool until college," Emma said. "So yeah, I guess. I think I'm easy to open up to. I know a lot of girls' secrets."

I could guess what the secrets were: complaints about your body, your crush, your relationship with your mother, your father's affair, the errant hand of a neighbor boy down your pants. Some of this language was universal. Maybe I was no longer fluent, but I was familiar.

Marcella had once told me a secret, that I, to this day, have told no one. It was a familial secret of the most horrible kind: an older cousin in a dark room, a hard candy in the shape of a strawberry, confusion, a whispered command to get on her knees, but in a sweet voice, a too-sweet voice.

Now when I thought of Marcella, it was sometimes that secret I thought of first: the strawberry candy, the sweet command, Marcella on her knees. On Instagram, Marcella so often posted her husband and small child—a little girl with glasses. Had she told her husband? How often did she think of the cousin, the hard candy, the command? Maybe not as often as I did.

Not so long ago, she'd posted a picture of a family reunion: the cousin smiling by a firepit. There in the very same backyard! Families could be unbearable.

After the spa, Emma and I ate on the floor in the café, our legs crossed. I felt relieved to be clothed again, to not have to avert my eyes from her nakedness anymore.

"Is my dad happy we're hanging out?" she said.

"Yes," I said, surprised she brought him up just then, on this isle of women. "Very much."

Just last night, he'd thanked me again. He acted like I was doing a good deed, or a personal favor for him.

"It's my pleasure," I'd said.

"You don't understand. I coulda had class. I coulda been a contender."

"What?"

"It's back on." He gestured to the gigantic flat-screen TV beyond my head—we were in the middle of *On the Waterfront*. He was introducing me to the Top Ten Best Movies Ever Made.

"What list is this?" I'd asked, thinking he'd borrowed it from something official.

"It's just my list," he said. "One I made up in my head." In exchange, he said he'd read my ten favorite books. But I already knew: he wasn't much of a reader.

"Do you listen to your dad's show ever?" I asked Emma now.

I had to wait until Emma swallowed. She ate in too-large bites, like the whole meal was being timed. "No," she said. "Why would I? So I can hear what kind of porn my dad watches?"

"Right," I said. "Makes sense."

On-air, he said the porn term he searched most often was "MILFs." When I'd asked him about it, he said he'd only said that because it sounded funniest. The actual porn he watched was very normal. "I search 'man plus woman romantic,'" he said.

"What about you?" he'd asked.

What I liked most in porn was a backstory. I liked to feel invested in the characters.

"I watched your comedy," I told Emma now. "I mean, I watched a set. I looked it up. It was hard to find," I said. "The different last name." I hadn't planned on telling her, but then again, I'd already seen her naked.

"And?"

"It was funny," I said, but I could tell the reaction wasn't quite what Emma wanted. I should've known that from my brother. "It was really funny," I amended now.

"I think I'm funnier when I'm dating men," Emma said. "I might have to start again. I'm snarkier at least. With women, I'm— I dunno, I get distracted."

I thought of Reid, who said he was much better on the radio when a woman was waiting for him at home. That was how he put it: a woman waiting for him.

People *think* they want to date a comedian, Jack had told me. They liked who they were that first time they saw you onstage: rapt. Then they got to know you, and found you to be very annoying: obsessed, preoccupied.

"And you?" Emma said. "Are you more creative when you're single or dating?"

"I'm not sure it matters," I said. "I haven't been very creative. Not for a while." Not for a few years. "And then I met your dad," I said. "I've been feeling differently lately. Better."

"Maybe he brings something out in people. You know what," Emma said suddenly, "the first time I remember performing, like actually making people laugh, was because of my dad. In high school, my friends and I would call his show, and pretend to be random people. I'd say I was a Viagra salesman or a director on a *Playboy* photo shoot. The stuff I could come up with! My friends would be dying. Just totally doubled over. We would lose our minds laughing. When he'd get home, he always knew it was me. He knew all the voices I could do. He'd already heard them."

32.

On my way to school the next morning, I decided to call Reid's show. I didn't stop to think about why, maybe I was still thinking of Emma—wondering if I could get away with pretending to be someone else, if Reid would recognize me. As the phone rang, I planned on inventing some elaborate character, but when the screener asked who I was, I simply said my name. I panicked, I guess. Or maybe I *wanted* Reid to recognize me.

"Speak up," Reid said, on the phone. "Who's this?" That's what he always said to begin every call: speak up. I'd never heard him say it off-air, though when fans recognized him on the street they'd sometimes shout it: "Speak up!" and he'd nod.

"This is Allison," I said. "First-time caller, longtime listener." I tried to make my voice go low, seductive. "I'm a huge fan of yours." Probably I just sounded like a lifelong smoker, someone who carried an oxygen tank, someone with mere months to live.

"Hello Allison," Reid said. "And where do you live?"

"Los Angeles."

"Me too."

"I know," I said. "Maybe you've seen me around."

"What's your question? I can't sit around all day and chat with strange broads."

"Maybe I'm not strange," I said. "Maybe we've met."

"What do you look like," he said flatly.

"I'm hot," I said. "Very hot. Curvy. Five feet tall. I have huge breasts."

"Now we're talking," he said. His voice had become more nasal, deadpan—the voice he took on when he was speaking to strange women on the phone.

"Are you fun in bed?"

"Real fun," I said.

"How fun?" he said.

"I've had a threesome," I said.

"Oh yeah?"

"Once," I said. "With a bartender, and a—" I couldn't think of a single other job. "And a teacher."

"How was it?"

"Great," I said. "Hot."

"I need a few more details for my listeners, sweetie." I could hear the impatience in his voice. I was bombing, I knew. "What did you say your name was?"

"Allison," I said.

"Beautiful name. So was it with two women? One woman, one man? Two men?"

"All men," I said.

"So you like to take a pounding."

"Yes," I said. "I like to be pounded right into the ground." Was that a saying? Did people say that to each other—that they wanted to be pounded into the ground?

"All right, sweetie, so what's your question. Or did you just call me to tell me about your sexual exploits."

I hadn't thought the plan through this far. I hadn't thought about the plan at all. "I wanted to do one of your quizzes. I wanted to win a prize."

"I'm sorry, Alice. We don't have time for a game."

"Allison," I said.

"But I'll tell you what, I'm gonna put you on with one of our screeners, and he's gonna send you a little gift. Because you told us a hot little story. You made all my listeners get hard in the car."

"Okay, ma'am," the producer said, all business. "Your address? Reid wants to send you a personalized gift."

"I know him," I said. "I know Reid."

"Ma'am," he said. "Can you repeat your address? I'm sorry but we have many calls."

I gave him my address in Van Nuys and thanked him profusely.

"No problem," he said. I could sense how little I mattered to him, how rushed he was to get to the next call. The interaction had drained the fun out of the prank.

"Wait," I said. "I am actually dating Reid. You can ask him. I don't know why I—" I tried to laugh here, breezy. "I just thought this would be funny."

"I'm sure," he said. "And he thanks you for being a loyal listener." I guessed this is what he was instructed to say whenever a caller turned odd. Suddenly it felt very important that this screener know who I was. I wasn't some freak fan!

"No, really," I said. "I'm with him. *With* with him."

"Check your mail in the upcoming weeks. A sweatshirt is on its way."

That night, in Reid's kitchen, I told him about the prank call. I even put the voice on again, pretended to be Sexual Allison, Smoker Allison. He had no idea what I was talking about.

"I don't remember any of the phone calls," he said. "I take so many of them." He gave an apologetic shrug. Then, pulling me close, trying to get something going, he whispered into my neck, "If I'd known it was you—"

"No worries," I said, which was exactly what people said when they were thronged with worries.

33.

Finally, my father called. I was at an outdoor mall, sifting through discounted dresses on a rack. This one, I thought, rubbing a cheap, cotton A-line between my fingers, looks like a dress I'd wear to some other mall, to buy another cheap dress just like it. And that, I thought, looking at a gauzy black number, is something I'd wear to a magician's funeral.

"Why don't you come visit for Thanksgiving," I said.

"That's what I was calling to tell you," he said. "I'm coming for Thanksgiving. I just have to make a stop somewhere."

"Where?"

"What are you, the police? To see someone."

"See who?"

"I have friends," he said. "I know people all over this country." He began to sing in a cartoonish baritone, "I have friends in low places—"

"Dad," I said. "I would just like to know where you are."

"I'm seeing a woman if you must know," he said.

"What woman?"

"None of your business!" he said happily. I was relieved to hear him in a good mood. "I know a lot of women."

"Well I miss you," I said. I was trying to be kinder. Couldn't he tell? Or was he going to make me announce it: I'm being kind!

I'd decided to buy both dresses: the mall dress, and the dress for the magician's funeral. Maybe I'd wear one on Thanksgiving.

"It wouldn't hurt to call your grandmother," he said. And so went the chain of dependence—the never-ending rope of phone calls.

My grandma was a Polish immigrant from, as she referred to it, "the old country," though she'd lived in Nevada for most of her life. Still, the eight years she'd spent in Poland as a girl had a profound effect. (She played with stray cats! And tin cans! She shat in an outhouse!) She didn't speak to her one remaining sibling, but not because they'd had a falling-out; rather, it was too painful to interact with this brother whom she'd left behind in Poland— not purposefully (she was eight years old!)—but left him, nevertheless. Yes, he'd followed her to America four years later, and now lived in Michigan, but that didn't seem to matter. The siblings didn't even send each other birthday cards. When I see him, my grandmother said, I'm reminded of the worst time in my life.

"Is there anything worse than having a family?" one of my students had said, when we were reading *Anna Karenina*.

You were always trying to solve the puzzle of your parents—what they did to you, what they didn't do.

"Have fun with the lady," I told my father. He broke out in song again, Frank Sinatra this time, "The Lady Is a Tramp."

"I'm hanging up on you," I said. But first I let him sing.

34.

Once, I saw a therapist in college. This was before my brother, when my concerns were less dire—who was I now that I was outside of my family's purview, away from my hot, claustrophobic town? Was it normal to have accidentally heard everyone in my family have sex as many times as I had?

The therapist had luxurious blond hair and earrings in the shape of Texas. "The greatest gift we can give our parents is not to continue to parent them," she said. It had sounded very wise at the time, though I wasn't sure what to do with the information.

"Do you often think people are angry at you with no evidence?" the therapist asked.

"Do you often overthink things?"

"Do you often have trouble regulating your emotions?"

She was reading from a list.

I found the questions difficult to answer. "I'm not sure," I said. "I'm not sure about any of those."

Recently, I'd rediscovered this therapist on Instagram. She now has a very popular social media account with the same number of followers as an NFL team.

"Are you open to herbal remedies?" she'd asked me back then.

"I think," I'd said, "I forgot something in my car."

35.

After the day at the Korean spa, Emma and I continued to send each other emails. It felt archaic, old-fashioned.

Dear Allison, she wrote, at the top of every email. At the sight of my own name, I felt a ripple of excitement.

We gave commentary about our days, about reality TV shows we had or hadn't watched, facts we'd saved up.

Orville Redenbacher died in his Jacuzzi after inventing popcorn, she wrote.

Have you ever heard of semen retention? I wrote back.

She sent a meme with a tall dog prancing next to a much shorter dog. *Us,* she wrote.

She wrote about giving out samples at the grocery store. Sometimes children ran up to her booth, begged for a taste. "Are you allowed?" she'd ask them, and they always said yes. Once, she'd given the wrong kid the wrong food. A terrible allergy, a terrible mistake. *It's funny now,* she wrote. *After the kid was fine.* Now, she told it as a joke onstage.

I wrote, *A lot of things are funny after the fact.*

Gradually the emails became more frequent. Then they became less funny, and more confiding. I told her about my ex-boyfriend, the graduate student, who sometimes visited me in dreams.

Are the dreams scary? she wrote.

Not really, I said. *More sad.*

He was always trying to show me something in another room, to speak to me in a language I couldn't understand. When I woke up, I always wished I'd asked the dream version of him the same question: *Do you hate me? I thought you hated me.*

Emma told me about when she first started going to the Korean spa: in Seattle, with the roommate she secretly loved.

She knew her roommate's body so well she didn't need to look, could hardly stand to look. She knew the flare of her hips and the shape of her breasts. She knew them as well as her own. At night, in their tiny room, their beds seemed so close together Emma had to hold her breath.

How long it had taken her to admit what she now knew with certainty: her crush—this longing—it had become unsolvable. It had become a problem!

The first woman she slept with was a barista at the university café. *She'd been there the entire time,* Emma wrote. *And I'd never noticed her before.* But that night, they'd run into each other at a party, which happened to be in October, or November, she wasn't sure, but definitely autumn, yes, definitely a time similar to the very one we were in now.

This woman came home with Emma, sat with her on the child-sized bed in which Emma had tossed and turned and longed and masturbated.

Emma let it all spill out for this woman—a woman who worked at the university coffee shop and whom she thought she had nothing in common— she told her about the Korean spa, about watching her roommate shampoo her hair, the sight of her delicate shoulder blades, the vicious command she gave herself: Don't look. Don't you dare look.

She'd told the story in a way she meant to be funny. She was surprised by the look on this woman's face, which was not amusement at all, but pity.

"You poor thing," this woman said. Now she spread her legs open and said, "Look." And so Emma looked.

I read it all and then read it again. Then I read it one more time. I felt my heart thump in my chest, making itself known.

*   *   *

When did you lose your virginity? she wrote.

I was at summer camp, I wrote. *He liked* Grand Theft Auto *and Will Ferrell. I can't remember his last name.* I should ask Marcella, I thought. Marcella was the person who knew.

I emailed Emma at stoplights, and in the classroom while I waited for students to file through the door, their pant legs wet and dragging. I emailed her while Reid was in the other room, and then when he lay next to me in bed, flipping through a magazine titled *Travel + Leisure.*

"We should plan a trip," he said. "We don't have to go on it. The planning is the best part."

The emails came and went as swiftly and silently as thoughts. I didn't tell Reid about them. I hadn't meant to keep our constant communication from him, but the longer I went without mentioning it, the harder it felt to bring up. I think they call this momentum. I felt guilty, then guiltier, and so I became a more attentive girlfriend.

In the evening, when we watched the sunset over the pool, diligently eating our Popsicles, I'd gently hold his hand and say something kind about how much I loved it there, being with him. I wasn't lying. I felt like one of those successful Hollywood types that referred to themselves as multi-hyphenated, or bicoastal. I lived in two different places at once. My life had become a prism, changing in the light.

36.

At the grocery store, Reid and I shopped for a Butterball turkey for Thanksgiving. Butterball was the brand I'd always had as a kid.

"Then that's the brand I want," he said.

I thought he'd hire a chef, or maybe we'd rent out a whole restaurant. But for the last three years, he said, he had dinner at home: just him, his daughter, and Kelly.

"Who cooks?" I said.

"All of us."

"What about your ex-wife?"

"She has a lot of friends," he said. "She doesn't need us."

"So it'll be you, me, Emma, and Kelly," I said.

"Yes," he said, "though Emma's annoyed with me. She says I don't take her career seriously."

"You don't," I said.

"She doesn't have a career!" he said. His voice had gotten loud. Quieter, he said, "I wish she'd just get a normal job." I couldn't tell if he was worried for her, or himself. My own father had trouble separating the two.

It annoyed me, when Reid and The Problem reminded me so much of each other. I'd had a health scare when I was young—a gastrointestinal issue that had at one point seemed very serious—and my father said, "I wish we could switch bodies. I wish you could take mine and I could take yours. That way I wouldn't have to worry about you." Body snatcher! I'd said to Marcella. He wants to absorb me whole!

But I also understood how badly Emma wanted her father's approval, though I wasn't sure she'd say it like that.

"It wouldn't kill you to listen to her," I said. "She knows what she wants, and that's to be a comedian."

"Trust me," Reid said, "she doesn't know. She thinks she knows. She won't like living in my shadow for the rest of her life."

But something about that hadn't rung quite true. Did he not want Emma to live in his shadow or did he feel he only had so much shadow to spare?

In the produce section, I said, "How would you feel about my father visiting for Thanksgiving?" I pretended to look at the grapes, to be fascinated by them. I'd said the words and now they couldn't be returned. That was the thing about words.

Reid was picking up apples and setting them down again. "When would he come?"

How to explain? "I'm not sure," I said. "I won't know until he...arrives." I had been trying not to picture what the visit might entail. It had too many moving parts.

"Well of course, he's welcome at my house," Reid said. "Will I like him?" I thought this was a strange question. How would I know who Reid would like or dislike? I thought maybe he meant: Will he like me? Or else, will he fawn over me in a way that doesn't make me uncomfortable? Still, the fact that Reid agreed to host him without knowing anything about my father moved me. I knew how particular Reid was, and this seemed to signal the depth of his feelings for me, that the importance of my comfort on Thanksgiving might topple his own.

"My dad's fun," I said. "And charming." I didn't say the rest—that a lot of my father's charm was his unpredictability, the way you never knew what stimulus would cause what reaction. Part of his charm and his trouble, both.

"He's about your age," I said. "Maybe a little older."

They were six years apart, both born in June. If I still had the horoscope app job, I'd write one for them both: *This month begins a new phase of your life. It's time to let your guard down and be open to all kinds of possibilities. The past is in the rearview mirror. Let bygones be bygones.*

Now Reid was poking an orange.

"When was the last time you were in a grocery store?" I asked.

"Why? Do I seem like I don't know what I'm doing?"

In the checkout line, a little girl in front of us squirmed in her mother's arms. "Hi," she said to Reid. "Hi, hi, hi, hi." She was reaching for a pack of gum, and Reid handed it to her.

"Insect betrayal," the little girl said, or it sounded like that.

Her mother turned around, let her mouth fall open when she saw Reid. "Sorry," she said. "This kid loves to talk."

"That's okay," Reid said. "I started it."

"Speak up!" the mom shouted, and then, suddenly bashful, "Big fan."

Reid said, "Thanks."

"My mom loves you too."

"Thanks," he said again.

"That must be annoying," I said, on our way across the parking lot. "People stopping you all the time." I'd driven, of course.

"It used to happen a lot more."

I remembered what Emma had said, about him wanting to be recognized. I felt protective over him, over the fragility of his fame. Though he was rarely in the tabloids anymore, I hated when someone misquoted him—got something wrong about Reid, or mischaracterized him. In the New York Post, they'd pulled a quote from his interview with the famous Allison in which he asked if she enjoyed giving blowjobs. The headline read SHOCK JOCK UP TO HIS OLD DIRTY TRICKS. That's just his persona!!! I wanted to shout. He's actually quite thoughtful!!!

The teenager in the car next to us had parked too close, her slung-open car door almost touching mine. We stood there waiting for her to get out, but she was busy kissing her boyfriend in the passenger seat.

"Ahem," Reid said primly. "If you don't mind." I liked that even when he was impatient—and he was always a little impatient—he still managed to be polite. "We don't have all day!" is what my father would have said. Sometimes, if Reid was waiting for me to get ready before we'd go out to dinner, he'd turn old-timey on me, say something like, "No rush at all, but I'm positively weak from hunger." It thrilled me, the idea that nobody who listened to him on the radio would ever guess he could be like that—formal, courteous.

When the teenager finally slid out of the car, I saw that it was my student Julie.

"Miss Cohen!" she said, because that was what the students called me.

37.

In class the next day, Julie said, "You didn't introduce me to your dad!"

"That wasn't my dad," I said. I couldn't help myself, though I knew I shouldn't have to explain anything to a nineteen-year-old; all I did all day was explain things to nineteen-year-olds.

"Ohhhh," she said. "Now I see. Now I get it. Not your dad."

I was relieved to change the subject. Luckily it was workshop day, meaning one student turned in a story for the entire class to critique. They enjoyed these days; they were their own kind of performance. The students were nervy, louder than usual, like the cast of a play warming up backstage.

I made them arrange the chairs in a circle so that we all faced each other. I thought the shape signaled safety, or secrecy.

"This is a closed loop," I said. "Nothing goes beyond this room. Beyond this circle."

We workshopped a student's story in which the protagonist had only one day left to live and had made a decision to kiss everyone he met on the mouth. The writer was a twenty-two-year-old premed student with prematurely gray hair. *Muah!* he wrote, each time there was a kiss. *Muah!*

Normally, I tried to give the students what I called a compliment sandwich: a compliment, followed by a critique, ending with another compliment. This time, I simply said, "Very creative."

✳   ✳   ✳

"Have a good weekend," I said, when the class was over.

"*You* have a good weekend," Julie said. "With your *man*."

But then again, maybe I only imagined the italics.

38.

In high school, Marcella came over to my house every Thanksgiving, after the meal, to have dessert. She wanted to come for the whole thing, but her mother wouldn't have liked how that looked—to leave your own Thanksgiving to attend someone else's. Her mother was very concerned how their family looked to other people. Marcella always wanted away from her own house, away from her mother, who was very different in private than she was in public.

I was jealous that her mother even knew the difference between good and bad behavior—that she cared about being embarrassing.

(Once my father had called the school to pull me out of class for an emergency. I came to the phone in the principal's office, thinking my grandma died, or my mother.

"Who won the NBA Finals in 1989?" he'd asked. I'd memorized these stats—he liked when I repeated them.

"That's not an emergency," I'd mumbled into the phone.

"It is to me," he said. "A guy playing baccarat asked and I couldn't remember."

The principal and her secretary were watching me with concerned looks on their faces. "The Pistons," I whispered, before I hung up.

"My grandma's in the hospital," I told them.)

❊   ❊   ❊

"It's not me she doesn't want to embarrass," Marcella had said about her mother. "She just doesn't want to embarrass herself."

In the privacy of her own house, her mother screamed at Marcella, said cruel things like "If you were kinder to me, I wouldn't have gotten breast cancer." In public, she laughed easily and told elaborate jokes. She'd pull her daughter close and kiss her hair. Marcella's mother was from Mexico City and had once placed second at Reina Hispanoamericana, a famous beauty pageant held in Bolivia.

Marcella was very good at the high jump, and at track meets, strangers would tell her mother how beautiful Marcella was, how much they looked alike, and her mother would say, Yes, yes, if only she'd clean her room!

At home, if Marcella forgot to make her bed, her mother would say in a low voice, If I was as ungrateful as you, my father would've put me on the street.

How protective I felt over her! If I could've, I would've followed her around with a bat. But who could protect you from your own mother? It was like one of those scary movies: the call is always coming from inside your own home.

When I slept over, at least, Marcella's mother was torn. I was half and half: half outsider, half insider. She'd open the door of Marcella's bedroom without knocking and hover at the door, a sudden tense smile on her face. "Allison," she'd say. "What a nice surprise. How are your parents? Your brother?"

I'd answer politely. "Fine," I'd say, "all fine."

We'd hear her walk into one of Marcella's sisters' rooms, to say something cruel to them, though she'd do it softly, what with me being in the room next door.

39.

Emma and I switched from email to text message.

Sometimes I couldn't remember if I'd just thought something in my mind or if I'd written it to her. Other times, I couldn't remember if I'd told the story to Emma already, or to Reid. What made Reid laugh might scare Emma, and sometimes it was the other way around. For instance, when I told Emma about the student who wrote a story about wanting to fuck me, she said, Now *that's* funny. Reid, on the other hand, was worried and disturbed.

"Did you report it to the dean?" he'd said.

"Report it to the dean?" I'd said. "I don't even know if we have a dean."

Now, seeing Emma's name in my inbox made a silvery pleasure surge through me.

Reid said he was happy we talked every day, though he had no idea how *much* every day.

"Yes," I said, "of course. It's the least I can do."

In one of our flurry of exchanges, a woman from a book club emailed me, interrupting the endless stream of communication.

She was confused about the time and date of the book club—all the logistics had become jumbled in her brain. Then, in another email, she seemed confused about who I was, asking me to order her capri pants from

Amazon. Maybe she thought I was her daughter, or her assistant. I'm just book girl! I wanted to say.

Then the woman added me to an email thread about playing mah-jongg. But when I reminded her of who I was, the woman wrote, *I know.*

I told Emma about the book clubs, about the women trying to set me up with their sons, then their brothers.

"You're running out of time," a woman had said, last week. We'd been discussing a Victorian novel, in which every happy character got married at the end and every unhappy character died.

"I'm seeing someone," I'd said.

"You're a woman approaching thirty," the woman said. "Seeing's not enough."

When I'd told Reid about the women, he'd told me I should quit the job—that I was too talented to have to lecture inane housewives about books.

"They're not all housewives," I'd said, "and they're not all inane," suddenly offended on their behalf. "And I need the money." While I appreciated his sentiment, he'd never read anything I'd written. Somewhere in our relationship, he'd simply decided I was a good writer. And for him, deciding was enough.

When I told Emma about the book clubs, she said they reminded her of her mother.

They sound impossible, she wrote.

Not all of them are bad, I wrote. And, *What's your mother like?*

Emma: *Jean is very beautiful. But that's not the most important thing.*
Me: *What's the most important thing?*
Emma: *That she's a failure. She failed at the thing she wanted to do.*
Me: *What did she want to do?*

Emma: *Be famous. She definitely didn't want to be a mother. She was an
actress.*
Me: *Would I recognize her?*
Emma: *She wasn't in anything big. Just small stuff.*
Me: *I didn't know your mom was an actress.*
Emma: *Nobody does. Except me. And her. And my dad. What has my
dad told you about her?*

I felt embarrassed that he'd told me nothing—that I hadn't really asked. I
had an idea of her, of course. This Jean, who committed to Reid before he
got famous—when the fame was but a freckle in the blue green of his eye
(he had very beautiful eyes; everyone said that). The only photo I'd seen
of her was from their wedding, shoving cake in Reid's mouth. You could
sense the joy in the photo—the noisy excitement of people just out of frame.
How could he trust any other woman beside her, this woman from his
before-time, who was attracted to that version of him, before he was rich,
before he was famous? Could he trust me? Could I trust myself? Would I
have been attracted to him if he was just any man my dad's age, alone at a
bar? Bald?!

I told Emma about my students, and that after every semester ended, they
tried to follow me on Instagram.

I never followed them back. Occasionally, I'd click on their profiles, see
a Maya Angelou quote captioned with a flame emoji. I liked to know what
they were up to, especially the smart ones. I wanted to know if they were
writing.

They must really like you, she wrote.

Yes, I wrote, *I think most of them do.*

Now, throughout the day, I felt the urge to tell Emma things. Or to retell her
things that had already happened. Then, I hadn't known how to talk about
my own life. The story of my life had become the story of my brother's life

cut short, and the story of my parents' grief. At that time, my life felt both minor and unwieldy, difficult to explain. Writing to Emma, it felt good to remember how I'd arrived here. Anything shameful I told her immediately became un-shamed—she wrung the shame right out.

She seemed to feel the same way. She told me about college, more about the roommate. How exhausting it had been—the staving off, the pretending not to want someone so badly. *Now I have a terrifying vision of myself then,* she wrote, *following her like a dog on a leash, constantly trying to find her in a crowd. I was always looking at her for cues. I can picture myself: very small and shrunken.*

I could picture it too. I knew how those things could shrink you.

Another day, Emma sent me an attachment: a video of her at work. She was handing out samples at the grocery store, wearing a red apron. She filmed herself offering a chip made of freeze-dried broccoli to a customer.

"Try it," she said, in a voice that sounded crazed with enthusiasm. "You'll like it! I promise!" At the end, she turned the camera onto herself and zoomed in on her frozen smile. She zoomed closer and closer until it was only the white of her teeth. Then the video ended.

I like the apron, I wrote.

People are mad when they don't like the sample. As though I freeze-dried the broccoli chip myself.

If only they knew who your dad is, I wrote.

I don't tell people about my dad, Emma wrote.

I didn't tell her that I'd watched the video of her doing stand-up many times. It had become a kind of ritual when I was alone in my apartment, away from Reid. Sometimes I'd fall asleep to Emma's voice, usually around the same joke, about a vibrator used for a shoulder massage.

That evening, Reid and I had sex in his beautiful kitchen, atop one of his gleaming, smooth countertops. I pretended we had an audience—that there was someone watching us fuck. It was something I'd started doing recently. Not Emma, but someone like Emma. Or like one of my students—young and impressionable, who'd be amazed by my moves, what few moves I had. I'd throw my head back theatrically as though there were a camera overhead, practically winking at it. The performance made everything feel more exciting, more pleasurable.

Afterward, I said, "Why don't we go see one of Emma's shows together?"

He looked surprised, maybe about the question, or maybe about me bringing up his daughter so soon after sex. "She wouldn't want me there," he said.

"Why not," I said, "you're her dad." But maybe he was right—she told dirty jokes, had a dirty persona, just like him.

"Did your mother listen to you on the radio?" I asked.

"I don't know," he said. He'd begun wiping the countertop with one of the disinfectant cloths he ordered in bulk. "That's not true. I do know. She hated the show. She thought it was vulgar. But she liked that I was famous. She liked when other people walked up to her and told her they liked me."

40.

The next morning, in the kitchen, Reid told me a guy from *Rolling Stone* was coming over to interview him.

"Interview you about what?" I said.

"My career. My contribution to radio. My fucking lifetime of contribution." He tried to slam the door of one of his beautiful cabinets, but it was too expensive, it only came softly to a close. He was in a bad mood, and I felt myself going quieter than usual. I'd seen him grow annoyed before, or become subdued, but I'd never seen him like this: petulant. How would I explain this to Emma, I thought, how her dad was acting. Like a teenager who didn't get his way, I pictured myself saying.

"What's wrong with an interview?" I asked. I'd been trying to type a syllabus at the kitchen table. So far I'd only written: *Week One: Read.* Now I closed my laptop and turned to him. I knew how badly he wanted my full attention.

"On the phone," he said. "My agent made it sound like—I don't know. Like I'm at the end of my career. Like they want me to look *back* on it."

"It's been a good career."

"Been!" he said. He moved so suddenly he bumped the table, splashing the coffee out of the mug in front of him. "It's still a career," he said. "I'm in the middle of it."

"I agree," I said, but he turned away from me then, walked into his study to do—God knows what, stare at the wall. How many times had I tried to soothe a man in my life, prevent him from stomping off in pain or anger, prevent myself from being abandoned. I'd failed this time, but I also felt angry—I'd somehow found myself here again, in the same position it seemed I'd been destined to play since birth.

In Reid's office, he had a row of framed records on the wall, awards of some kind. I hadn't looked at them very closely. He had a photo album in there too, with photos of his late mother, and Emma as a smiling baby, splashing in a pool. That was where I'd seen his ex-wife, too, shoving cake into his mouth. I'd been caught off guard the first time I'd seen her: the woman he never mentioned. Had he not thought to remove this photo from its little plastic case? Was it laziness or sentimentality?

The next morning, when the journalist arrived, Reid answered the door as though he'd forgotten the guy was coming.

"Oh right," he said, like he was expecting a package instead.

I hung back in the living room, hovering near the arcade game. I'd said I would leave last night, go sleep in my own bed, away from him and his awful mood. I went cold, like a gray slab of concrete, and in doing this, I managed to out-sullen him—turn more morose, and it worked. He apologized profusely. In fact, he was a very good apologizer.

"I'm sorry," he said, "I was just taking my insecurities out on you. On anyone in the room. My stupid insecurities that aren't that important after all. Even Kelly got it," he told me. "Even she had to listen to me bitch and moan." I liked when a man could admit something like that: when he could debase himself with vulnerability. I felt closer to him after, like I'd finally seen a side of him he'd been working to conceal.

Now, he stood looking at the journalist from *Rolling Stone*, pretending to be surprised, wearing jeans I knew he'd spent a lot of money to have tailored—he liked the cuff to hang over the top of his shoe just so.

Also, I knew his agent had given the journalist a specific two-hour window in which he was allowed to come over. Reid had certain hours he liked to "conduct business." He also had hours he liked to watch TV and hours he liked to play piano. Every morning he ate the same brand of oatmeal with blueberries sprinkled on top. Every night he ate one sugar-free Popsicle for dessert. Would the journalist ask him questions like these—What do you eat for breakfast? Do you ever allow yourself an extra Popsicle for dessert? (No, the answer was no.)

The truth was, I was more like Reid than unlike him. Reid took great pains to keep his obsessions—his incessant hungers—at bay. It took a lot of careful routines to hem him in, hem in the constant yawning maw of him. Me: I had no routines. I hungered and yearned and never grew full. If I found a TV show I liked, I watched it all in one night. I'd put off the rest of my life to attend to my desires. Maybe that's just a lack of self-control. Or maybe immaturity. Forget hobbies—I had none. I could not muster the reasonableness needed to maintain something like pottery or chess, anything I loved became my life. That's why the graduate student boyfriend had been such a perfect match: he maintained hobbies. When he liked a TV show, he watched one episode every Sunday until the show was finished. But after he went to sleep, I'd watch the whole season. He was never angry with me. Instead, he'd said, I know it's hard for you to resist.

The journalist had his hands stuffed in his pockets. His hair was long and stringy-looking, like the drummer of a rock band.

"Is this not a good time?" He seemed disappointed that Reid hadn't remembered.

"No, no," Reid said. "As good a time as any."

Reid wasn't a very skilled actor. He was good on the radio—good at being a heightened version of himself, a dirtier version. But his put-on casualness wasn't convincing. Or maybe it just wasn't convincing to me.

The journalist had a trio of photographers with him, and they took photos of Reid in front of his record collection, and standing by his pool.

"Look off at the hills," the photographer said. "Look off into the distance."

"Don't make me look stupid," Reid said.

"We couldn't if we tried," the journalist said. I could tell by his questions that he admired Reid. "Don't you think podcasting wouldn't exist if it wasn't for you?" he'd asked. "Do you agree you changed the face of radio?" I imagined him telling his girlfriend or his parents about the interview. I imagined him on his way over here rehearsing his questions.

I kept offering to make myself scarce, but Reid said he wanted me around—he felt more comfortable with me there. I didn't want to be asked a question about myself, or for Reid to have to answer a question about me. I was surprised when Reid introduced me to the journalist as his girlfriend.

Ask her anything, he said wryly. I was surprised to feel disappointment when the journalist took no interest in me, in my presence in Reid's home. He must have thought I was just one of many girlfriends on the long conveyor belt of Reid's endless supply, a conveyor belt of girlfriends that ran through Reid's beautiful kitchen and right up into his bed.

They sat at the kitchen table and the journalist asked, "If you could do anything else besides radio, what would you do?"

"I don't know," Reid said. "Be a teacher maybe? I'd live a quiet life. Play piano in my spare time. Get some reading in."

Ah-hah! I thought. I'd like to see him try.

41.

The first time Emma called me, I was in the teacher's lounge with Chris, the adjunct who taught studio art. I saw her name flash on my cell phone screen and I felt wings in my chest.

"Someone's smiling," Chris said.

"Pardon me," I said, like I was somebody else, someone polite, whom he had never slept with. "I have to take this in my office." I went to my barren cubicle and whispered hello into the phone.

"I don't have anything important to say," Emma said. "I just called to chat."

"That's okay," I said. "Say whatever." I was used to reading her words; I was not used to hearing her voice in my ear, and now I regretted the eagerness when I spoke, how bald my excitement must have sounded.

Over email and text message, we'd built something private—a different room, in a different building in my mind. I pictured a warm, yellow light through the window of a cozy apartment. It was a place I'd admire from the outside. I'd not had a close friend like this since college. No, not since Marcella.

"Do you want to hang out tonight?" Emma said into my ear.

"Sure," I said. The next day I was picking up my father from the airport. That is, if he managed to get on the plane. He'd decided not to drive, he said. The long hours on the road had begun to take their toll on his back. (A new worry to keep me up at night: my father aging.)

* * *

I agreed to meet Emma at a pool hall. I called Reid to check in on my way, and he said, "I wish you were here! I'm nervous about the *Rolling Stone* thing."

The article was supposed to come out any day now, but he hadn't heard anything from his agent.

"It'll be good," I said. "I'm sure of it." I liked that he wanted me there. It made me feel useful, desired. It had become tricky to parse the two feelings apart.

"God I miss you," he said, though he'd only just seen me. Then, he called me a private nickname he'd only used when we were in bed. I won't write it here. It's not that it was dirty. The opposite, actually: it was very sweet.

"Cancel your class," he said.

I had lied, and said I was teaching a night class. I don't know why I didn't tell him about Emma—that I'd made plans with his daughter instead. One of my habits from childhood: secret-keeping. It had felt necessary in my house. There was always the threat of The Problem storming into my room and opening all my drawers, overturning the shoe boxes beneath my bed. Not because he thought I was hiding anything, but because he was sure he'd misplaced something there.

Maybe Reid had been right. I was a private person after all.

42.

I had never been to a pool hall in LA, but I already knew it was the kind of thing Emma was proud to know about, proud to show me. She liked feeling as though she were on the inside.

As soon as she started chalking her pool cue, I launched into a story about one of my students—the premed major with gray hair. Today he'd told me he was writing a book.

"What's the book about?" she asked.

"He said he didn't know. He said he was making it up as he went along. I'd wanted to say to him, Can't you just be a doctor?"

"Couldn't he be both?" Emma asked.

"But isn't being a doctor enough?" I made a long showy sigh, to indicate that I knew I was being unreasonable. "Probably I'm just jealous," I said. "He wants to write a book, so he'll sit down and write one." It was pretty simple when I put it that way.

"So could you," Emma said.

"I know that," I said, "maybe I will. Maybe I am." For the first time, there was something uncomfortably taut between us. We'd done so much talking—so much constructing—that hadn't been face-to-face.

"I'm sorry," she said. "I feel like I came on too strong."

For the next three hours, we drank and played pool poorly and the ease returned. We told each other stories about when we were younger, dumber. We told the stories as though our bad decisions were now very far away.

I'd thought Emma would be good at pool, but she was worse than me.

"I just like being around it," she said. It was true—the constant clatter of pool balls had a kind of meditative effect on me. She turned away from me then, and asked if I could tighten the straps on her dress. I wasn't used to seeing her wear anything other than a gigantic T-shirt, and now I wondered if she'd worn this with me in mind. I tried to make my hands feel light on the small of her back. I wanted to give the impression of lightness—like my hands meant nothing to me.

"Perfect," she said, and we went back to playing, which was mostly talking.

Emma told me about visiting her college roommate one summer, the one she had a crush on. The girl lived in a ritzy suburb an hour outside of Seattle. As soon as Emma entered the house, she felt unmoored. They had a bunch of photos in the hallway, her roommate at all ages. There was one in particular: her roommate as a toddler at a baseball game, eating ice cream from a giant helmet.

"I couldn't stand to look at those photos," Emma said. "I felt totally bereft. I can't say why exactly. It just made me realize I'd never get to be close to her in the way I'd like to be," she said. "Something about seeing her as a kid. I don't know, it made my heart ache." I liked the frank way she explained her own feelings—she didn't downplay it for me, or cushion it. Maybe I just liked hearing her talk about heartbreak.

"But still, I was glad to be there," she said, "in the inner circle of someone I loved." The family joked together, played board games at night at a long wooden table that had been passed down through generations of Scottish family. They drank large glasses of wine and got louder as the night wore on.

"I remembered feeling jealous of them," Emma said, "you know my dad doesn't drink and he's so anal about his routines. Bed every night at the same time. Every morning waking up to the same stupid Bruce Springsteen song. And he and Mom in the same room together! Not very relaxing. Neither of them would ever make a fool of themselves for a board game. Especially my dad—he's too concerned with coming off in a certain way. Cool, I guess."

I wanted to say, But he's old! How can he be cool? Though I knew she was right. And it *was* hard to imagine Reid playing a board game in which you had to act out words for someone else to guess, pretending to be a bird maybe, flapping his arms wildly, teeth stained with wine.

But, nothing is as it seems, and it turned out the roommate's father wasn't so great after all. He had what Emma called "a major drinking problem."

"After everyone went to sleep," Emma said, "he got so drunk he wasn't able to find his own bedroom." Instead, he'd wandered outside and fallen off the balcony down a small thistle-covered slope. When he found his way back inside, he'd accidentally gone through the wrong door, into the guest-room, and got into Emma's bed, confused and bleeding.

"When I woke up," she said, "I saw him lying next to me and thought he was dead. Seeing him all bloody, I thought he'd been murdered. And you wanna know the weirdest thing? I thought, They'll think I killed him."

I thought of the true crime shows my mother watched every night. She once told me, no matter what kind of mistake you make—no matter how bad it is—you can always tell me. You can always come home. By home, she meant, to wherever she was, which was as good a home as any. I missed my mom then, the tomboyish way she walked, with her arms swinging. The way her voice was a little too loud for every room.

"In the end," Emma said, "her dad apologized, said he just got too drunk, and asked me not to tell anyone."

"Did you tell anyone?" I asked.

"I tried to talk to my roommate about it the next day, to say something like 'Your dad got into bed with me covered with blood,' but she refused to hear it. Or she couldn't. 'People fall,' is what she said. 'Don't be weird about it.'"

The brain works miracles to protect you, I thought. The brain runs circles around itself. The brain does not want the child to know the parent is unsafe. The world can be unsafe, the child even. But not the parent. The brain hates that!

*　　*　　*

"Did you ever tell your roommate how you felt?" I asked.

She'd pulled her hair back to shoot, tossing it in one of those effortless buns I'd never quite mastered, and then missed the cue ball completely. "I told her one day in the dining hall, while we were eating salads. I just blurted it out: I think I'm in love with you."

"And?"

"And," she said, "she didn't agree."

"Did you think she would?"

"I don't know," she said. "Probably not. Probably I just needed to say it." In the dim, tinny lighting of the pool hall, she made her mouth into a little comma—a sort of half grin. She reached for the cue I was holding, let our hands brush together. Or I let them brush. "Let me try your stick," she said. "I think mine's unlucky."

"Sure," I said. "That must be it."

"Thank God my dad chose you," she said.

I hadn't really thought of him as choosing me, as much as the two of us meeting, and choosing each other. But I'd been wrong before, at least about choice.

"He could've done a lot worse," Emma said.

43.

Finally, I was picking my father up from the airport. Before I saw him, I spotted his cowboy hat bobbing among the commuters.

"Let's call your mother on speakerphone," he said, when he got in my car. "But if Raj answers, you talk."

"You won't talk to Raj?"

"I'll talk to him. Why wouldn't I talk to him? But why does he have to answer her phone? They have separate phones. They're not conjoined twins. Hey," he said, "you know the dealer—"

"Yes," I said, before he could finish. There had been a dealer at the Peppermill who'd given birth to conjoined twins. They were our town's version of celebrities—they'd been featured on the nightly news several times. Recently, they'd gotten married to one man. They had a big party; my father officiated the wedding. He brought it up constantly.

"Elle and Sandra got married," I said. "And you were there. I remember."

"Only Sandra got married," he said. "Elle's just along for the ride." This might've been rude or grotesque coming from someone else, but not my dad. He preferred Elle—found her funnier, smarter. Same body, smarter mind, he'd said.

"Where to?" he said.

"First I have something to tell you."

"Wait," he said, "let's call Mom." He still called her Mom, like we shared her.

"Hi Car," he said to her on the phone.

"I see you've got him," she said to me. She was on FaceTime, and my dad kept trying to show me the screen as I drove.

My mom talked about Peter: He'd swallowed a chicken bone, but he was fine. Yes, she'd send photos. He was lounging in the sun as we spoke.

"Isn't he handsome," my father said.

"The most handsome," my mother said.

They were much friendlier—divorced—than they were toward the end of their marriage. Now they'd grown more tender toward each other. Why not? The worst possible thing had happened: their son was gone. What else was there to hold against each other? They agreed it was best to take the long view of the marriage—hadn't it been a wild ride? Joyous at times and tragic too. Marriage was like life, I guess.

"Our girl's giving me the grand tour," he told my mother now.

He'd visited me in LA once before, about a year ago. I'd just moved here. I took him to the pier in Santa Monica. We'd watched the Ferris wheel rotate against a smeared orange sky.

"I hate it here," he'd said. But he wasn't really talking about the place.

44.

I decided that night we'd get dinner just the two of us.

I took him to a steakhouse on Beverly—all dark wood and red leather seats. Framed photos of celebrity patrons decorated the walls. I wanted to please him, to give him a taste of the classic version of Hollywood I knew he'd idealized. Maybe I wanted him to think that was where I lived: not in Van Nuys, but in a place he would've chosen for himself. I thought that would impress him.

"You know you got it pretty good here," my father said. He was leaning back, resting his clasped hands on his belly. After all, it wasn't that hard to impress him.

I wondered who would pay. Probably we would split it, unless it was a night he'd decided to make a show of being generous—a show of being my father. And yet, he was my father whether or not he paid for dinner. He was always my father, regardless.

"I got it good in LA?" I asked.

"Sure," he said. "The land of the sun and the free."

I knew that wasn't a saying anybody used, but I nodded. I had never been able to argue with him. He was a man whose thoughts came out like facts.

"Listen, Dad," I said. "I want you to meet someone on Thanksgiving."

"Oh?" Impossibly, he leaned back even farther. "Thought it would just be the two of us."

"I'm seeing someone," I said.

"You know, I loved your mother," he began. "I've never loved anyone more." I waited. References to my life reminded him of his life. This was how it was—how it had always been. "But she wasn't always easy to be with."

"I know," I said. "Dad, I know that."

"Not that I was easy either."

"Yes," I said. "I think that's true. Neither of you made it easy on each other."

This assessment seemed to please him, and he regarded me over the white tablecloth. The waiter brought the check and I grabbed it, determined not to be disappointed.

"I got it," I said.

"Listen to this girl," he said, to an imaginary audience, or to the whole restaurant maybe. "My daughter. She gets the check. She's amazing." I felt the warmth of the compliment despite myself. This warmth, too, felt like a fact.

"So you got a bloke," he said, trying briefly for a British accent.

"I started seeing someone I like, yeah."

"I wanna hear about him."

"You'll meet him soon," I said.

"Sure," he said. "I can't stay in town very long though."

"I know," I said, though it hadn't been discussed. This, too, was usual.

"But I'm happy to meet anyone important to you," he said. "Important to my daughter."

"It's someone famous," I said now. "The guy I'm seeing."

My father lurched forward in his chair. "See?" he said. "You're livin' the good life out here." He didn't ask who, so I didn't say. I signed the bill and my father looked over my shoulder, as though he were checking my math.

That night, in my studio apartment, I put my father on the pullout sofa. Then, I texted my mother, who still liked to hear that The Problem was safe, horizontal, ready for sleep. In bed, I could hear the sound of my father's rhythmic snoring from across the room. It almost made me lightheaded, the way the sound moved me back in time, when he used to take me on long-haul trips in the big rig. We'd spend nights in motels and occasionally, if we'd saved enough money by the end, a Holiday Inn. We'd eat at a Sizzler nearby, and I'd go back for seconds, then thirds, then fourths.

"Have as much as you can eat," my father would say. The world felt buffet-like, then—a spread to be devoured. Why hadn't we invited my brother? Had he not wanted to come? I hated that I couldn't remember.

In my next life, I thought, I'll write everything down. I won't forget a single thing.

45.

The next day, I readied for work in the bathroom while my father sat in the kitchenette eating the Lucky Charms I'd bought specifically for him.

"Do you know what you'll do today?" I asked. "You could come to school with me."

"What would I do there?"

"I don't know. Or you can stay here, in the apartment."

"I don't need looking after," he said. "I have a whole list of things I wanna do today. People to see."

"Who?"

"I have friends here! You think you're the only one who can hobnob with celebrities? All right, my friends might not be celebrities to you, but where they come from? In certain circles?"

"Okay, Dad," I said. "Well you know how to get ahold of me. And after school we can meet up wherever you are."

"What school?" he said suddenly, though we'd gone over the plot points of my life many times before.

"It's a junior college," I said. "You want the name of it?"

He shook his head, smiling. "A junior college. I have no idea what that means. We were lucky with you, your mom and I. You came out fully formed."

"I guess you're right," I said. It must have seemed that way to him.

* * *

My school day passed in fits and starts.

The first class felt like a hostage negotiation, trying to get the students to pay attention. When a class went badly, it felt like I'd happened into teaching, like stepping into a puddle, in which I splashed uselessly around.

And my father's proximity only made it worse. All day, my stomach churned. The old tether had been reestablished, or rather, repaired, because it had never disappeared.

A few times I texted him, "Doing okay?" or "Just checking to see where you are now!"

He answered with a thumbs-up emoji, or "Hollywood Walk of Fame, baby! Just took a photo with Superman!"

This reminded me of a report I'd written in sixth grade about my dad, the hero, who—like a magical, invisible force—transported everything people needed to live. Sometimes food, sometimes livestock, sometimes mops and bandages and lamps, you name it, he drove it. The rest of the report resulted in me answering questions from my fellow classmates, one by one, about if my father had ever transported that. Birds? No. Books? Yes, I think so. Batteries? Definitely. Christmas trees? Probably.

"And he is hardly ever thanked, either," I'd said emphatically, in front of the class, reading from my script. Later, when I found the report in a box in my mother's garage I realized that it was my father's constant refrain being parroted out of my mouth: I'm hardly ever thanked. Then, this is the most thankless shit job on the planet, shouted through the house as he packed his things, but I must have known enough in sixth grade not to repeat the last part.

"Then stay home and deal cards," my mother would say, but that was a shit job too. Drunkards who think they'd put twenty-five dollars down when they'd only put down ten. You got my odds wrong; you're against me; you're working for the casino; you're working for everyone but me. You asshole, they'd say, though the female dealers had it worse. Sometimes they were bitches. Sometimes they were whores.

"What about when they win?" I'd asked.

He laughed. "Oh then they love you. You're the best. You're their friend. But they never win for long." That was the whole problem: they never knew when to leave. Not my father, he was perpetually leaving. When he was around, he devoured all the air in the place, but when he was gone, we weren't quite sure what to do with ourselves—my brother and I—we didn't know quite know how to act. I thought of a documentary I'd once watched about a Ukrainian tennis player, who, after her mom died, no longer wanted to compete, though she was ranked as one of the best in the world. "What was the point," she said, "if my mother wasn't there to watch me."

And anyway, two shit jobs were better than one, at least according to The Problem. Variety was the spice of life, even if you were sprinkling salt on a steaming turd.

"He just likes doing jobs he can complain about," my mother said. "That allow him to feel underappreciated. He could do a lot of other things. He could do anything he wanted." It was true, my father was smart in the way mobsters were smart—resourceful, innovative. He could spin anything. He could turn straw into gold.

In my last class of the day, the kids were learning poetry—writing haiku— and they stood, dramatically, to read them aloud. After they were done, I clapped so enthusiastically my palms stung.

"You're poets now," I said. Reading aloud had loosened something in them. They whooped and hollered at each other's words. I couldn't forget these moments, I told myself. The times when they seemed least self-conscious. I couldn't forget that I had brought it out in them—led them back to themselves.

It was pouring rain as I left work, and Emma called to tell me about one of her shows the night before.

"You won't believe—" she began.

"My father's here," I interrupted. I'd developed a habit of talking over her. It was something I only did when I felt very comfortable with someone. I never talked over Reid.

"Is that good?" Emma said.

"Sort of. He's coming for Thanksgiving."

"Great!" she said. "So is Bones. So last night, while I was telling some stupid joke about Seattle, a drunk guy wandered onstage while I was performing. I thought he was gonna attack me."

Rain had been sloshing over the windshield, pounding against the car, but suddenly it stopped, and so I rolled the window down. I liked the smell of the asphalt, slick now. I'd stayed at the college late, and it was lonely down Burbank Boulevard, the gates pulled down over storefronts. In a boxing gym, a lone woman threw punches at a bag.

That man who rushed the stage at Emma's show had just wanted to shake her hand, she said. "Not because he was a fan of my dad, either," she made sure to say. "Just because he was hammered and enjoying my set."

"Weren't you afraid?" I said. "Some guy jumping up there while you're defenseless."

"I wasn't defenseless," Emma said, "I had a microphone. No, but really. It didn't even occur to me to be scared."

Strange, I thought, what does and doesn't occur to people.

46.

When I arrived home to my apartment that night, there was a woman I'd never seen before on the couch. This wasn't a surprise: my father often befriended women out in the world. Sometimes, they stayed his friend—he received more Christmas cards than anybody I had ever known. He had a girl in every city, or however the song went. The woman sat on the edge of the unmade bed, which was really the pullout couch, her legs politely crossed.

"This is Ellen," my father said.

"Pleased to meet you, Ellen," I said. She wore her hair in two long pigtails, like an elderly preschooler.

"Your father was just telling me about you," she said. "You teach at a fancy college. You teach people how to write."

"Sort of," I said. "Dad, do you want me to go to my boyfriend's? Give you some privacy?" I'd never called Reid my boyfriend out loud before. I thought it sounded too young for what he was. But what other word could I use. My beau? My gentleman caller?

"The boyfriend!" my father said. He turned to Ellen. "Apparently he's famous."

"Who?" Ellen said. She turned her head so fast the pigtails swung.

"She won't tell me," my father said.

"I'll tell you," I said. "I'll tell you right now." I said his name. I said it right there in my studio apartment.

Ellen's face fell. "I don't know who that is."

"You're joking," my father said to me.

"I'm not." *Jeopardy!* was playing on the television. My father knew a lot of trivia. He'd picked it up in the casino. Now he turned the volume down.

"Reid Steinman," he said. "From the radio?"

"Yes," I said. "That very one."

"Well I wanna meet him," he said.

"You will," I said. I'd wanted to stave off this moment for as long as possible. I couldn't imagine the two of them in the same room, the way my attention would be shorn in two.

He sat back on the couch and looked at me primly. "So where is he right now?"

"He's at his house."

"Reid Steinman."

"Yes," I said.

"From the radio."

"Yes. I just wanted to warn you beforehand."

He pursed his lips. "Do you want ChapStick," I said, but he didn't hear me. "Dad," I said.

"What?"

"I don't know, you're not saying anything."

"Well, that's wild is all. Not what I was expecting to hear." He turned the TV up. We'd missed the question. "What is Mongolia?" a contestant said.

"Are you upset?" I asked.

"Why would I be upset?" His voice was higher than usual. "You're an adult. You can date whoever you damn well please."

"I'll let you have the apartment tonight," I said, like we were longtime roommates. "Ellen, please help yourself to anything in the fridge."

She was busy googling something on her phone. "Ah," she said. "This guy. I remember him. Filthy, dirty. Real short."

47.

Thanksgiving Eve. I suggested we go to the bar where I first met Reid, and then later, where I met Emma. I thought it would be a good idea for my father to meet Reid on neutral territory.

"Let's go early-ish," Reid had said. "It gets too crowded there later." Did he think it would be too crowded for a famous man to navigate comfortably? Or did he worry it would be crowded and nobody would recognize him? Maybe, I decided, a little bit of both.

Also having too many eyes on him would make it hard for him to be himself, to speak and act like Reid the man, as opposed to Reid the radio guy, Reid the shock jock. And he wouldn't just be Reid the man, he'd be Reid meeting a woman's father. A father who happened to be around his age.

It had been a long time since I'd introduced my father to anyone. Once I became a teenager, I'd prepare people. "He's a lot," I'd say. Or, "He just says whatever comes into his head." This was my role as the daughter, to trail my father, to apologize for him.

"Fancy," my father said when we pulled up. "Doesn't look like my type of place."

"Dad," I said. "You're fine. It's fine."

I opened the door for him and he had to duck slightly through the doorway that had made Reid seem unusually small. My father was six four, which made the weight he carried seem somehow purposeful, or at the very least, manly. My mother had told me this was what attracted her to him when they met—the way he carried himself, like a man, a *real man*. That my mother would be so taken in by something as simple as manliness embarrassed me, but women had been attracted to worse, I knew.

Reid was hardly manly, at least not stereotypically. He didn't like sports or drinking beer with other men. He liked watching reality television at home and playing the piano. He liked going to bed early after he drank a seltzer. But on-air, he talked about tits, how he loved all of them, every size and shape. He talked about strip clubs. He talked about fucking women from behind. Suddenly I wondered if my father would be disappointed—if he expected to meet the crass womanizer and instead, would just meet an average guy his own age.

But did I even consider my own father "manly"? He loved sports, yes, but he also loved musicals. He never spoke of his feelings with any sort of self-awareness, but cried with such regularity it felt like he'd scheduled it on a calendar. We were all large, we all contained so many stupid, fucking multitudes!

"There he is," I said. Reid was sitting at the bar alone, with a book in front of him. It was the book I'd been reading when we first met, a book I'd set down that night and never picked up again. I was moved to know he remembered the name of the book—that he'd bought it somewhere or, more likely, asked someone to buy it. Reid wore another plain sweater and stylish thick-framed glasses: his uniform. I remembered the way he looked that first night—calm, unassuming—sitting alone at the bar. I had no idea he'd been looking for someone, that he was worried about a daughter.

"Dad," I said, guiding him gently forward. "This is Reid."

"Je-sus," my father said, hauling himself onto the barstool. "Doth my eyes deceive me?" I was still standing and Reid gestured for me to sit down at his other side. I wished he'd gotten a table, but I didn't say anything. This happened around my father, too. My own needs—no, my own good sense took a back seat to some other, more pliable part of me.

"So the two of you," my father said. "Together." He was slowly shaking his head.

Reid turned to look at him squarely in the eye, though he had to crane his neck to do it. "Yes, sir," he said. Sir! "I really like your daughter," he said.

"Well, she's easy to like," my father said, doing his customary lean back, as though he were a cowboy on a horse, considering another rider.

"I know we haven't known each other that long; I'm sure she's told you that."

My father sat, not poker-faced exactly, but in the neighborhood. I knew a grin was beginning to form but only because I knew his face that well. I knew all of its expressions, even the pre-expressions.

"And I know I'm probably not what you had in mind," Reid continued. "Age wise, or"—here he faltered—"reputation." My father was nodding seriously to everything Reid said.

"Any concerns you have," Reid said, "I can certainly try to assuage them."

"Say," my father said. "I got a question for you."

"Sure," Reid said.

"When Paul McCartney came on, I'm talking that first interview. I'm talking a long time ago. And those bartenders were in the studio because one had slept with Bobby." He laughed a little. "Or so Bobby said." Bobby was a staff member on Reid's show who provided a lot of storylines through his bumbling antics.

"Yes," Reid said. "I remember." He seemed only a little surprised at this line of questioning.

"Was it true that Paul stayed an hour after the interview to hang with the staff in the back. That he even tuned a—"

"—a PA's guitar," Reid said. He said it like someone who wanted to get to the end of the story as quickly as possible.

"I don't remember where I heard that," my father said. "I thought, man that's gotta be the coolest feeling in the world, sitting across from him. You seemed a little nervous during that interview? Am I right? Maybe you said you were nervous that day, or maybe I'm just imagining it. A little more… hesitant," he said finally.

Had my father listened to anyone else as closely as he'd listened to Reid over the years? Could he distinguish when his own daughter was nervous, or excited, or embarrassed, by the way my voice changed?

"I guess I was a little nervous," Reid said. "Though I probably didn't say it on the radio. But I guess you could tell." I felt grateful for this, for his generosity. I put my arm through his, pulled myself a little closer.

"I'm a big fan," my father said, suddenly bashful. "A huge one." I was surprised to see him admit it so plainly, to offer himself up, unprotected, on the bar for Reid.

Reid sat up a little straighter. I could sense him retreating, pulling back. I didn't like him as much just then. It was so hard not to see the world—to see Reid—through my father's eyes. Give my father what he wants, I wanted to say. Give him something. Anything.

"That's very kind of you," Reid said, like a celebrated novelist on a panel during a Q&A.

I remembered the name of his autobiography just then, the one my father had purchased in hardback so many years ago.

"Did I tell you he had your autobiography," I asked Reid. I hooked a thumb toward my dad. "It was our coffee table book for a long time."

"You read it?" Reid was looking at me now.

"I read it," my father said. "Twice, if I'm honest." That wasn't true, I knew. He read it more than twice, because he often took it to the bathroom with him to pass the time.

"I've read parts," I said.

"She probably doesn't consider your book real art," my father said. He wore another expression I knew well—exhausted by our differences, or the gulf between who I had been when I was under his care and who I was now. "Books gotta win awards for her to like them," he said. "They've gotta be a little boring." He smiled at me now, as though to say even he knew this was an unfair categorization. Sometimes we had to play our roles, I thought—it was hard not to play them. If we didn't play the roles, who would we be?

Reid held up the book that lay before him on the bar. "I bought this because of her," he said. "It's boring as hell."

My father laughed now. They'd found some common ground, talking about me.

"I bet," he said. "I can't get through anything she recommends. Unless she's written it." I guess I hadn't known my father had read anything I'd sent him. I felt the familiar warmth. I couldn't help myself. "And you have a daughter too," my dad said.

"Yes," Reid said. "She turned out good. Ask Allison. Allison's friends with her. She's like her . . ." He thought around for the word. "Her mentor," he said.

"I'd hardly call it mentoring," I said.

"I can believe that," my father said. He pointed at me with his dead hand. Reid had been doing a very good job of not looking at it, but now he couldn't help himself. My dad had drained his first beer, and was now on his second. He was drinking faster than usual. I guessed because he was nervous.

"I used to take her on long hauls. Can you believe that? And we listened to you. And look at her now. Tell me—can *you* believe *that*?"

A realization seemed to be dawning on Reid. I'd so carefully down-played how *much* I'd listened to him after all this time—how not-so-well I knew the radio version of him. All the things he knew about me: about my childhood, about my brother. But he didn't know that. He looked at me now with the same face he'd looked at me when we first met: like I was puzzling him somehow. Maybe he wondered if all the versions I knew of him were currently colliding. Maybe he wondered if I liked what I saw.

"If you told me to picture this," my father said, "the three of us here. I couldn't have. I wouldn't have believed it."

The drinks didn't last much longer. I said I had work to do, and Reid, for his part, seemed to pick up on how desperately I wanted the meeting to end. I was awash in gratitude for Reid then, that he should be so attuned to me. He could sense that I needed out! He let my father ask a few more questions about the show, the staff. Even Kelly his driver.

"I know her," I'd told my dad earlier. "I might even say she's a friend." Kelly told me I could call her anytime. If I needed her, I could call her.

Reid looked at his bare wrist, claimed it was late.

That night, I put my father back on the pullout couch across the room. He still percolated with excitement, bubbling over. There had never been a time when my father's emotions hadn't dominated every room we'd ever been in. He controlled the weather in every sky I was under.

I was on my computer, and my bedside lamp was the only light in the room. I was reading another story Julie had sent. It was about a woman who was dating two men at the same time—one was rough, and one was tender. My father was saying something about the way Reid looked in person.

"What, Dad? Sorry, I'm reading."

"Oh, okay," he said. "I'll be quiet."

But I couldn't leave him alone too long with his unspoken thoughts. They made the air in the room feel heavy, dense.

"Did you like meeting him?" I asked finally.

"I did," he said. Then, slowly, "Do you think he liked meeting me?" The way he said this, in the quietest voice I'd ever heard him use, made me look away from my computer and directly at him.

"Yes," I said, "I'm sure he did."

"It's strange, to match the voice with the person finally. To see him talk in real life."

"I know," I said. It had been strange for me too.

"I don't know what I was expecting," he said. He sounded a little sad, across the street from sad. "I guess I should give you some fatherly advice. About dating someone older."

"If you want," I said.

"Here's some advice in general. Don't date anyone who doesn't make you feel like he couldn't go on without you."

"That seems a little hyperbolic," I said.

"Say," he said. "Wanna know who I ran into on Hollywood Boulevard? Right there on the stars? On the famous walk?"

"Sure," I said.

He said the name of an animated character I used to like as a kid. We'd watched him on the tiny television in the Motel 6, on one of our trips.

"Did you say hi?" I said.

"I waved," he said. "Shoulda gotten his autograph." I could hear the smile in his voice. How long ago that had been, me on a tiny twin bed, my brother still alive, while my father scrolled through the channels, searching for something that might entertain me.

"Jack would've been amazed," he said now. "To see who you're ending up with."

"Let's not jump the gun," I said. "I'm not ending up with anyone."

"Come on," he said. "The way he looks at you!"

Before long, he wore himself out and began to snore. I got up and out of bed and turned the television toward him. I put the remote on the coffee table, just in case he woke up and felt adrift, wondered where he was, and wanted to watch something.

"One guy was rough and one guy was tender," Julie had written in her story, "but sometimes the tender one was rough and the rough one was tender, so the whole thing had become very confusing."

48.

On Thanksgiving, Kelly did most of the cooking. She was wearing a polka-dot wrap dress that made her look like a sitcom wife from the fifties, and the same dangly earrings as usual. I was not used to seeing her out of a baseball cap, her hair teased, helmetlike, around her head. She fussed over me and Emma like we were her children. She even made Reid go upstairs and change his shirt.

"Wear something nice," she said. "It's Thanksgiving!"

When she met my father she said, "How do you do," and my father bowed, like he were a lord and she were a lady.

I led my father around the house, showing him what I thought he'd like to see. "Here are the records," I said. "Here is the pool."

Eventually he stopped exclaiming every time something amazed him. There were simply too many things to be amazed at.

"Let's call your mother," he whispered. "She's gotta get a load of this." My mother and Raj were out of town for Thanksgiving. They'd gone to Hawaii, finally.

Emma had brought Bones over, and now my father put Bones's paws up on his shoulders and pretended to slow dance with him. Reid, on the other hand, didn't care much for dogs. And anyway, he had been making himself scarce all night.

✻   ✻   ✻

That morning, he'd seen proofs of the *Rolling Stone* article.

"This idiot," he'd said, pacing the hallways of his beautiful home and smacking the pages against his thigh, over and over. "This idiot. This loser! This motherfucking loser."

Even I'd been wrong about the interviewer. If he'd been trying to manipulate Reid—make him feel like he admired him, respected him—he'd been successful. He made me believe it, too.

The article was titled TWO HEADS MIGHT BE BETTER THAN ONE. Reid had had a sidekick who'd recently retired, his opposite in every way. They'd hated each other toward the end, or that's what everybody said. When I asked Reid about it, he'd said, "I wish it were that interesting." They didn't hate each other, or at least, not that Reid knew of. Mostly, they didn't talk much off-air. They didn't have anything in common. His sidekick had just grown tired of the early morning schedule, and listening to Reid's same old stories all the time and faking the same baritone laugh. He wanted a normal life. He wanted to ride off on a horse into the sunset and play solitaire on his phone.

Sure, Reid assumed the guy was envious of his career, assumed the guy thought his life would've turned out a lot better without Reid lording over him. But the guy had never said it out loud.

Might be time to hang up the microphone, the journalist had written. *What did Reid have to say that was relevant anymore? The last twenty years, he's just been rehashing the first half of his career.*

I looked for Reid in his office, where he was sulking in his very expensive chair that looked like it could take you to space. I thought about what my father used to say when I was a child, and something had gone wrong for me: "Go outside and look at the trees." Of course, my father wouldn't say that today. He wouldn't say that to Reid.

I could hear my father and Emma in the other room, talking to Bones.

"He's my big man," I heard Emma say. "Yes he is," my father said. I knew my father would like Emma—he liked girls that reminded him of me. And most girls under thirty did.

I put a gentle hand on Reid's shoulder. That's how I thought of my hand, anyway: gentle. "Do you want to come out and socialize?" I said. "We need you to mash potatoes."

Reid held his finger to his lips, shushing me, like I was his child.

He had his agent, Bob, on FaceTime. Bob was mild-mannered, like an accountant. I thought Reid would've picked someone louder and more aggressive, someone to bellow at people on his behalf. Probably I'd just seen too many movies.

"It's humiliating," Reid said. "I would never have agreed to this. It's like the Rock and Roll Hall of Fame all over again."

Apparently, he'd been inducted into the Rock and Roll Hall of Fame one year ago, but the audience had only been half full. He'd screamed at Bob then too. Bob had said, "The camera won't pan over the empty seats" and Reid took a mirror off the dressing room counter and smashed it on the ground. He'd told me this all in a timid way, ashamed.

"I'm an asshole sometimes," he said. "And I hate that about me."

I'd been a little charmed by the admission, by the self-awareness. Sometimes what was good about you was also bad about you. I think the term is called a "double-edged sword."

Now I looked at Reid's phone—at his agent, Bob. Probably Bob wanted to get back to his own Thanksgiving. He had kids. He had a grandchild, even. He looked exhausted.

"Can you pull it?" Reid said. "Can you refuse to let them publish it?"

"I don't think that's possible." Bob rubbed his face and I saw he had an artsy wedding ring with a turquoise inlay from a place like Taos, New Mexico. His wife must have picked it out. I wondered if she was cooking in the other room. From what I could see, his house looked very expensive. There was a lot of marble flooring in the background.

"Fine," Reid said. "If you can't do anything I guess I'll just hang up. I'll let you enjoy your Thanksgiving."

Bob said nothing.

"Enjoy your little mashed potatoes," Reid said. "Enjoy your little boat of gravy."

Probably Bob would go find his wife in the kitchen, put his face in her hair, breathe in whatever expensive perfume she wore.

"This fuckin' asshole," he'd say. "This asshole's never happy. No matter what I do for him." At least I hoped he had that kind of relationship—one where talking to his wife was like putting down something heavy.

You don't become famous if you're normal, I thought. Hadn't a comedian at the Tropicana told me that?

At the table, Reid was quiet, sullen. My father did most of the talking.

"Kelly," he said, "you made a feast." I could tell he was flirting with her, that he found her attractive. It had something to do with how much effort she'd put into her hair. I hated that I knew that, but I did.

"You're too much," Kelly said. I had to assume she was flirting back.

"Dad," Emma said, "we missed you in the kitchen. We needed your cooking skills."

"I don't feel well," Reid said. "I think I'm gonna have to go lay down."

"It's Thanksgiving," she said. She'd taken on a new tone, too: a cajoling uptick in her voice I recognized in myself.

"I'm sorry," Reid said. "I have a headache. Aren't I allowed to have a headache?"

I saw the disappointment on my father's face. Maybe he was wondering if he could do something to change the course of the night. Did my father know he was charming? Did he know the way his charm could affect people? Same with when he pulled the charm away?

"Say," my dad said now. "Shall we go around the table and say what we're thankful for?"

"Bones," Emma said. "And friendship."

"Family," Kelly said, though she wasn't with her own. When I'd asked her about them, she said her grown children had their own families. This was where she liked to be—with Emma, with Reid.

"I want to say both of those," my dad said, "friendship and family. Mostly my daughter," he said, as though I wasn't in the room. "My daughter is on the top of the list."

Reid gestured at the potatoes with his fork. "Pass those over." Then he said, "Potatoes. I'm grateful for potatoes."

*　*　*

After dinner, Emma said, "Let's go in the Jacuzzi. You could borrow Reid's swimsuit."

"His swimsuit," my dad repeated. I knew what he was thinking: my schlong where Reid Steinman's schlong has been! But Reid's mood had subdued my father, and I wasn't used to someone else subduing The Problem. I was used to being the one who felt subdued. Maybe, I thought, he was understanding something about Reid he hadn't wanted to know. I felt grateful for Emma's presence, that I had an ally.

Kelly was washing the dishes, and I wondered if she got paid for this. A while ago, I'd asked her where she was from and she said, "Around here," as though that explained everything.

"Reid and Emma are like family to me," she said, when she was setting the table. And maybe that was true. And here she was like so many mothers: doing the dishes, opting out of the fun.

I even thought of the women in my book clubs. Their catered dinners, their elaborately set tables. I hoped their families were living up to their expectations, at least this once.

In the Jacuzzi, Emma asked, "So are you seeing anyone?" She said it to my father like he was just another pal, someone she might meet at a bar, or the pool hall.

"I'm seeing a lot of people," my father said.

"Good lord," I said. "Dad. Come on."

"What," he said. "She asked!" In his bad hand, he held a brand of beer he'd never heard of before tonight. He'd made a big deal out of that: even the beers are fancy!

Emma laughed. "Me too," Emma said. "I'm seeing a lot of people too."

"Variety is the spice of life," he said.

"Yes," Emma said, laughing, charmed.

I didn't argue. I didn't say: he misses my mother every day, that he'd told me that many times.

Reid had long since gone to bed, so I suggested we play poker: Texas hold 'em. I'd already taught Emma, after all.

"I refuse to deal," my father said. "I'm off the clock."

"I'll deal," I said, though I wasn't good at it. Every time I shuffled, cards sprang out of the deck like they wanted away from my hands.

"I hate this game," my father said, before he folded his cards. "It's a great game but I hate it. My son," he said, gesturing at Emma with his beer bottle. "He loved it. He was very good at it."

That wasn't true, actually. He did love it, but he wasn't good at it. He mostly lost. At least he'd been honest with me about that. He liked gambling too much. He'd go all in with junky hands, pray for a good flop. "I never learn," he'd said.

"I wish I could've met him," Emma said.

"I wish he could've met Reid," my dad said. "And seen this house." Then, I think, sensing how rude that sounded, "And you."

I wondered what they would've made of each other—Emma and my brother, Jack. They probably would have had chemistry. Probably, I would have felt left out.

In one of the last conversations I'd had with my father about my brother, I'd said, "You can't tell me he didn't have something wrong with him. Something mentally wrong. Or something was *going* wrong." I hadn't known what tense to use.

"That is the dumbest thing I've ever heard," my father had said. "He had an accident." We were at the pier, standing outside of the arcade. He'd been gripping my arm so tightly that the next day, I could see the imprints of his fingers, a grayish bruise. I didn't tell him that—he would've been humiliated. He would've cried. It would've been my job to console him.

Now, I wondered why I was so intent on my father seeing it my way—on him seeing the truth. Wasn't he the one who always told me it was okay to lie, though he didn't call it lying, he called it "telling stories." Let him believe whatever he wants, I thought now. Maybe I'd been part of the problem.

49.

The next morning, my father was gone. I'd thought he'd want me to take him to the airport. I wasn't even sure he knew how to use Uber, but maybe he did. Or maybe one of his many "friends" drove him. He'd slept in one of Reid's luxurious guest rooms. He'd left the blanket in a heap on the bed, atop which sat a note in his surprisingly tiny lettering. He wrote in all capital letters, so that even his notes were adamant.

> TO MY BEST GIRL: WHAT A TRIP. GIVE MY LOVE
> TO THE OLD MAN. YOURS, DAD.

Was the old man Reid? Wasn't he—my dad—my "old man"? Now did I have two old men? Two?!?! I could barely handle one.

He'd taken the signed copy of Reid's autobiography that Reid had left on the kitchen counter. I was grateful Reid hadn't forgotten, that he'd thought to do this before he'd stomped off to bed alone.

I texted my mother that my father had left, because I knew my mother would want to know, would want to track his whereabouts in the way she always had, as though having been married to him for so long had installed in her a tiny GPS with his constant coordinates. It was a GPS that had, at least during my childhood, continuously failed, continuously made my mother fret and worry and yell. Time and space had tamped that all down.

* * *

When Reid came out of his office, I said, "My father left." I'd been sitting on the floor in the living room, touching the soft carpeting.

"I know," he said. "I told Kelly to drive him. Otherwise I thought we'd worry."

I let the word "we" move through me. It was a relief I didn't have to explain more—that my father leaving unexpectedly and without saying goodbye was common, if not expected. It was a relief to feel, in that moment, known.

"Let me take you to dinner tonight," Reid said. "On a date. I feel bad about Thanksgiving."

But I knew that wasn't really true. Or yes, he felt bad, but I assumed he also felt that it was his due, getting in bad moods. It was part of his process.

This was true about writers I'd known, too: they were very into "process."

The restaurant was called Frankie's. It was a small, Italian place, and while it had white linen napkins, the plastic menus were smudged with fingerprints. It was a place I knew we wouldn't see anyone notable, no celebrities or paparazzi, not that I ever saw any paparazzi hunting Reid down. Reid chose restaurants that offered privacy, though I had begun to realize he didn't actually need very much privacy. If anyone ever came up to him, it was only a stray, polite fan. Still, it was easier to assume he'd successfully evaded fans than to find out there weren't that many fans to begin with. The truth was, I preferred staying at Reid's to going out. I loved being in his luxurious home—the pool! The kitchen with the invisible fridge! I could go out to middling Italian restaurants with any middle-aged man.

When the host arrived, he addressed only Reid. "Where would you and your daughter like to sit?"

"She's not my daughter," Reid said and then forced out a laugh, though I knew his laughs by then, and this one meant: I don't find that funny at all.

The waiter faltered, "Of course. Please, we have a table in the back." He pulled out both our chairs, recited the specials. When he walked back into the kitchen, I imagined he'd retell the story, the blunder he'd just made. The kitchen staff would shake their heads. "This is LA, idiot. How do you not know what it's like here?"

We both ordered the fish and Reid said he'd had a good talk with his agent. "I probably overreacted," he said. He looked younger, just then, when he apologized. I liked being reminded of how uncertain he could be, how timid. I thought of the first walk we took: the way he gingerly took my hand. Now, he laid his hand on mine in a way that struck me as very old-fashioned, though not necessarily in a bad way.

"I want to tell you how much I've been enjoying our time together," he said. So formal! As though we hadn't had sex in his Jacuzzi a total of seven times. "And I even enjoyed your father." I didn't like the word "even" there, but I let it slide. I thought I should be the only one allowed to be critical of my father.

"Having you around me," Reid said. "These have been some of the happiest months."

He sounded so serious, I thought he might be gearing up to end things. As in, These have been some of the happiest months, but I know it can't continue. Or something like that.

Instead, he said, "There's a wedding coming up. My brother's only child. If you wanted to come with me, as my plus-one. Emma will be there too. You could meet some more extended family."

"Your ex-wife," I said, and he looked surprised.

"Sure, she'll be there. I didn't know you wanted to meet her."

"Of course I do. She's the woman who supported you when you were starting out."

"Who said she was supportive?"

I realized I didn't know. Hadn't I read it somewhere? Or had I just assumed? It seemed like common knowledge: he and his young wife, making ninety-six dollars a week, yet she believed in him—in his talent and his drive—despite everyone (the whole world!) telling her not to.

"Well then why did you marry her?"

"I dunno," Reid said. "I guess I liked that she had very strong opinions. And she said them loudly and confidently. She'd argue with anyone. She wasn't afraid. I wanted some of that to rub off on me."

"And didn't it?" I asked. "You made a career out of saying whatever you wanted."

"Sort of," he said. "I guess that's how people think of me. In reality, I think of myself as pretty shy."

I couldn't tell if he was waiting for me to refute him. Either way, he was looking at me expectantly and so I said, "I keep waiting for you to change your mind about me."

"Why," he said.

"I don't know," I said. "Maybe you don't know the whole story."

"What do you mean?" he said.

"Where's the wedding?" I asked.

"Lake Tahoe," he said. "Have you ever been?"

"Yes," I said. "I grew up going."

50.

In fact, I'd been to Lake Tahoe many times.

Some summers, when Marcella and I wanted out of our small town so badly we'd have agreed to be abducted by aliens, we worked at what we referred to as the Death Camp.

The Death Camp was a free summer camp for kids who were grieving. The camp consisted of a collection of small, utilitarian cabins that overlooked the lake. The kids could canoe, do archery, horseback ride, white water raft, that kind of thing. We wanted the kids to forget about their lives for a little while, to risk those young lives over rushing rapids while they tried to forget about whatever loved one they'd lost.

The camp was a nonprofit, started by the richest man in Reno, a man with the largest cowboy hats you've ever seen, who worked in the elevator installation business. He'd lost a child at a cousin's graduation party (the kid had drowned in the Jacuzzi of a mansion, her long hair sucked into the pump), and I remembered being especially disturbed by that setting—the mansion—the money that offered no protection. Maybe I'd thought that if my family had more money, or when I grew up, if I cracked the code on getting money, that the money would form a protective barrier, like the shell of a snail that housed its gooey insides. But no, for the richest man in Reno, money only seemed to make it worse. The town could be cruel. Hadn't that family had it coming, they said, throwing lavish parties, the mothers sipping margaritas instead of watching their kids?

In fact, the mother had been watching. The mother watched the whole awful thing.

The richest man in Reno found the hardest part (beside his own blinding grief) to be his surviving child's grief, his elder daughter, who now felt isolated, because she had nobody to talk to about her sister other than her parents, who kept walking into rooms forgetting why they'd entered and then dissolving into tears.

At camp, all the kids were dragging themselves through their days as though moving through syrup, but also doing archery and paddling in canoes and eating ice cream sandwiches. They would bring up tragedy constantly, offhandedly: "I want a pet kangaroo. And my father killed my mother last month." The camp psychologist believed that it mattered very much how we counselors reacted to statements like these. If I acted distraught, let's say, or pitying, that might make it worse.

It made sense to me: Other people's reactions taught you how to feel, how much shame you should carry. So we were taught to respond in a neutral, but empathetic way, without judgment or overt surprise.

"Would you want a baby kangaroo or a full-grown kangaroo?" I asked the little girl in response.

"Baby!" the little girl said.

In the summer, yellow and violet flowers split the hillsides like rips in the fabric of the earth. You couldn't look at the lake without wearing sunglasses—it glittered that violently.

It was at the Death Camp that both Marcella and I lost our virginities, in the same room in fact, on Halloweenie, a made-up day in which the counselors blew off steam by celebrating Halloween in the middle of August after the campers had gone to bed. The boys we'd chosen were also roommates. Or maybe they'd chosen us.

Marcella and I were dressed as sexy Oompa-Loompas, and the boys were a priest and a cowboy, respectively. In retrospect, this might've been the most exciting part, the fact that we were all in costumes. It didn't matter that the next day, at the morning meeting, they were themselves again: Nate and Bradley, two boys who loved *Grand Theft Auto* and quoting Will Ferrell movies. They were two different boys, sure, but the distinctiveness mattered less to us than the fact of their friendship—that we could so easily lump them together as one. And anyway, they wanted to be lumped together, that's why they were best friends, because they liked so many of the same things.

Nothing could be more perfect, we'd said, than two best friends sleeping with two *other* best friends. I imagined the experience would bind us together inextricably. We'd brought the boys to our cabin, to our neatly made beds, and stole glances at the other side of the room—watched each other bravely take off our clothes with a determined lack of passion. I don't remember much of the sex, but I remember that Marcella and I both moaned theatrically, pornographically—"yes, yes, yes, more yes, more, yes"—but the performance had been for each other, not the boys. In Tahoe, we'd become adult women together. We'd moved through a door that we could not return through.

The boys even looked similar—two brown-haired boys of average height, except the priest (Bradley) had a touch of vitiligo around his eyes, so that when he winced in pleasure as he entered me, I thought the discolored patches looked particularly poetic. I even said that in my head, to remember to tell Marcella: his patches looked poetic. I was much more focused on his pleasure than on my own, and much more focused on Marcella's pleasure on the other side of the room than everyone else's pleasure combined.

At that time, I felt like looking into my best friend's face was more useful than looking into a mirror. When I looked at Marcella, I could see my own feelings reflected back at me. That's what I remembered thinking during the sex: I wish I could see Marcella's face right now.

51.

December. No snow falls in LA, of course, but the wind was biting.

It reminded me of my first few months in Los Angeles.

Every night, I'd eat a slice of pizza in the same one-room pizza parlor on Ventura Boulevard and then lay in bed naked with the windows thrown open. I liked to listen to the harsh blur of traffic, the car horns and rumbling buses and someone shouting at their friend to hurry up, get in the car, hurry up. I liked the smell of grilled meat, the bougainvillea, the salsa music coming from someone's tinny car stereo. I liked wondering when I would feel less alone.

The truth is, the city never seemed that way again: lonely, yes, but never as welcoming in its loneliness.

After class, I found myself in the usual tiki bar, drinking with the other adjuncts. Chris wanted to talk about Reid. For once, I wanted to talk about myself. I'd been writing well lately. Or if not well, more. I'd take long walks in Reid's neighborhood, in Laurel Canyon, and carry a notebook with me, pausing like a mental patient in the middle of someone's driveway to scrawl a frenzied paragraph. Later, I'd spread out in Reid's comfortable bed, the sheets with their abundant thread count, and reread what I'd written and think, it's something. It's definitely something!

"The kids don't get it," Chris said. "They don't get his appeal!" Who were the kids? I wondered. Our students? Or just everyone younger than us? Anyone who wasn't, at this moment, standing here under a fake parrot?

"He still has fans," I said. "Don't worry."

"You're right," he said and then launched into some theory about the algorithm and cognitive dissonance. I'd forgotten how much he liked talking about the algorithm.

By the bar, I met a man who'd just moved here this week from Chicago to teach Chicano studies.

"Do you like LA?" the man asked me. He had an appealing way of rocking back and forth on his heels when he talked. "I'm finding it hard to get used to."

"I think you'll like it eventually," I said. "There's a lot to do."

"Like what?"

"You could go to a pool hall. You could go see a stand-up comedy show."

He offered to buy me a shot, so I agreed. No, I'd said, it doesn't matter what kind. I was spending so many nights at Reid's—letting myself get tangled up in his routines, sedated by them—I now had very few nights to myself. It felt like something to celebrate, being at a bar, having written. Probably I'd already had enough to drink. My sentences were beginning to run away from me like rabbits into their holes.

There was so much to like about alcohol! Why had it taken me this long to realize that? All during my childhood, I had played the role of the responsible one, and I was tired of the person I used to be. No wonder people wrote poems and ballads and lullabies about drinking.

How many shots did I have that night? Three? Four? I understood that I wouldn't be able to drive, that I would need someone to pick me up and take me home. Kelly? I thought, and then chastised myself. She didn't work for me. I could call an Uber, but I didn't want to sit with a stranger in a silent car. I wanted to talk to someone!

I wandered out of the bar and the dark palms against the charcoal sky suddenly appeared beautiful. At that time in my life, drunkenness made me poetic. Probably it still does.

I wanted to call someone and tell them about the sky, how meaningful it looked. And the moon. You didn't want to get me started on the moon! How wise and all-knowing. Should I call Reid? But no, I would have a difficult time explaining what I meant. I wanted to speak to someone who would understand. Someone around whom I didn't need to try that hard to explain myself. I wanted to call Emma, I realized. I wanted to see her. So that's what I did—as simple as that. I had a thought and I acted on it. It used to be that I'd have a thought and act on it ten years later. But not today. Today, I was making my life happen. Or else, I wasn't thinking of my life at all.

52.

When my mother called me and told me about my brother, I'd just begun a master's degree at a fancy Ivy League school. I had made friends with a group of writers, girls like me, hardworking, quiet. I remembered I had been upset about something petty—a professor hadn't liked my writing, had called my stories "wan little husks." I'd been making fun of the professor with my knot of friends, imitating her at the frozen yogurt machine. That night I had a date planned: the graduate student boyfriend with the easy-to-draw face, at least if you knew how to draw faces.

The next thing that happened was this: I met my parents in Vegas, at the precinct, and the cops told us my brother had fallen off the track of the monorail. Or maybe he had jumped. There really was no way to know.

"What the fuck is the monorail," my father had said.

"It's a tourist-type train," the cop said. "It goes over the Las Vegas strip."

"He jumped? Or he fell off? He might've just been goofing off," I said. Trying to impress a group of people—that guy Tommy? Trying to make everybody laugh.

"Maybe," the cop said. He wore the brim of his cap low, so that it was difficult to see his eyes. He wanted to know if we had any information about Jack that might be useful.

My mother talked about the pool where Jack lifeguarded, that she told him to eat three square meals every day, though she wasn't sure if he did. She wasn't even sure he saw a doctor, and if so, when was the last time?! Why hadn't she kept up with him better? She'd been busy. She'd been distracted. And he so rarely called her back! She should've forced him to call her back.

For once in my life, my father didn't cry. He cried plenty later, but not then.

The cops looked to me, and so did my parents. Didn't I know the most about him?

I tried to explain: he loved stand-up, was obsessed with it, obsessed with the weight of the microphone in his hand, the heat of the spotlight, the suspended drip of time before he uttered a word, while the audience waited to see if they could trust him, waited to see if he was any good. And he was good!

He hated schmoozing, he didn't want to send suck-up emails to bookers who didn't care if he lived or died. And he definitely didn't want to talk "industry" with greasy men in trendy bars, holding their phones in front of his face. Or at least, that used to be true. Yes, he drank too much. Yes, he gambled. He was a little bit impulsive, wild. Had I said any of that? Probably words had failed me. There weren't enough of them, or else, I couldn't find any that were useful.

I tried to explain Tommy, the money in the cooler, but somehow—when I spelled it out for all of them, it was like what Faulkner said, a tale told by an idiot, signifying not a whole hell of a lot.

"If you're suggesting he might've been into drugs," the female cop said, "that seems pretty clear according to friends we've talked to." I remembered the cop was unusually pretty. She had high cheekbones and wore the cakey foundation that reminded me of the cocktail waitresses who worked in the Peppermill, forever bringing gamblers their drinks.

"But I think this... cooler of money, as you put it, might've just been a cooler of money," the male cop said. "Maybe for drugs. Maybe for who knows what. Maybe for nothing. For a show," the cop said, though that didn't make any sense at all. "Didn't you say he did comedy?"

"He was a comedian," I said. "That was his job." Suddenly, it seemed like that was very important. He was on the edge of greatness, I wanted to say. He was on the edge of fame. He mattered, was what I was trying to say. I thought maybe that would make them try harder. "But if you found the cooler," I said. "Wouldn't that be a clue? Wouldn't that lead to something?"

"Maybe," the female cop said, "maybe not."

The cooler was long gone. And when they tracked down Tommy, he had a warrant for outstanding child support, but nothing useful to say. He liked Jack. Around him, he'd felt a little less depressed, a little less like his life had been falling apart.

I remember seeing Tommy in the back of Jack's funeral in his cowboy hat and suspenders, head bowed. When he hugged me, he said, "Your brother helped me through my worst days." Maybe I'd had the wrong impression of him.

My students always wanted me to assign them mysteries, and so did the women in my book clubs. At that time, I refused.

Now I read plenty of mysteries. I like the classics. Who doesn't want to see order restored by some detective with craggy features and a dark past—a savior who restores the paradise that's been lost.

But my brother lived in Las Vegas, not paradise, and there was no mystery to be solved, apparently, other than whatever was going on inside of him. And even that now seemed minor. It might've been a tumbleweed blowing through his life. In a week, he might've felt better. Or a month. He could've waited it out.

That's what I kept thinking: he could've just waited himself out.

53.

Emma picked me up from the tiki bar and in the car, she was oddly quiet.

"Why didn't you call my dad?" she said finally.

"I don't know," I said. "He's already asleep."

I'd texted him, *Getting a ride home from the bar* because I didn't want him to worry about me when he woke up. But also, I liked having someone worry about me—I liked having a man at home who might wake up in the middle of the night and check his phone, grateful to know where I was.

"And," I said to Emma, "I wanted to see you."

I showed Emma to my complex, led her through the broken gate, to the filthy pool.

"Should I get in?" she said.

"If you want." The moon was sword bright. It was almost Christmas.

"I wish this pool were heated," she said.

"Poor little rich girl," I said. "She'll freeze to death in a body of water that isn't warmed perfectly to her liking." She stared at me blankly and I worried I offended her, but after a moment, she laughed. It seemed difficult to offend her, at least for me. We rolled up our jeans, put our feet in the pool. We sat so close our legs touched.

We sat quietly for a while and the air pulled so taut with expectancy, I was aware of every sound. Eventually she put her hand to her own mouth. "I bit my lip," she said. "I keep biting it over and over and now it's swollen.

Here," she said, taking my hand and placing it there. "Feel," she said. So I did. I felt my pulse in my fingertips. I felt the curve of her lower lip.

A big, complicated insect buzzed brainlessly around our heads.

"Can we go inside," I said, as though it were her apartment and she had the key.

54.

In the darkness of my living room, nothing had happened yet.

I didn't want to turn on my loud overhead light, so I lit one of the fancy, scented candles Reid had bought me, listened for the sizzle of the wick catching fire.

We were standing very close to each other in what I referred to as my living room, but was really just the center of my studio apartment. I couldn't hear anything over my own oceanic pulse in my ears. I was trying not to breathe too loudly. I didn't feel nearly as drunk anymore.

"It's freezing in here," Emma said. And then, "excuse me," as though she was trying to get by me in the grocery store. She kissed me on the mouth then, chastely, before stepping abruptly back. It was a quick, firm kiss—tiny and intact—like a period at the end of a sentence.

"I like you," she said. "Do you like me?"

"Yes," I said. "How can you ask that?" It was a surprise to access how I felt so readily. Usually I'd have to shout the question to myself from the rooftops: how do you FEEL?

Now it was me who moved forward, quickly, before any thinking might stop me.

The kiss became deep, plunging. She put her hands on my waist, in my hair.

"We should stop," I said, but in a whispery way, my nose against her cheek.

"Of course," she said. "Of course we should stop."

"Yes," I said, "stop." Though the word "stop" sounded more like a come-on. And we didn't stop. Of course we didn't. Would I be writing this down if we had?

"Jesus Christ," Emma said, when I peeled my T-shirt off. Then, "Are you kidding me?" when I unclasped my bra. "I can't stand to look at you," she said.

Men had been excited to see me naked, but this was different. Emma looked pained, as though the sight of me was almost too much to bear.

I thought of Marcella. I wanted to ask her: Did you ever—had you ever? What was the question on the edge of my mind? It didn't matter, Emma was pressing her fingers into me, driving every thought from my brain.

I'm not sure what I expected—softness? Sensuality? Instead, we rolled around a lot, jammed our fingers into each other, mashed our boobs together. What I liked about it was how our bodies fit together—almost fused—but I would have never called it soft. I thought of Reid in bed, how there was something about him that was a little too skilled, a little too smooth. Maybe desire should make you clumsy, foolish. I felt very much like a fool.

After, in my bed, Emma said, "You don't have to say anything corny like, 'It's never felt like that before.'" It hadn't ever felt like that before—that strenuous and messy and slick and pleasurable.

I said, "I won't say that then."

"Should I leave?" she said. "I should probably leave."

She slept over. At one point she held my face in both hands and said, "I've been jealous of my dad for many things but not anything as much as having you."

"I have wanted you the entire time," I said.

"Is that true? How would I have known?"

"I don't know," I said.

"And him?" she said. I couldn't answer that, so we started up again.

*   *   *

The next morning, when I drove to Reid's, planning to end things, to bring the whole wild experiment of the two of us to a close, it felt like looking down a cliff—terrifying, sad. I couldn't imagine how I'd get to the bottom. I didn't have the right equipment, the necessary shoes!

I thought of our evening Popsicles and the sweetness of our mornings in bed, our cheerful toothbrushing, his serious, Clark Gable goodbyes. I thought of the books I bought him to read, which he'd fall asleep with, splayed open on his chest. Our private nicknames for each other, what we called my favorite chair (Mr. Chair), and the neighbor we didn't like (BG for Bad Guy)—all of it a language that would go extinct with us, that nobody would use again. Bizarrely, I thought of my dad, of his awful disappointment if I left Reid. He'd already been disappointed by so many things! I was between a rock and a very hard place, I thought. I wondered if I'd ever be comfortable again.

Christmas was next week, then New Year's. Then, I hoped I would turn over a new leaf. Finally, finally my leaf would turn.

55.

Some months passed. I don't want to bore you.

For those months, I tried not to see Emma. Her texts and calls piled up, swelling in my inbox, all unanswered. She'd come for dinner at Reid's and I'd treat her like an uncle whose politics I disagreed with: politely, but with a kind of formal distaste. I felt I'd opened a box I was now trying with all my might to shut, to stomp on with my feet, to tie down with industrial chains. I missed her in a visceral way—I walked through the world as though I were battling a heavy wind, a little stooped.

Reid asked if we'd gotten into a fight.

"No," I said, "I've just been busy."

And I was busy—I was teaching more, and continuing to write more too. I was dedicating myself to Reid, to being someone's girlfriend. And I enjoyed our routines! They became more and more entrenched. We watched four whole seasons of a critically acclaimed show neither of us had seen before. It was a show about a failing garment factory, and by season five we decided to stop watching because it made both of us too sad. I even liked that we shared that—a sadness that descended on us at exactly the same time. When he felt his agent was turning on him, I listened carefully, with the submission of a mirror: his anxiety was my anxiety.

Still, I felt tired all of the time—it took a lot of effort not to think about what Emma looked like naked every day.

* * *

One night, I asked Reid if he'd ever been with a man—had ever even thought about it. I doubted it. Was it a generational thing? A lack of open-mindedness? Maybe he just wasn't uncertain enough.

But he surprised me. "Of course I've thought about it," he said. "But I don't even like the look of myself naked." He fell asleep with the lamp on. I lay staring at the wall. I tried not to imagine what other bodies felt like.

A gossip magazine published a photo of me with Reid, in which I was called "unnamed woman." We were walking out of a Starbucks, something we did most mornings now, though nobody had ever cared before.

In the photo, he was holding the door open for me. I'd turned toward the camera—my face in motion—so that I looked like I *could* be beautiful if only they'd captured me straight on.

Marcella sent me a text message: *ARE YOU FUCKING KIDDING ME— YOU'RE DATING HIM?????*, which got Marcella and me back in touch. We began to talk weekly, and not just about my brother, or our parents, or our town. We talked about what we did every day—what her kid said at school, what my book clubs were like. We talked about Tahoe.

"I'm trying to write about some of it," I said. "About the way we grew up."

We talked about everything but Emma.

On one of our long rambling phone calls, I said, "I think I'm attracted to women." Then I amended it, "I shouldn't say think."

"Will it hurt your feelings if I don't act surprised?" she said.

If we never knew how we looked to other people, then why did it come as such a shock to hear what other people saw? Maybe I was a bad performer. Or a bad liar, though now I see, we don't always know that we're lying. Sometimes we just think we're turning the light off in a room we shouldn't enter right now.

"I was scared in our town," I said to Marcella. "Scared to say anything."

"There were a lot of things for us to be scared of," she said.

*   *   *

Reid ripped out the page from the gossip magazine and taped it on the fridge.

"My unknown woman!" he'd say as a joke.

My father called to tell me he was having the same photo framed.

My mother called and said, "Raj wants to know if Reid actually hated his sidekick, Mark, or if it was Mark who hated Reid?"

I told her I hadn't known Raj was a fan.

"Of course," my mother said. "You never asked!"

I taught five different classes: The Literature of Los Angeles, Intro to Composition, Intro to Creative Writing, California Noir, and Books!: A Survey, though the last had to be canceled—not enough students signed up.

"Don't take it personally," my boss said. "The sun comes out and they don't want to read." People were always saying not to take things personally. Meanwhile I took in every piece of news like it had been planned with only me in mind.

Julie transferred to a four-year liberal arts college. She gave me a tearful goodbye, asked if she was allowed to hug me.

"No," I said, "but do it anyway."

I'd begun to think of myself as a writer again. Every day, I wrote. I wrote on my long walks through Laurel Canyon, and in front of the filthy pool in Van Nuys, and in my tiny office in Glendale, where I still had nothing on the walls. I had made one decor choice: I put a few tchotchkes on my lone Ikea shelf, objects my mother sent me: a small pyramid, a cactus in a bright, blue bowl. And I was a teacher, too. I now thought of myself as one. I was a person who said useful things to students who wanted to hear them.

"I could prescribe a book for whatever ails you," I told my classes. "I'm like a book doctor that way."

*   *   *

The premed student with gray hair finished his novel. I read the first three pages, which made almost no discernible sense.

"Did you like it?" he said.

"It was very creative," I said.

56.

I made it to spring relatively unscathed, until it was time for the wedding of Reid's only nephew in Tahoe.

Kelly drove, in her usual baseball cap (Cubs that day). Kelly had also been invited to the wedding. Reid sat in the front and Emma and I sat in the back, like we were their kids. It felt jarring to be this close to Emma after she'd existed so wholly in my mind. In the car, her lines were unusually sharp.

Kelly and Reid argued playfully about the music—who should DJ. They had a sibling quality, I'd decided, more than employer-employee. Then again, who knew what Kelly would've said if I asked her.

My dad always said: Bosses always want you to forget you work for them. They want to trick you into thinking you are family.

When Emma set her hand on my knee, my heart threatened to fly from my chest, to wring her neck with its little heart hands.

"You went dark on me," she whispered. I didn't want to have this conversation so close to Reid, who was locked in some debate with Kelly about a Don Rickles joke neither one could actually remember.

"That one was about Italians!" he shouted.

"I got busy," I said to Emma idiotically. What else could I say? "I watched a lot of stand-up though." I wanted her to read my mind, to understand that this was my way of saying "I thought of you constantly."

"It hurt my feelings," she said. I couldn't believe she'd put it so plainly! Shame filled me all at once, like salt water filling a lung. She was wearing a new bracelet—a delicate gold chain. Later, I would touch it and notice it had warmed in the sun. I looked out the window.

"Deer," I said, when I saw one.

I wanted to blame my brother. Or my father. Or her father! I blamed so much on everyone else. I was astounded by the way other people were able to process things, like loss or childhood. Why couldn't I ever get *over* anything? It was all still at the tip of my fingers, or on the tip of my tongue.

"I was scared," I said, and she let it go.

This weekend, at least, I vowed to act naturally. Normally. "Be loose!" I told myself. "Be natural!"

It was a seven-hour drive, and on hour five, Emma told us a story about the sugar daddy she met online.

"He was my sugar daddy for two years when I was in college," she said. "He never asked for much. He just wanted me to be happy. And occasionally, he wanted to see pictures of my feet. Sometimes he'd ask for videos of me rubbing the soles together."

"Did you send them?" Kelly asked, from the front seat.

"Of course," she said. "My feet are public domain."

I could tell she was trying to shock her father. Meanwhile he was staring out the window, at the pine trees flipping by like cards in a deck, refusing to be shocked. Reid had told me his attitude about parenting: he wanted Emma to know she could tell him anything. Like my mother, I'd thought, who told me I could always come home.

"You're allowed to be shocked," I'd said, "if she's trying to shock you."

"Maybe that's harder to do than she thinks," he'd said.

"Did this guy ever want to meet you in person?" Kelly asked now, about the sugar daddy.

"No," Emma said. "I can't even remember where he lived. Somewhere random, like Kentucky. He had three kids and a window-siding business. He sent me terrible poetry sometimes, and photos of the countryside at night. Big open fields."

"He must have been lonely," I said.

Emma looked at me, like she was surprised that I had finally joined the conversation. I thought maybe she'd take it as my version of a truce. I guess, in a way, it was.

"Maybe," she said. "Or maybe he had a full life and wanted to make it even fuller."

Somehow in hour six, we got on the topic of our favorite fast-food place. Reid had no opinions; he hadn't eaten fast food in twenty years.

"I worked at In-N-Out in high school," I said, and Kelly said, "I worked at Hardee's!"

"I can't believe we were paid so little," I said. I remembered it being hard, greasy work. You'd leave smelling of French fries, of beef patties left too long on the grill. "I can't believe people are still paid so little!"

"Well it's a minimum wage job," Reid said.

"You should make enough money to be able to live," I said. "I think you should be able to earn a living wage even if you're just flipping burgers."

"I don't think fast-food jobs were ever meant to be adults' primary incomes. It was meant for high school kids. For summer jobs."

"Maybe in the fifties," I said, and he laughed sharply, like I was trying to insult him—to remind him of his age. But I'd forgotten how old he was at that moment; I was just trying to make a point.

I remember this: somewhere along the line, it escalated into an argument between us. Reid pretended it wasn't, but it was clear to me that it was. Or at least, I felt clear that I was upset. Sometime in the last string of months, I'd begun to have an easier time naming my feelings for what they were.

"Don't get me wrong," he said, "I don't mind paying taxes and having those taxes going to help the greater good. God knows I pay a lot of taxes. And I'm a Democrat for God's sake." I'd heard him say this same line on the radio: I'm a Democrat for God's sake. It was jarring, to hear him say it to me now.

"But if my taxes are so high that other people don't need to work nearly as hard as me," Reid said. "That they can work a high school kid's job and then take money from the government when it's—surprisingly, I guess—not enough money to make ends meet." He made an exasperated face in the rearview mirror. "I guess I just think that's not fair."

"I'm not saying you don't work hard," I said. "But the amount you get paid. I mean even you'd agree you're lucky."

"Sure, of course, I've been lucky. But I've also *made* myself lucky due to talent and work ethic. I've made a great living in a nearly impossible field."

"True," I said. "But what about a fast-food worker or a...I don't know, a truck driver." I said the words "truck driver" like I'd never known a single one in my life. "Are you saying they don't work as hard as you? Do they not deserve a living wage?"

"Well you're getting into something complicated," he said. I heard the subtext: too complicated for you. "How do these small businesses— these mom-and-pop restaurants—how can they afford to keep their doors open if the minimum wage is so high? It's supply and demand," he said. "Supply and demand," he repeated, as though that explained everything.

"I wasn't talking about mom-and-pops," I said. My voice had grown louder, and a little whiny. I hated how I sounded just then. "I'm talking about places like McDonald's. I'm talking about huge corporations."

"All right, everyone," Kelly said. "I think you've all made your points." How much does she make? I wondered.

Reid shrugged theatrically, craning around the seat to face me. "I get what you're saying," he said. I knew when I was being lectured—I was a teacher after all.

"I get what young people say now," he continued. I'd never heard him put me in the category of "young people"—the category of the back seat.

"Hey," he said. He settled back into his seat, looked at me in the rear-view mirror. "I'm not trying to fight with you."

"We're not fighting," I lied. I worried he'd see it on my face: just how angry I was. When we stopped for gas, I said I needed a walk. "To stretch my legs," I lied.

"Sorry my dad was being an asshole," Emma said. She'd followed me to the snack section. I felt calmed, looking at the rows of beef jerky in their familiar places, right where they should be. I'd always found the sight of groceries calming—everything tucked into their neat little shelves, in their neat little homes. It reminded me of precious time spent with my mother in the grocery store, picking out the foods my father and brother loved.

"It's not your job to apologize for him," I said.

"I was gonna come to your defense, but you didn't look like you needed it."

It occurred to me then that maybe she was a little afraid of him, or at least, afraid to piss him off. I almost said: It's not your problem. Or, He's not your problem. She was wearing another baggy shirt that said *R-E-L-A-X*.

That night, in our luxury cabin that was really more like a hotel suite, Reid apologized.

"I shouldn't have taken such a hard stance," he said, which didn't mean that he thought he was wrong.

We tried to have sex, or we did have sex, but I couldn't finish. I thought of Emma and Kelly sharing a cabin only a Frisbee's throw away. I wondered what they were talking about—if they were laughing together in the dark. Before tonight, the pleasure with Reid had been relatively effortless, pried from me without my control. Now it felt as though my desire was far away, in a different cabin.

I'd felt distracted by his dry breath on my cheek, the way his lips parted in concentration, his buffed fingernails on my thighs. How different Emma's fingernails were (bitten), and the pressure of her hands (much harder than Reid, who was so often overly gentle).

"It's not happening for me tonight," I said. I wouldn't fake it, I decided. I wouldn't find another way to be dishonest. "But let me finish you."

*   *   *

After, he said, "Everyone's not in the mood all the time. Don't worry about it."

"I know," I said. "I wasn't worried." I resented the fact that he thought I would be.

57.

The actual wedding was small and enchanted-feeling—string lights and a live quartet's long-held violin notes. At weddings, my father would bring a blank check and decide how much to gift the couple based on the food, the band—how extravagant it all was. Then, depending, he'd fill the check out in the bathroom, or sometimes at the bar.

We were encircled by trees. The air felt charged. Everywhere, women in dark dresses and men with slick hair. I was closing in on twenty-nine, and I'd attended very few weddings. Marcella's was one. My father had no siblings, my mother a single sister. The only family wedding I could recall: my aunt's son, whom we all called Cousin Danny, as though it were a necessary title like "rabbi" or "sir."

Looking at the other guests, I realized I'd underdressed. I'd mistaken "summer cocktail" for "summer dress." Why hadn't Reid corrected me when he saw me just hours ago, after he'd twirled me around in front of the mirror and said, "Don't you look good"? That should have been his job, as my boyfriend—to find out what his girlfriend should wear. It was always easier to dress as a man, to be a man: suit with a tie, suit without a tie, blazer, jacket, coat, it all worked, it all looked the same. In floral pink, I stuck out like a brightly colored thumb.

Emma wore a dark green velvet suit, which even now, I can picture very clearly. I wasn't used to seeing her dressed in something so tailored, so expertly fit.

"Pink," she said to me, by way of greeting. "It's good," she said, seeing my miserable face. "We needed color."

At night, the lake rippled like the dark fabric of a dress.

After the ceremony, Reid introduced me to extended family members, family friends, friends of family friends.

"She's a writer," he said. "Her stuff is really, really good." He looked at me like he meant it, and I felt he did, though he still hadn't read anything. Did it matter if he read it when he knew he liked it? That was still important to me at that time, for Reid to be impressed by me. Or maybe, for someone my dad was impressed with to be impressed. Awe twice removed.

Right as the reception began, I finally met Reid's ex-wife.

She had presence, which shouldn't have surprised me. And what is beauty if not presence? She did not look like she belonged on the cover of a magazine; rather, she looked like the person who chooses the woman to put on the cover. In other words, she looked powerful. She was wearing no makeup or jewelry, not even nail polish, though she talked constantly with her hands. She looked like the kind of woman who found the idea of enhancing her beauty boring. Some of the women in my book clubs were like that, women whose whole wardrobes looked soft and expensive. At any moment, they might board a plane to Greece for a little rest and relaxation.

Emma introduced me, while Reid was nowhere to be found. This, too, should've been a boyfriend's job. (Later, he'd said, he'd taken Kelly to see how beautiful the lake looked.)

"Mom," Emma said, "meet Allison."

"Hello Allison," Jean said, sticking out her hand obediently, like Emma was the mother and Jean was her child, doing as she was told.

If Jean knew I was her ex-husband's girlfriend, she pretended not to. "If you'll excuse me," she said now, "I'm wanted in wardrobe."

Soon the bride showed up in a different dress for the reception: short, like the flappers wore, the fringe swinging as she corralled everyone onto the dance floor. By then, Reid had returned and so the two of us danced.

I danced like I imagined a younger, easier person might. I laughed and panted, and sweated so much I felt refreshed, like I'd been through a baptism, like I'd gotten rid of something I no longer wanted inside me. On the dance floor, Jean's proximity to Reid only made her seem brighter, more significant. She drew every eye in the room.

Maybe because of this, I danced with Reid with unusual intensity, pressing my waist against his. I didn't mind if people stared. I saw Emma from the corner of my eye, watching. I pretended like she didn't exist.

"I met your ex-wife," I whispered hotly in his ear.

He'd been singing along to the Motown floating up into the trees, claiming I sent him. Honest I did. He was a very good singer, though I wasn't surprised. He was obsessed with music, and he had a talent for all his obsessions—piano, radio. Was he good because he got obsessed, or was he just obsessed with whatever he was good at? It was a chicken and egg scenario.

"And was my ex-wife nice?" he asked. He'd had nothing to drink, as usual, but there was an uncommon looseness in the way he spun me, in the way he shimmied his hips.

"She was fine," I said. "It was brief."

"Well whatever she tells you," Reid said, "believe half of it."

"What would she tell me?" I asked.

"Who knows," he said.

After the wedding, Reid retired to go smoke cigars with Kelly.

"Am I allowed?" Reid asked me, which felt strange, to be asked permission, especially when he'd been so scarce for so much of the night. I didn't want to say: I had assumed you'd want to be near me at a wedding, a time when people thought about the person they loved.

"Of course you can go," I said. I almost said, I'm not your mom.

And anyway, when Emma volunteered to keep me company, I must have sounded ridiculous when I said, "I guess," like I could go either way—with her, or back to my cabin alone. How ridiculous, when I wanted her company so acutely, I could feel it in the joints of my hands.

✻   ✻   ✻

I suggested we take a walk down to the lakeside. We used the light from our cell phone screens. As we descended, I felt the pull of the woods—the cool, shadowy smell of them.

"Maybe we'll see a bear," Emma said.

When we were finally alone, she pushed me against a tree, the bark scratching the tender skin of my inner arms. I thought maybe she'd kiss me, or at least put her hands on me.

Instead, she said, "Why am I being punished for what happened? What we did. And it was we. It was both of us."

"I'm not trying to punish you," I said. Really, I think I was trying to punish myself. "I'm sorry," I said. "I've been—messed up."

We walked more and didn't say anything for a while. Among the trees, the air was dense with anticipation.

"I used to come here growing up." I'd said it to change the subject, but then I couldn't figure out how to easily explain the Death Camp, and Marcella, and all the kids who'd seen so much bad luck before they even turned eighteen.

Instead, I told her about the Haunted House near my childhood home—about the guy who killed his parents.

"Why did he do it?" she asked.

"I don't know," I said. "Who knows why people do what they do." *The awful thing about life is this—everyone has their reasons.*

We kept walking. All around us, nighttime sounds: frogs and insects and very far away, music at a wedding.

"I had a stalker once," Emma said. "Well, he was my dad's stalker, really. I was just easier to get close to."

"That sounds terrifying," I said.

"Sort of. I mean, until I met him. Then it was more sad. He used to send my dad these long, creepy letters and then he found my address at college and started sending me letters. But they weren't like sexual. They were more just. I dunno. Lonely. Sometimes they said interesting stuff. Like, did you know cruise ships have morgues? Three to four passengers usually die every cruise, and they just put them down in the morgue so they don't dis-turb everybody's vacation. Once, he showed up at my dorm room."

"No way," I said. I was happy to hear one of her stories again, to let her talk and talk uninterrupted.

"It was true," she said. "He was standing outside of my dorm room, wait-ing for me to get back from class."

"Are you Emma?" he'd asked.

She didn't even consider lying. "Who are you?" she asked.

"Jared," he said, like she should know the name. "I'm a friend of your father's." Of course, she knew that wasn't true, and not just because of the stained, rumpled sweatshirt and the sleep still in his eyes and the fact that it was cold and he didn't seem to notice the single drip of snot making its way down his face, but because her father had so few friends, if he had a friend named Jared, she would've known.

She'd backed away from him in tiny incremental steps, afraid to spook him, like he was a bull about to charge. She didn't think he was dangerous—he didn't have the threat of violence emanating from him.

"Though," she said now, "I've always thought of myself as a bad judge of character. Maybe my dad is right about some things." When she told Reid that the stalker came to see her, he was furious—apoplectic with worry. Another time, she said, in college, she'd let a man use the bathroom during a party and he stole the television. "Everybody in the building was mad at me. Only my roommate laughed." I hoped I would've laughed too, that I would not have gotten hung up on the price of the TV. I liked that about Emma—the way she let people in, her openness to the world.

"Anyway," Emma said, "that same stalker had shown up at the hospital when I was born." Security wouldn't let him in, but he left a teddy bear. The bear was more for Reid, of course, a way to say, I'm thinking of you and your new daughter. "The guy didn't see himself as a stalker," Emma said. "But they never do."

They think of themselves as "superfans," or worse, Emma explained, true friends Reid just hasn't had the chance to meet yet. They'd listened to him for so many hours alone in their cars, some strange transition occurred. They'd begun to feel as though he was communicating directly to them, for them.

Hadn't that happened to me? To my father? Not to that extent, but still. Didn't we feel a special sort of connection to Reid before we'd ever met him? Because yes, he could be crass and disgusting, but he could also be vulnerable. Once he said to his hundreds of thousands of listeners (or was it millions then?)—and also to me and my dad in a big rig moving through Colorado—"I'm worried I'm just some loser they put a microphone in front of. I'm worried someday you'll all figure that out. That I'm nobody important. But I guess we all worry about things like that." Yes, my father had said aloud, yes we do.

"I'm glad your stalker wasn't dangerous," I said.

"No, no," Emma said. "He wasn't dangerous. And also, anyone *can* be dangerous. I think you have to recognize some of yourself in a person like that."

"A crazy person?"

"Sure. Though maybe I wouldn't call him crazy. Maybe I'd call him 'a person who has been stripped of the safeguards that keep the rest of us normal.'"

Hadn't there been a string of months after my brother died when I hadn't even bothered to look in the mirror? When I, too, must have had sleep caked in my eyes? When I was acting off, abnormal? Maybe I still was. Acting a little off, I mean.

Emma still had the last letter the stalker sent her. *If you knew me, you'd understand*, he'd written. *This has all been one huge misunderstanding.*

In a clearing amid more trees, where we could see the lake through a gap in the greenery, I asked if we could rest. We sat inches apart, close enough that I could hear the whisper of velvet when Emma moved.

"I thought you hated me," Emma said. "After you know what."

"No," I said. "The opposite."

In the dark, I could hardly see her. Her voice seemed to drop down suddenly from the trees and land at my ear like a soft black cat.

"It's always awkward when my parents are together," she said.

"Was it awkward tonight?" I asked. "It didn't seem like it to me. They hardly spoke."

"Yeah well," she said. "When he wasn't with you, he was hiding out with Kelly. And my mom would never say anything rude in front of Kelly. In front of anyone, really. She's not that kind of person."

"So she just doesn't like him?" I said.

"More than that," she said. "My mom thinks he ruined her life."

"Why?"

"He made her stop acting, give up her dreams. And she was obsessed with acting."

I had trouble picturing Reid forcing anyone to give up anything—With what? His sulking?—let alone an obsessive dream, and certainly not Jean, who seemed much too self-assured for that. Then again, it might've just been her persona, a version I'd met tonight.

"It all happened before I was born anyway," Emma said. "My mom thinks my dad ruined her life and my dad thinks my mom's life took its natural course and now she gets to blame him for that. So I guess it depends on whose story you're following. Like if you think about a dog getting bitten by a flea—you're mad at the flea. But let's say you were watching a documentary about that flea—you'd be so happy he found a dog to bite."

"Who is who in this scenario?"

"It doesn't matter," Emma said.

"My mom cheated on my dad," I said now. "When I was young. In junior high I guess." I'd never told anyone that. This had been around the time of the Christian girls, before my first kiss—before I'd been expelled from the group. My father had found an email a man had sent my mother with the subject line *To my darling*. It had seemed like a joke—to my darling?! My father had walked around the backyard screaming, *To my darling, to my darling*, until it sounded like a nursery rhyme.

"It's always a surprise to people who know them both," I said. "It seems like my father would be the one to cheat."

After I left for college, my mother wanted to confide in me about it, to explain herself: the man she'd cheated with was The Problem's opposite. Wasn't that the whole point of an affair—to get a window into an entirely different life, an alternate dimension if only you might've made a different choice.

This man was an auditor for the city of Reno. He liked to go to bed at nine o'clock every night to a rerun of *Frasier*. He only drank alcohol on the weekends—wine, never hard liquor. He never cursed; he said "oh my gosh."

In the end, he was still difficult in a similar way that my father was difficult—needy, easily set off. My father was troubled by the way the wind blew some days (so fucking hard!), like it was out to get him. But this man, too, was a complainer. Once, at a restaurant, he said the waiter made him feel weird by the way he took his order, by the way he repeated, "Did you say medium or medium rare?" The waiter had made him feel small.

"So I figured," my mother said, "why not just stick with the hand I was dealt. With the problem I already had."

I'd never talked to my father about it. He liked to pretend it never happened—or at the very least, that it was an ill-fated hobby my mother had taken up for a little while, like curling, some wacky diversion: the time she considered leaving my father for another man.

"And me," I said now. "I've cheated before." I thought of the graduate student with the soft voice. After he'd found out, he'd cried on my wet front lawn in the middle of the night and told me I was the love of his life, that I was despicable, that he would miss me every waking moment from here on out, that I deserved whatever was coming to me, fuck you he said, fuck you, I loved you so fucking much. Now, on social media, he seemed to be thriving. He and his fiancée made blueberry muffins and walked their German shepherd mix to the beach. I'd done him a favor, it seemed. I think if it hadn't been for my brother, our mutual friends would've turned on me—maybe even called me a bad person. But I'd suffered the death of a loved one, so they treated me gently, which was somehow worse.

That's when I'd moved to LA for a new job, out of Palo Alto, away from everything that had come before.

For a while Emma and I were still, quiet.

"Why did you cheat?" Emma said.

"I was so, so sad," I said. "I wanted an escape hatch. I wanted to feel anything else but sadness." It felt good to be honest—to state something as plainly as she so often did.

"And now?" she said.

I laughed. "I still feel sad," I said. "But in a different way. About different things." I thought my brother would appreciate the sentiment. He thought of us both as artists, as two people who had a certain intensity of feeling— our friendly little sadness that we could always carry around, slung over our shoulders like a backpack.

"Sometimes I wonder if my mother thinks I only date women because I'm not beautiful enough to attract men," Emma said. "But men are easy to attract. And nobody should know that better than my mother."

"That can't be true," I said. "Hasn't she seen you?"

"So we're friends again?" Emma said.

"I'm trying so, so hard not to touch you," I said.

58.

A few weeks later, summer school began. The students were distracted by the good weather outside—its tantalizing presence through the window. They could be out there throwing Frisbees. They could be lying in the grass, getting all-over tans.

We'd been studying genre.

"According to the genres," I had said, "tragedy ends with a death and comedy ends with a wedding."

"What if it ends with both?" a student asked.

"Then I guess it's like life. Comedy and tragedy dovetail."

At the end of every class, I forced a student to give a "mini lecture" about their favorite genre.

A student stood at the front of the class, looking meaningfully at me before he began.

"I pose a question," he said, "are comedy and tragedy lovers or enemies? For me," he said, "they're lovers. They fight sometimes, but that's natural." Now he directed his eyes at the empty space in the back of the room above the other students' heads. His note cards trembled in his hands.

"And," he continued, "the lovers—comedy and tragedy—need to have good communication or else they'll break up and go their separate ways."

I'd been nodding in and out of concentration and now I couldn't remember whom he'd been presenting on—George Saunders? P. G. Wodehouse?—but I could tell he put in the effort.

The fact that the presentation didn't make much sense mattered less to me than the fact of his caring (his trembling hands!). Also, I liked that he so eagerly read the books I suggested for him outside of class. In the end, like so many other unquantifiable assets, likability made a difference, sometimes *the* difference. And I liked him.

When he finished, the class clapped in a half-hearted way, like water dribbling from a turned-off faucet. I knew I'd raise his grade as much as I could, give him the "likability bump," as I referred to it in my mind.

After class, he hovered by my desk.

"Great job," I said, and when he didn't walk away, I asked, "How are you otherwise?"

"Bad," he said, "my parents are splitting. I know I'm an adult, and I shouldn't care but I still do."

"That's not true," I said. "You can care. You can care forever."

Somebody is always going through something, I thought. Somebody is always reading a book and finding himself there.

Or herself!

59.

At one of my book clubs, I made a cardinal mistake: I picked a book for the women that I hadn't read. According to my boss, this was very much against the rules. The books needed to be vetted! The women were very particular.

But I'd been scattered—my thoughts like bits of paper in the wind— and pressed for time, split between two people, at least in my mind. I'd read about the book online, and it had sounded good. The women hated it.

"Is the character gay or straight?" Cher-hair asked. "Gay or straight?!" she asked again. They loved categories—needed them like you or I might need water, or sleep.

"Neither," I said. "Or at least it's never mentioned. So in this case, I think neither."

"Or both," a woman said.

"Yes okay," I said, "or both."

"We didn't understand it," one woman said. "It seemed like a book for millennials. Or...what's the younger generation? Gen X?"

"All the young people are gay now," another woman said. "So all the books are gay too."

But then later, as I was gathering myself to leave, the corporate lawyer who was actually very thoughtful said, "You're our favorite. We've had other book girls and you're our favorite one."

I had known some of the women who used to work for the company—they'd moved on, secured better jobs, sold their novels.

Well, I thought, it is something to be the favorite. It's certainly not nothing.

60.

Emma and I began to talk on the phone again. We were trying to be *friends*. We started calling each other a few times a week, but that quickly ramped up to daily. I had never been formally addicted to anything, I didn't think— not to gambling, not to drinking. But this—her—was as close as I'd ever been.

Sometimes I'd talk to her on the floor of Reid's gigantic walk-in closet when he was downstairs in his office. He had rows of identical cashmere sweaters, all fresh from the dry cleaner, still in their plastic sheets.

Emma would tell me about visiting him in the studio as a kid, watching him do his show, awed by the equipment, his huge presence in the room. How deferential everyone was! How the staff clapped and laughed at everything he said.

When it was over, Kelly would take her to get an ice cream in Studio City, let her talk about what she'd say on the radio if *she* had a show—let her talk way more than her own mother ever did.

"I thought I'd do a show about animals," she said. "A show about dogs."

"So maybe you should blame your father," I said. "Maybe he did plant the seed."

I told her about seeing a cell phone commercial and recognizing the actor as a friend of my brother's, another comedian I'd met when I visited him in Vegas.

"He used to be kind of famous," I said. "He was once in a big TV show."

In the commercial, he was a put-upon dad trying to secure a better phone plan. He had only four lines! And yet I knew, if he was anything like my brother, he'd taken ten years of acting classes, had suffered so many humiliations both small and large, had his heart broken by the industry in a thousand minor and major ways, but also had seen his name on several screens, big and small, had attended movie premieres, had meetings with agents across broad steel desks, had thought his life was about to change—finally now, finally!—over and over and over again. Did he feel his career had shrunken down to the size of the cell phone he held in his hand as he looked directly to the camera and said, "Where's the Wi-Fi?" You assumed your career would be a ramp, going up and up, when in fact, it was the freeway after a natural disaster—after Godzilla stomped all over it—up and down and down and down and up again.

"I think," Emma said, "that a lot of people would kill for that commercial."

She put a new stand-up set online.

That's what you're supposed to do, she told me. You're supposed to market yourself.

This girl sucks, someone wrote.

Hurts my ears, said another.

A few commented *ha-ha*s and one wrote, *She's not bad—just needs to work on stage presence.*

"People are always rude online," she said on the phone. I was doing paperwork in my office at the Glendale Community College. "People are especially rude to women."

I made a fake user name Jackie696969 so I could comment, *She's hilarious.*

Reid stienman's daugthter??? someone else replied, and so Emma deleted the whole thing.

*   *   *

"I can never escape him," she said on the phone. "I can never get away from him. I know what you're thinking. Poor you. Poor little rich girl. Poor little daughter of a famous rich guy."

That's not what I was thinking. "Come over," I said instead.

61.

We started meeting regularly, in my apartment. I'd find a sweater of hers in my closet, and she'd find one of my bras in her drawer. It was like cross-pollination. I asked to come see her mother's house, to the room where she spent so much time away from me.

"I'm embarrassed for you to see it," she said. "It looks exactly like it did when I was a kid. It's like a little girl's room. I like meeting at your place. It's an adult apartment."

It's a shit box! I thought. It's a hole in Van Nuys! Though I'd been trying to make it more personal, just like my office in Glendale—I'd been placing objects on shelves, or as I called it, "curating the space."

Every now and then—idiotically, carelessly!—we met at Reid's.

(I wish I could find a way to tell this so that I seem less villainous, less diabolical.

It was not that I didn't feel guilty. Quite the opposite. The guilt felt karmic, like something I had long deserved.)

In bed with Reid, I would look over at him, reading some magazine, and he'd look back at me and say something odd and sweet, like, "I could eat you with a spoon."

On those same nights, I'd sometimes get a text from Emma, something like, "I want you to crush my head in your legs like a vise."

These two! If only they knew how much they had in common. Or maybe they already did.

"Is that Emma texting?" Reid said. "Tell her 'hi.' Tell her 'kisses.' Tell her Dad says, 'Hi baby, kisses.'"

No, I thought. I will not tell her that.

When I was with Emma, I thought of Reid, and when I was with Reid, I thought of Emma. Always an alternate life rumbled beneath the life I was leading, like a sewer beneath a city. I could lift the manhole cover of my mind and see the other life rushing by, I wondered if there would ever be a time when I was not fantasizing about a different life.

I felt sick and stressed, like I was coming down with some disease—mononucleosis maybe, which felled at least two of my students every semester. And yet, when I wasn't feeling nauseated with some nebulous dread, I wrote more than I ever had before. I wrote to escape myself, to escape the exceptional mess I'd made, the one I was rolling around in like some corpulent prize hog.

On a Monday when Reid had meetings scheduled, I brought Emma over to hide out in his expanse of bed. I'd offered to go to her room, but she said that bed reminded her of childhood, of her father.

"And his bed isn't reminiscent of him?!"

"No," she said, "not in the same way."

I wore an old pair of underwear from Victoria's Secret that said *Sexy Thing* spelled out in tiny rhinestones, many of them long gone in the wash. I still have the underwear, believe it or not.

"When did you buy these?" Emma whispered, pulling them down, putting her face between my legs. She rubbed her cheek against the patch of downy hair I'd carefully shaved into a small triangle. I'd seen a naked woman online do the same.

"I got these before you were born," I said. This had become a joke between us—because we were so close in age.

When we switched, and I went down on Emma, she covered her eyes.

"I'll be too fast if I look at you," she said. "I have to pace myself."

She'd dressed for the gym, and now I licked her through her spandex shorts. I'd had ideas about sex. Now those ideas paled in comparison. She made me feel brave, creative. I pulled the spandex shorts aside. She made a pained noise when I held her like that, let the cold air-conditioning in Reid's apartment do its work on her.

Afterward, when we were panting and slick with sweat, Emma said, "You look upset."

"I'm not," I said. "I'm exhausted." More than that. I felt out of it, out of my mind. That's the only way I can describe it.

Had I ever felt closer to my brother than in those moments—closer to his imagined end? (Oh, how I hated to imagine it. And how often I did!) Maybe he'd been like me, trying to pull the car of his desire over. But he couldn't. His was a runaway car, screeching, careening off a cliff.

"I feel insane," I said.

But it must have seemed to Emma like a compliment, because she said, "So I did my job."

Then we heard a voice from somewhere downstairs: "Babe?"

At the sound of Reid's footsteps echoing against his custom wood floors, we sprang away from each other.

"It's my dad," Emma said. She looked panicked, though maybe a little excited too—like something interesting was about to happen.

I had picked Emma up on the way, so there'd be no trace of her. Now that only seemed more suspicious. Why wouldn't she just drive herself? We were friends, after all. We were very good friends. A friend could drive to see a friend.

Reid's voice rose up from the kitchen again, "Babe?! Where are you?"

I heard him coming up the stairs. I thought of my lesson on genre: we were in a sitcom now, or a horror film. Possibly a porno.

Emma struggled back into her spandex, her matching sports bra. "I'll go," she said. "You stay here."

Now Reid was at the top of the stairs, confusion on his face.

"Babe!" he said, talking to his daughter now. I appeared behind her, saw his delight.

"I'm so glad you're here!" he said. "What a nice surprise."

Emma smoothed the back of her hair with her hand. "I thought I'd come join you guys for dinner."

"You said you had meetings," I said. Did I smell like her? I tried to make it sound casual. Instead, it sounded sarcastic, like I was an underappreciated housewife, mad at how long he'd been gone.

"They got out early," he said. He made a move to kiss me and I made an artful dodge, put my cheek to his cheek as Emma watched. If only he'd known where my mouth had been.

"What shall we make," he said. "Burgers? Or try the new pizza oven?" He'd recently had one installed. He wanted to make the most of the summer, he said. He'd been trying to relax. He'd been trying to *enjoy* himself.

"And you relax me," he'd said, just last night. "Even my agent says so."

I had been rifling through excuses why Emma might have shown up here in the middle of the day, unannounced. But I saw now, she needed no excuse. She needed no reason to be here other than the accident of her birth. She was her father's daughter, and she belonged.

62.

My parents called over and over and I didn't answer.
My mother texted, *Just tell me you're alive.*
My father texted, *Have you forgotten I'm alive?*
Yes, I said.
And no, I could never.

63.

Another night in my studio apartment: me on all fours, and Emma behind me. She'd made her hand into a credit card to swipe between my legs.

"Don't—" I began. Don't—" The word "stop" was lodged in my throat, I couldn't get to it in time. But Emma didn't. She didn't stop, I mean.

When we were done, I told her I wanted to build a fort around her vagina, live there like it was a summer camp, somewhere I could swim with my friends, where I could be myself. Emma kissed me gently, and got up to do her makeup in the mirror, dramatic swipes of eye shadow. She was looking at me in the reflection when she said she wanted to tell a joke about the two of us having sex. She'd started leaving more T-shirts behind, whole bags of makeup and fancy face cream. How much did those cost? And who paid for them?

She'd been thinking this joke through, she said, and right then, she'd come up with the punch line. She was talking faster—I could hear the excitement in her voice. I knew this voice: before we'd ever seen each other naked, when we only talked on the phone, and she'd call me after a great set. The elation.

It reminded me of my brother too. But so did sunflower seeds. So did tigers. So did brooms.

"What's the joke?" I said.

"I can't say it now. It won't sound right offstage."

"Is it flattering?"

"It's not *not* flattering. It's about me," she said, "not you."

I felt taken aback. I thought I'd only have to worry about this with Reid—Reid, who never mentioned me by name on his show, nor did he mention any identifying features. The most he'd ever said was, "I'm seeing a nice woman. Even my daughter likes her."

"Well I'm not gonna tell you that you can't tell a joke about me," I said.

"I won't if the joke makes you uncomfortable."

"How will I know if it makes me uncomfortable if I haven't heard it?"

"Nobody will know it's about you," Emma said. "Obviously. For obvious reasons." We went around in circles like this, treading over the idea of the still unformed joke until it was flattened and we were both annoyed.

"How is this any different than you writing about me?" Emma asked.

"Well I've never done it," I said. Which was true then. "And I write fiction. It's different. There would be no way for you to know it's about you."

"My jokes are a kind of fiction. At least some of the time. Some of them."

"But this isn't fiction," I said. "Because something we did in bed made you think of a joke you wanted to tell. Or something *I* did."

"It's not whatever you're thinking."

"Well you don't know what I'm thinking," I said. "And won't know unless you tell me."

"Now it's *really* not gonna be funny. And I still think it's the same for you. I mean where do you get anything you write about? If not from your life?"

"It's not the same," I said. "My writing's different." Tears had sprung to my eyes and now I felt embarrassed. What I meant was: my writing is private. Private for me, anyway. My writing always had been—secretive, aside from my life.

"I won't tell the joke," Emma said. "I'm sorry." She'd come to put her arms around me.

"Say whatever you want," I said, turning away from her. "And I'll write whatever I want." I started going about my life, putting my dirty clothes into a hamper I'd carried from apartment to apartment. I'd had it before my brother died. "You tell your jokes."

"Fine," she said.

"Fine."

I almost shook her hand, like we'd just made a crappy deal.

My father, who was not formally educated in business in any way, was a big fan of the show *Shark Tank*, and every other show on MSNBC. He liked shows about finance and real estate and making money. He liked to say, "If the deal's good, both sides leave a little unhappy."

Maybe that was true about relationships, too. Weren't they just negotiations? Even this one? Especially this one.

Life was a series of concessions, big and small.

64.

On a day when I had no classes to teach and no book clubs to facilitate, and Reid was at the studio and Emma was at the grocery store delivering samples to people who didn't want to try them, I visited the Korean spa by myself.

Next to me in the Jacuzzi, a woman with enormous breasts closed her eyes in relaxation.

"Mmm, mm," the woman said. "Does this feel good."

"It does," I said.

"It sure does," she said. "It feels damn good."

Her eyes were still closed, her mind probably on a different, private planet, when I blurted out: "I'm sleeping with two people at the same time."

"Oh, lord," the woman said blinking a few times, her eyes adjusting to the steam, to my big shiny apple face beside her. "I've been there. It'll be okay. No, no," she said, seeing my face. "I swear it will be." I must have looked scared. "These things have a way of working themselves out."

I felt a pinch in my nose, like I could weep from the gentleness in this woman's voice.

"Now do you lean more toward one or the other?" the woman asked. "If you close your eyes at night." Her white hair was twisted into a pristine French braid.

"It depends on the night," I said.

"Oh, yes," the woman said. "But soon, enough nights will pass that one of your lovers will start to pull ahead. Not that it's a race, but sometimes you have to keep score. You have to keep track of it in your heart."

I liked the fact that the woman used the word "lovers." Would she be surprised to learn one of the lovers was a woman? But this was LA, after all. This was not the middle of Mississippi—a place I had never been, but had ideas about.

"They know each other," I said. "The two people."

At this, the woman burst out laughing, disturbing the water in the Jacuzzi so that it frothed around her shaking breasts. "In that case," she said, "you're in a real pickle."

But even this cheered me, thinking of it as a pickle—no big deal, just a simple salty snack. In ten years, I'd tell the story at dinner parties. I'd say, I'd gotten myself into a pickle. I'd say, I was coming out of a difficult time in my life.

"I've been married four times," the woman said now. "And I still have a hard time picking my favorite."

65.

On a Sunday morning, I was still in Reid's bed when the little *ding* of his fancy keypad chimed. I hadn't slept well the night before. Lying next to him, I'd felt dread rise up in me. I watched him sleep, stared at the hollow in his cheek. A hollow that used to thrill me! Now I wanted to unzip my skin and slither out. I can't stand myself, I thought. I can't stand it in here.

"Emma's downstairs," he said. "She needed to pick something up." I could feel her presence downstairs—a little charge of electricity, the air lightening. I checked my phone, surprised to see she hadn't told me she was coming.

She needed a dress from her old closet, the one in her childhood room.

Reid was puttering around downstairs—the way older men putter—and I barged into the closet and said to Emma, "What do you need a dress for?"

I'd meant the question to be dull and harmless, but it sounded too sharp. It gleamed under the closet's warm light.

"I have plans tonight," Emma said. "Is that okay with you?"

She picked a shimmery dark dress that looked like an oil spill. I had never seen her wear it—it looked low-cut.

Reid asked Emma if she'd like to stay for lunch. Kelly had picked up chicken salad from the deli she liked.

We stood at the counter together, scooping the chicken salad onto plates, careful not to touch each other as we washed lettuce, shook bottles of dressing.

"Here," Emma said, handing me a container of grape tomatoes. I touched Emma then, an accident. I pulled away. We both did.

"Just toss them in," she said.

At the kitchen table, Reid kept trying to stab a grape tomato on the end of his fork and it kept slipping away from him, again and again. I was afraid Reid could see it on us. I thought sex would paint the space between two people a different color—make the air vibrate in a different way. But maybe it was different with two women, two girls, because I still thought of myself as a girl at that time, as someone's daughter. Girls could touch each other's lower backs. Girls could whisper in each other's ears. Girls could ignore each other pointedly.

"What's the dress for," Kelly asked.

"A date," Emma said.

This must be hell, I thought. A hell of my own making. And there are no worse kinds of hell, as far as I'm concerned. I tried to keep my eyes on my plate, to stare at the tomatoes as though I could char them with the intensity of my gaze.

"Boy? Girl?" Reid asked. He raised his eyebrows and I knew he was putting on a show for me, for Emma too—demonstrating his open-mindedness. Live and let live, baby! Love is love.

In private, he'd told me that he sort of liked the idea of Emma ending up with a woman. "I've spent my whole career listening to the perversions of men," he said.

"You've given voice to some of those perversions," I'd said.

He'd laughed. "Sure, sure. Better to have them voiced aloud than hidden."

This was his motto—his life's work—to untaboo-ify the taboo.

"And women can be creeps too," I'd said.

"But there are far fewer of them."

I'd agreed. Who could argue with that?

"What would your father say?" Reid asked me.

"If I was with a woman instead of a man? I don't think he'd care," I said. The only thing that would be truly upsetting to The Problem is if I was lost to him—if I was *really* someone else's.

"I'm seeing multiple people," Emma said now.

"Anyone serious?" Reid asked.

Emma looked away from me in a very deliberate way that reminded me of the acting class I'd taken in college. You try hards!, the teacher had said. Trust the other actors! Trust them to pick up on your subtlety! She did not trust me to pick up on her subtlety.

"Nobody serious," she said. "People I like, but nobody serious." She said the word "serious" slowly, like it was actually three words: *ser-i-ous.*

"Girl or guy?" This time I asked. I could feel my pulse quicken.

"Both," Emma said. "I'm seeing both."

"You're seeing someone?" I said. I'd opened the gigantic fridge for no reason and now I slammed it shut. Reid was outside, with Kelly, dutifully cleaning his grill with a special brush he ordered just for that purpose. I was trying to keep my voice down.

"Aren't I allowed?" Emma said. "You're also seeing a boy. Well a man, depending on who you ask. My mother would say he's neither a man nor a boy, but something in between. A kind of man-child—"

"Jesus," I said. "What is wrong with you?"

"What's wrong with me? What's wrong with you?"

"I didn't ask for this."

"Neither did I!"

"Girls," Reid called from outside. "Do we have time for a dip in the pool?"

66.

Finally, I answered my father's call.

"Thank God," he said. He wanted to talk about the Tropicana, a hotel-casino we used to stay in when I was growing up, where Jack eventually got his first paid gig, where he was passed as a club regular.

Back then, they didn't have rules against animals in casinos; or else, Vegas was free from those rules, a lawless place. There were parrots who would eat birdseed out of your hand, an ape who would take a picture with you—his arm slung around your shoulder with a big, toothy smile on his face. Best of all, there was a tiger on a leash.

"You could pet him," the trainer would say, "and if he's in a good mood, you'll keep both your hands." My father always made the same joke: it must depend on how much money the tiger lost.

"You remember going there," my father said now. "To the Trop."

It was a question that required no answer. He was gearing up to talk, I could tell.

"Jack loved the ape," he said into the phone. "He didn't like the tiger. He didn't like it being on a leash."

"I remember," I said. But it was the parrot he'd loved, because of the bright colors, and the fact that you could feed it, that you could feel its cool, plasticky beak against the palm of your hand.

* * *

"He bites," Jack had said, laughing. How old was he then? Eleven? "Do it again," he told the bird. "Go ahead and bite."

What had he wanted? To break skin? To distract me from whatever our parents were doing?

Somewhere nearby surely they'd been fighting. That's when I remembered the fighting being at its worst—when we were young, after my mother had made her mistake, after she'd considered an escape. But maybe your parents fighting always seems worst when you're a little kid. It always seems worst when you're powerless.

Your father causing a scene, my aunt Gena had said. He's always causing a scene.

And yes, I remembered a scene in that very casino, in front of the animals, and all the other tourists, my father hysterical, screaming at my mother, at the ceiling—what about?

My parents had so many of these fights my brother named them: the Tropicana Tumble, or something like that. He'd use his best announcer voice, like we were ringside at a wrestling match.

"And now," he said, "in one corner, at six foot four, with almost no ability to control his emotions, our father!"

I no longer remembered many of the names we gave the fights, I mainly remember being humiliated—watching other people take in my dad. I must have thought people were looking at me and feeling bad for me.

Look at that guy, they must have thought. Look at that asshole yelling in front of his kids.

They're misunderstanding you, I'd wanted to tell my dad. They think you're bad. They don't get it. They think you're something you're not.

67.

I read a study that said even people on death row think of themselves as good people who have made a terrible mistake.

Does anyone think of themselves as a bad person? I thought.

68.

Outside of the tiki bar, the other adjuncts watched Emma and I yell at each other. She'd come to pick me up, and I'd introduced her to everyone as one of my closest friends, though we must have seemed like enemies just then.

"I'm breaking up with him," I told Emma.

"Hold on," Emma said. "Hold on. Relax." She put her hands on my shoulders like she might need to physically restrain me.

I pushed her off. "What do you want then? A little sliver of me? Some fucked-up thing you share with your dad? Because he won't talk to you about what you really want to do with your life? About who you are?"

"What the fuck," Emma said.

I'd meant it as a compliment—she was talented! Why wouldn't Reid say so? And why did she insist on grappling for his approval like a little kid! Emma's face was distraught, until it turned derisive. She never held a mood for long.

"This is rich," she said, "coming from you, a person with a very normal relationship to her family."

"That's different," I said. "My brother."

"The rules are always different for you."

"I'm just trying to do the right thing," I said, "for everyone." I'd once heard a writing professor say, a good story should make the pendulum of your sympathy swing back and forth between characters. Wasn't I swinging now?

"I'm not saying not to break up with him," she said, "but don't do it on my behalf."

"Why?" I said. "Why not for you?"

"I'm just saying," she said. "That's a lot of responsibility."

That's what a daughter does, I thought. She takes responsibility for her father.

69.

Reid took me to a charity gala benefiting something specific and terrible—pediatric cancer? He couldn't remember. Bob, his agent, made him go every year.

It was at a trendy museum, and we posed for a photo in front of an installation made up of blinking stoplights. In fact, I still have it. I haven't shown it to anyone in a long time.

"Aren't you a handsome couple," said a woman in long, white gloves.

Bob put his arm around me like a kindly uncle and said, "I call you Xanax. Because you make him so much easier to be around."

Reid's ex-wife, Jean, was the MC. She was on the board, Reid explained, and part of the organizing committee, whatever that meant.

"I thought Bob made you come," I said.

"Bob was friends with us both," he said. "Is friends with us both."

It was true, I saw Bob shaking hands with everyone at Jean's table. He clapped at something she said. I think he prefers her, I thought. That seemed very clear to me then.

Over the unfolding of small talk and clinking silverware, Jean coughed lightly into the microphone.

"Excuse me," she said, from the podium. She gave a tinkling laugh and spread her arms wide, looking radiant. It was easy to see how much she liked the spotlight.

"It's with great pleasure I tell you that this year has been our most successful yet, or I should say, you all have been your most generous. Now I want you to turn to the person next to you," she said. "And tell them what it would mean for you to find a cure for juvenile arthritis. Go ahead, do it, tell them."

A low rumble emanated from the crowd as they did what they were told. "It would mean a lot to me," I said, to the elderly man sitting next to me.

Then I turned to Reid and said, "I would love a cure."

He laughed, kissed me lightly on the mouth. "Wouldn't we all!" he said.

Before we left, Jean gave us each a kind of half hug with one muscular arm.

"You've made quite the impression on my daughter," she said.

"Me too," I said. "Or her too."

I'd wanted to stay longer, to talk to Jean more, but Reid was anxious to get in the car and go home, to his television and his Popsicle, to his comforting routines.

"Kelly's waiting for us in the car," he said.

God you're old, I thought.

70.

Every week, it seemed, Emma and I found new places to yell at each other. When we fucked, it sometimes morphed into something else: angry, hard, like the fucking was only a way to extend our arguments.

It was hard to find time to be alone together, so we'd gotten in the habit of meeting at work, driving each other home and yelling in the car if we had to. We yelled outside of classrooms, outside of wealthy women's houses, outside of grocery stores where Emma gave out samples, saying "Enjoy!" over and over again.

This is what happened in love. One of you cried a lot and then both of you grew sarcastic.

"Let's tell him," Emma said. We were outside of one of my book clubs— a gated community of luxury condos.

"What if he's upset?" I said.

This is how it went between us—the volleying of who's on truth's side. Or maybe who's on Reid's side, though you could argue that meant someone was on the side of breaking his heart. Didn't I tell my students morality is complicated?

"Books are not for taking a moral grandstand," I'd said. "Books are for teaching you what it means to be alive." Then I'd quoted someone smarter than me. I was always quoting people smarter than me!

"So what if he's mad," Emma said.

"So what if he's mad," I agreed.

But I was thinking of my own father then, the times when he'd become so upset he wouldn't speak to me for weeks, and I felt walled off from the whole world. I worried Emma had more to lose—that to be walled off from her father would be akin to a death.

What did you do, when a whole planet suddenly dropped you out of its orbit, threw you into free fall? Did it matter if you were an adult woman?

Then, Emma said, "Don't do it before his birthday."

"That's weeks away," I said.

"But still," she said. "He gets weird around his birthday."

When I finally entered the book club, a woman in a weird French beret said, "I saw you arguing with your sister. I hate it when my daughters fight."

"Well," I said. "Sometimes it can't be helped."

Then she started talking about a surgery she was about to have. "They're moving my skin around," she said. "They're taking skin from up there and putting it down here."

For once, I'd let them choose the book. They picked a schmaltzy romance. I'd found it surprisingly enjoyable.

"So how did we feel about the novel?" I asked.

"Crap," a woman said. This was another woman with eyebrows that were unusually high—not in the normal eyebrow place—and now they looked surprised. "It was crap. We should just let you pick them."

Okay, so not all the women in my book clubs were blindly wealthy, nor were they all simplistic readers, incapable of depth or nuanced understanding. Some were extremely smart. A few were extremely kind.

But that wasn't as good of a story.

I see that now, how much I've probably twisted things, made them—if not easier—more interesting. Writers aren't trustworthy. They fold your life inside of themselves, crunch up your secrets with sharp, jagged teeth. They bloody the people who love them.

✻   ✻   ✻

"We'll read your book in the club," beret woman said, "when it comes out. If you want us to."

"That's sweet of you," I said.

I hadn't remembered telling them that I was writing a book. It might have just been something I said to keep them off my back, to sound like less of a loser.

But I had been writing something. Maybe it was even a book.

At the end of the hour, one of the women pulled out a wrapped gift from underneath her chair. I unwrapped it slowly, only to find a vintage edition of a book I'd told them was my favorite.

"Why the gift," I said.

"You've been our facilitator for a whole year," she said. "So we thought we should get you a gift." I hadn't known any of them had been paying attention to dates—to anniversaries!

"You mentioned it at our first meeting," the woman said. "So we thought we'd pitch in and get it for you."

I blinked my eyes as a way of convincing the tears back in. When I started to speak something happened to my voice and I had to clear my throat and start again.

"Thank you," I said. "That's so thoughtful."

71.

I looked at the Instagram of the therapist I'd seen in college—in the before-time—the famous one who once wore dangly Texas earrings.

Now, she wore small tasteful hoops.

In one post, she'd written, not making a choice is so much more painful than making the wrong one.

I wrote a comment: *Hi Dr. G! Do you remember me?*

She hearted it, but did not reply.

72.

I took Emma to a tropical-themed casino an hour outside of Los Angeles called Hawaiian Gardens. She said she wanted to play against *real* people, not just me and her dad. And I wanted to be alone with her somewhere other than my apartment, somewhere other than work. We sat at a table filled with grim-looking regs (regulars) and degens (degenerates) as my brother used to call them.

Waiting for the cards to be dealt, we held hands under the table. I felt a little self-conscious there, surrounded by men who reminded me of the men I'd grown up around, with a meanness blooming inside them, but I made a decision to hold Emma's hand anyway.

"No funny business," the dealer said, but he was smiling.

"Who's the better poker player," he said, "of you two?"

"She taught me," Emma said. "But I'm ready to surpass her."

"How long have the two of you been together?" a young Asian guy asked. He had multiple rings on every finger.

"Awhile," I said.

"It feels like forever," Emma said.

"How did you meet?" the dealer said. I looked at my cards. I had an ace and a king. Big Slick, is what the poker players called the hand.

"We met through my dad," Emma said.

"I wouldn't trust my dad," the dealer said. "He'd set me up with the kind of woman he likes."

"What kind of woman does he like?" I asked.

"Ugly," he said.

"That's funny," Emma said, which is what she said when she didn't think something was funny at all.

"Who would your dad pick for you?" Emma asked me. I raised the hand pre-flop, flicking in two five-dollar chips.

"I don't know," I said. "Probably a version of him."

"I think Allison is my dad's type," Emma said to the dealer. The bets had gone around the table, back to Emma. The pot was around sixty dollars by then, and we all waited for her to do something.

Emma looked me up and down, and said, "All in."

I knew she'd done it mostly for dramatic effect, and when she lost all her money, she only laughed. I never quite knew how much of her money was her father's money anyway, it was something we never discussed.

"You went all in with a jack and a three," I said. "That isn't a hand." But I hadn't won either, the pot had been stolen by a pair of eights. I, however, knew when to fold.

"You're lucky you're cute," the dealer said, and we didn't know to whom he was speaking.

"You're not good at poker," I said, on our way to the car.

"I was just trying to have fun," she said. "But I always have fun when I'm with you."

"Except when you're mad at me."

"Well, yeah," she said. "But still. I'd rather be mad at you than be mad at anybody else."

Emma, like her dad, didn't like to drive. I'm not good at it, she claimed. When I'd asked if her father was also a bad driver, she said he just preferred having women drive him around.

"Like you," I said.

"Sure," she said. "Like me."

At my own car, I kissed her urgently, like one does at the beginning of a movie, before everything goes awry.

"I want more than fun," I said.

"You want to play poker professionally?"

"No," I said. "I'm saying that I've made up my mind. That I want to be with you." She didn't say anything at first, and all I could think of was Reid's catchphrase, the one he used at the beginning of every radio show: Speak up! Speak up, I wanted to say. But she just got in the car.

Finally she said, "Let me think about it."

But I knew that was a bad sign. It was not good to spend too much time thinking about your own life. Your own life became a wormy, writhing thing under that kind of attention. No life looked good in such harsh, unforgiving light. No choice seemed right.

73.

I wouldn't wait around and let her think. I was tired of waiting myself out.

I'd decided it would be easier to break up with Reid if I did it by surprise. If he knew I was coming over for a "big talk," let's say, he could prepare himself. He could try to talk me out of it. And I didn't trust myself not to get talked out of it, especially by him, a professional talker—one of the best in the world.

I'll do it like a Band-Aid, I thought, I'll just suddenly pull it off. But that didn't really make sense. The person *wearing* the Band-Aid pulled it off. Not a woman trying to break up with you.

Either way, I knew I had to shock him with the bad news. Or maybe what I needed was to shock myself. I needed to break up with him as though I were the hero in a thriller, rolling out from beneath the garage just as it was closing.

Because I didn't want him to know that I was coming, I'd told Reid I was going out of town to visit my father. I had been doing that often—lying, making excuses—in order to see Emma. I'd used every possible excuse by then: I was facilitating extra book clubs, I was teaching extra classes, I was writing before school, I was writing after school. He never questioned me. He trusted me explicitly.

This wasn't a total lie: I decided I *would* visit my father. After I broke Reid in two, I'd get out of LA. I'd go stay in the town outside of Reno.

Maybe I'd even go and see the old house where I grew up, or the house Jack painted the wrong color, or the house where Marcella's mother still lived.

Reid's Prius, or rather, the one in which Kelly drove him around, sat glumly in the driveway.

Why didn't he buy her something new? I thought it was very rude, to make someone drive you around in an older car when you could afford something so much better, so much more luxurious. Didn't he wonder what she did all day, away from him, alone in that car? Didn't he want her to be comfortable?

When I pressed the keypad—the numbers that were Emma's birthday—I thought about where she and I might be next year, on that very day. Maybe we'd go on vacation to Hawaii. Maybe we'd go to Vegas.

Inside, the house was oddly quiet, undisturbed. I yelled Reid's name and heard nothing, just my own voice echoing in his beautiful home. I yelled Kelly's name. I looked in the living room, saw the pristine rows of records, untouched. I looked in his study. I looked in the kitchen. One of Kelly's baseball caps was sitting on the kitchen island. So, too, were the dangly earrings she always wore. I looked out by the pool.

Yes, Reid was by the pool. And so was someone else.

I'm not sure how much I should tell.

It was Reid and Kelly out there, and I'll say this: the two of them were naked. I was shocked by her body—how much more toned she looked than I'd expected. Her high ass! I'm sure that says something misogynist about me, that I assumed an older woman's ass would sag, but I've never claimed to be free from prejudice, from my own blinding expectations.

The strangest thing: they weren't engaged in any sexual activity, at least not at that moment. They were just lounging, nude, by the pool—like they were chatting about the weather, or lunch, or Reid's new grill.

When they turned to look at me, they did it at the same time, in a way that made them look related—like lovers, or brother and sister.

So Kelly wasn't just a driver. Yes, she'd been driving him a long time, but it wasn't just that. Their relationship was complicated. In fact, it was nearly impossible to explain. It wasn't just sex and it wasn't just love and it wasn't just companionship. It was something else. Or maybe it was all three. Who could understand that which cannot be defined better than me? (And trust me, Reid tried.)

But no, she wasn't just his driver. And no, she never had been. He'd given her the earrings on the tenth year she'd worked for him. She'd worn them almost every day since.

I pretended to be very angry. I didn't actually need to pretend. I *was* angry, even if I had no right to be.

"You have to let me explain," Reid said, now a towel around his waist. He'd gotten down on his knees, put his hands together in prayer in front of his Adirondack chairs.

Kelly was using the guest bathroom, making herself back into someone else.

"I've been an idiot," I said.

"You haven't," he said. "No you haven't."

"I have," I said, "I've been terrible." But I didn't explain why.

Now, in retrospect, I think the person I owe the apology to is Kelly. She was the person I so clearly had wrong.

This, I think, is the defining characteristic of youth: we assume we see people for who they are. The older I get, the more I'm astounded by how rarely I get anyone right the first time, or the second, or sometimes even the third.

Of course, when I started writing this book, I was tempted to tell the story a different way: that I broke up with Reid because I was the woman scorned. I could've said I was never unfaithful, I never lied. I could've said there was no Emma at all! Instead, I've decided to tell the truth, whether or not you believe me.

*   *   *

After I'd calmed down, Reid and Kelly took me into the living room and sat across from me on Reid's expensive sofa, Reid still with a towel around his waist, Kelly now in her usual utilitarian blue jeans. They stared at me with gentle faces, like we were having a fun-house version of a family meeting, in which they'd evenly try and explain.

"It's not a romantic thing between us," Reid said.

"Yes," Kelly agreed, "not exactly."

"We've known each other for so long," Reid said. "When you asked before who was the one to support me . . ." He trailed off then, not bothering to explain.

It turned out, they'd known each other since childhood. They knew each other from the before-time.

"Why do you think I first agreed to work for him?" Kelly asked. "I'd known him for so long, I knew he was someone I could trust."

"Jesus Christ," I said. "I've been sleeping with someone else. You're not the only one." I wanted to be honest. I wanted to give myself that.

Reid stood up. "That guy," he said, "that teacher at the party."

I didn't correct him. He started pacing around in his blue and white striped towel, the kind you get at a hotel pool. He was mumbling to himself. He must have been debating whether he had a right to be mad, or at least, to show that anger to me. He should feel betrayed, I thought, he just didn't know what about.

"Reid," Kelly said softly, and when he looked at her, I saw something I hadn't seen before: an immediate retraction of his anger.

"You're right," he said, "you're right."

He was still surprised when I said I didn't want to continue this. He was surprised when I was not open for any negotiations, when I said there were no concessions to be made.

When Emma got off work, I was waiting for her outside of the grocery store, hanging around the shopping carts.

She came out with her apron still on, with this look on her face like she already knew.

I opened my arms wide and she walked into them. "It feels good to be chosen," she said.

That night, we stayed at my place, and then for six more nights after that. I designated two drawers for her big shirts, lined up her face creams by the bathroom mirror. We barely left the bed. It felt like a honeymoon, like we were my parents in Niagara Falls. My thighs ached. I called in sick for every class.

On the eighth night, she got restless. She had to do stand-up; she had to visit her dad. Go, I said, because I was planning to see my own.

Over towering pastrami sandwiches at the Peppermill Casino, I told The Problem, "I'm not with the Old Man anymore."

"What the hell?" he said. "Did he leave you?"

"I left him," I said. If my father didn't believe me, he had the decency not to show it.

"Almighty," he said. He took off his cowboy hat and set it on the table, a sign of respect—of mourning. "I'm sorry. I was looking forward to a party."

"We can still have one," I said.

"There are plenty of people," he said. "Plenty of people we haven't met yet." He was scanning the buffet line, the hungry people maneuvering tongs, piling up their plates, reaching for rolls of bread and oysters and the tails of large prawns.

"It might be a woman," I said.

"What?"

"I'm trying to be honest."

"What," he said again.

"I might end up with a woman."

"Fine." He broke into laughter. "Did you come all the way to tell me that? What kind of odds are we talking? Fifty-fifty? Do you want to put a bet down in the sportsbook? Man oh man," he said. He was still looking at the buffet. "You want the whole world I guess."

We drove by the gray house—the one my brother had painted—my father steering with his off hand, but it was renovated now, a serene, forest green.

But I was happy to see nobody had touched the Haunted House. The porch was cluttered with old beer bottles and red Solo cups and shattered glass. Kids were still haunting the place.

"It's not a bad town," my father said, though he'd never said anything positive about it when I was growing up there.

"A lot of good people came from here," I said.

I never told Emma about seeing Kelly and her dad together. I didn't think she'd want to know. I thought of it as a kindness then, keeping that from her. Karma or guilt, either way, there were things I didn't want coming back to me.

Emma and I didn't last much longer. When her father was out of the mix, it was like a rope had been loosened—something went slack between us. We met half-heartedly at my apartment, at the pool hall, at various dive bars around town. She didn't want her dad to know that we were still seeing each other.

And I understood where she was coming from. She was her father's daughter. She was her father's daughter before anything else. Later, she became very successful. Not as a comedian, but as a TV development executive. How much her father had to do with that—I'll never know. But I can picture her behind a desk, convincing a writer to see it her way.

I got a raise at the junior college. And I wrote more than this: more than you're seeing here. I dated five more people in Los Angeles: three women, two men. I slept with several more. I even slept with Chris again, in his bedroom filled with art. He kept asking what Reid was like. He even asked what he was like in bed.

"Someday I'll write about it," I said. "But I'll disguise it. You won't even know who you're reading about."

By then, I liked Chris better. I liked how hard he tried. Even when I stopped sleeping with him, we'd walk around the Silverlake Reservoir and talk about art and fame and whatever legacy we were hoping to leave behind. Then we got a little older and talked about how dumb it was that we ever thought about "a legacy" at all.

☆　☆　☆

I hope I didn't spare too many details or tell too many lies. I've tried my best to remember things clearly. Hopefully I haven't said too much.

Marcella even said that at my wedding, when she gave a toast. She said, "Once you get her talking, she might tell you too much."

My wedding was on a beach, by the way. At first, I thought I wanted something small, but I kept accumulating guests. I knew a lot more people by then. I'd taught so many classes. I'd made more friends.

That night, we all drank champagne and I had seconds of everything. My parents were both there, and Raj too. My father brought a date named Susan who got raucously drunk and fell asleep in the sand. We toasted my brother over and over. It became a kind of motto—saying his name.

"How about his toast?" my father said. "Think how funny it would be."

When it was my father's turn to talk, he said, "I love my daughter more than I love life itself." My mother and I both wiped our eyes. I can't say I didn't believe him. I hugged him for a long time, my beloved problem.

After people tossed handfuls of rice in our hair, we shut the door of the limo, red-faced and sweaty and doubled over with glee. I put Reid on the radio. I wanted to fill the limo with his voice. The episode was a rerun, as they all were by then, but it was a thrill to hear him after so many years.

We were on our way to a beautiful hotel in Santa Monica, and I felt sick from happiness, and from having eaten too much.

You won't want to eat at your wedding, people had told me. But that hadn't been true at all. I wanted everything in front of me. I wanted to feast.

ACKNOWLEDGMENTS

First Time, Long Time started out as a thirty-page short story, rife with all of my usual preoccupations. First and foremost, thank you to my agents: Mollie Glick and Anthony Mattero, who gave me the confidence to take those thirty pages out into the world and see how they might be transformed.

This novel wouldn't exist without my genius editors at Grand Central Publishing, Jacqui Young and Maddie Caldwell, who helped me build a house from a few planks of wood. Thank you for your patient guidance. I'm sorry I was late on every single deadline I was ever given.

My many years at USC have been a gift, mostly because of the invaluable mentors I've had the pleasure of working with: Aimee Bender (who has generously read so many of my short stories), Judith Freeman, Mark Richard, Percival Everett, Dana Johnson, among others. The workshops—and the peers I've met through those workshops—made me into a writer.

I've had so many dear friends—writers and non-writers alike—listen to me fret about finishing this book. Thank you all for the space you gave me to worry aloud, and for your constant reassurance. I won't name everyone, but here's a list: Roxane Gay, Rachel Kaplan, Whitney Ralls, Maddie Connors, Blair Socci, Dana Bell, Rachel Hall, Kaitlyn Tanimoto, Jasmine Tejwani, Laura Peek, Karolina Waclawiak, Olivia Friedman, Carly Roukos, Lisa Mecham (& the whole Studio 69 Group Text), Alex Wallachy, Christine Medrano, Neha Potalia, The Rat King Group Text, Mica Unger, Carly Passovoy, Jen Passovoy, Lindsay Adams, Katy Fishell, Danny Palumbo, Dean Bakopoulos, Thomas Renjilian, and many others. I can't forget to thank the comedians who let me shout about my novel at stand-up shows. And of course, Dr. B—thank you, thank you.

Sara Rooker and Andrea Bartunek hosted me in Reno and introduced me to the Peppermill Casino: my time there became a centerpiece for this novel.

To the women whose book clubs I've so enjoyed facilitating: I hope you'll let me continue, even after what you've read here. Your raucous opinions remind me why I write. It's a pleasure to be surrounded by women who always want to turn the page.

If I ever meet Howard Stern in person, I'll tell him: you were the inspiration for this book, though not the source material. The times I spent listening to Howard in the back seat of my mother's car are cherished memories. Howard made me realize what kind of parents I had—utterly open-minded. I've always been fascinated by Howard's complexity, that he might be so inwardly sensitive while so outwardly crass. How misunderstood he's always seemed to me! I've long since considered myself to be two things at once: a writer and a comedian—a literary person with a filthy sense of humor—among other dualities. It's been a great source of solace to have Howard in my ear for so long. He reminds me that people are allowed to be more than one thing at a time. Also, Howard, you remind me that people are allowed to evolve. Bababooey!

An urgent thank-you to my Danny—your unconditional love has allowed me to become the truest version of myself. It is a love that's made me brave.

And finally, thank you to my family. My grandmother, Virginia Lee, an artist in her own right, taught me how to paint, and more so, taught me that the life of an artist looked better than any other life I could imagine. My brother, Jon, is so unlike most older brothers—he always acted happy to have me around. Your constant support has made me feel cooler than I am.

Lastly, thank you to my parents, Larry and Nancy Silverberg. Mom, you were my first trusted short story reader. Dad, thank you for giving new meaning to the phrase "number one fan." If I had a fan club, and there was only one member, I know it would be you.

What can I say to you both? Without you—nothing.

ABOUT THE AUTHOR

Amy Silverberg is a writer and comedian. She holds a PhD in Creative Writing & Literature from USC. Her fiction has appeared in *Best American Short Stories, The Paris Review, Granta, The Idaho Review, TriQuarterly, The Los Angeles Review of Books,* and elsewhere. She was selected as a "New Face" in stand-up comedy at the Just for Laughs Comedy Festival in Montreal. Her stand-up has been featured on Comedy Central, Hulu, and Amazon Prime. She also writes television, most recently for *The Movie Show* on the SYFY channel. This is her debut novel. She lives in Los Angeles.